THE PAPER BOY

JOSIAH GOLOJUH

For:

Coleman Hough.
Mom & Dad.
Judy, Penny, & Prim.

CONTENTS

EARLY PRAISE FOR THE PAPER BOY

"The best horror book you will read, funny, dark, referential and clever, Josiah isn't clowning around with this very real tale of terror."
- **Stephen Chiodo**
writer/director,
Killer Klowns from Outer Space

"*The Paper Boy* is a clever and suspenseful contribution to the superhero genre. Josiah Golojuh will keep you guessing and you make think at the same time."
- **Tom Perrotta**
writer,
Little Children, Election, The Leftovers

"Scary, intriguing and exciting all wrapped up into one amazing debut novel from Josiah. If you love horror, comic book heroes and interesting stories this book will not

disappoint. The southwestern Pennsylvania setting lends itself perfectly to the movie that will soon be following the novel we hope!"
-Dawn Keezer
Director, Pittsburgh Film Office

"An adolescence shaped by a small town upbringing, a longing for adventure, and a love for all things counter-culture have served Josiah well in his efforts to share his experiences, interests, and gifts with his audience. I hope you enjoy reading his book as much as we all did living it."
-Kim Snair
Childhood crush
Actual owner of the Jim Morrison birthday cake

"The Paper Boy is nothing less than a veritable time machine of nerd culture in the 90s."
-Steven Kung
Writer, *Dear White People*
Director, *Fresh off the Boat*

"There's a reason Josiah Golojuh calls his YouTube channel, Josiah is Write - this fella can really write!"
-Stephen Stern
Co-Creator, *Zen: Intergalactic Ninja*

CHAPTER 1
THE BOY WHO DELIVERS THE NEWSPAPER

You really need to grow up.

It was a strange thought. A foreign thought, so foreign it was alien. Aliens! An alien thought, a thought actually implied alien control, at least to Daniel and his nearly 15 years of experience. He would have preferred that, actually. At the very least, mental alien invasion would've made life more interesting than his own tended to be. In reality, it was a thought handed down from generation to generation as age made them increasingly less happy. It was also very Daniel-like. He thought big, of the future, of the past, of the future-past, of life and death, what came beyond and everything in between, and if he were honest about it the whole thing frightened him because he had no answers. He had no desire to think beyond himself, but he often did anyway.

Daniel stamped out the mental brushfire as he carefully slid an X-Factor comic book into its mylar bag and then into a folder — for extra protection — before finally returning it to his backpack. He wouldn't admit it, not even to himself, that he'd pulled it out hoping someone would notice the comic, yet fearing that exact scenario. Did he want contact and connection? Sure. But the contact and connection he typically got were swift punches to his plump stomach.

Daniel looked around at the other kids on the school bus; they didn't seem to be troubled by thoughts like this, at least as far as he could tell simply by looking at them. He liked that. It made him feel smart. There was the kid with the overbite, next to the kid with the underbite. Nothing was inherently wrong with either of these things, but their parents (and later themselves) would never bother to fix these issues, so they would haunt them into adulthood.

The worst physical offender? Wonky teeth kid. Daniel always thought those things looked like the entrance to a fun house designed by Tim Burton. Thankfully, his own parents took care of his own dental issues. He failed to consider the fact that his teeth had once been equally wonky with a prominent gap peeking between his two front teeth every time he grinned. No, it wasn't a *great* look, but on the upside, it was super-easy to floss. The fix wasn't necessarily because of his parents, though. It happened after a friend carelessly swung his hooded sweatshirt around and a lone zipper collided with a previously mentioned wonky tooth. Emergency dental surgery blessed Daniel with two perfectly matching front teeth. And yes, one was totally fake, but even he forgot which one it was. He assumed he'd be the same when he grew up, even though he loathed the idea he'd grow up.

Daniel distracted himself from the thought. His focus was now on the miserable expressions of the other kids, nary a smile shared between them. It was a beautiful Western Pennsylvania fall day, an Indian summer. He pictured summer stretching its arms and legs, caught in an extensive yawn as it quietly refused to yield control to autumn, instead overtaking and holding the muddy brown of fall at bay. Daniel grinned. It was as perfect as perfect weather can be. They should have all been smiling, beaming with youthful laughter and mirth and joy. They were about to go home, watch TV, maybe play a few video games and generally avoid doing any and all homework. Well, everyone but Daniel. Daniel had to go to work — *real* work, like working in a factory of a salt mine. He'd find a way to avoid that stuff later.

Indian summer or not, the past half mile stretch of bumpy back roads had firmly shifted into fall. Sneaking gray clouds crept up and now hid the sun, an airy mist moistening the grass and softening the soil. The rolling hills sparked despite the lack of sun, the shades of Kelly green only enhanced by the light rain. Thinly spread houses gave way as an emerald green forest, thick with underbrush, threatened to take over. The green section in Daniel's 200 Crayola pack didn't do justice to the number of shades in the woods. No, this was a breathtaking green that would soon turn to the blandest brown, but not before a rainbow explosion of reds and oranges and yellows, an array that would make Crayola itself insanely jealous.

Daniel's mind raced as his imaginary self, Super Dan, darted through the forest at the speed of the school bus, sometimes even overtaking the huge vehicle as he zoomed in and out of the trees along the road. He pursued some unseen evil, laying waste to villains, trees, and even the occasional building. Daniel flew and leapt, dashed and darted, moving so fast the bus had no hope of keeping up. His mind had escaped the confines of the school bus and was on a great adventure. An adventure where Super Dan, young and untested, would rise to meet the challenge. Where Super Dan would cease to be a boy and become a true hero. Daniel quietly mumbled to himself, narrating his fictional heroics, adding in surprisingly accurate sound effects when necessary. When he sensed a nearby bully staring at him, he sank in his seat and quieted himself, but the adventure of his mind never stopped. It would just go on and on, awake or asleep, his quest continued. Outrunning the bus, outrunning planes, rockets and his real life. Real life bored him, but his imagination? Totally epic.

In his backpack, nestled right next to his precious X-Factor comic and the homework he'd soon forget to do, rested a notebook, jam-packed with scribblings of his adventures. Truthfully? Daniel's ability to imagine far exceeded his ability to draw. Undeterred, he'd nonetheless decided long ago he wanted to be the next Stan Lee. Granted, the younger version of Daniel thought Stan *drew* the comics. That same Daniel also naively believed writing comics meant you just sat around and drew panels and made up a story as you went along.

Daniel now knew better. Being very aware of the utter and absolute greatness of Jack Kirby, he drew and drew. He'd be a one-shot deal, Stan and Jack in one. Which he later realized was Jack. For better or for worse, Daniel had to admit he had way more Stan in him than Jack. His lack of artistic ability stopped him from drawing all day long in class, but there on the bus he was free to let his imagination rule the trees and buildings as they passed by. The world outside the bus moved like an IMAX movie, like the one at the science center, set around Daniel as he conjured details on the stage of his mind. Just as quickly as they popped into view, he grew tired of them. He always knew the *next* idea, the still undreamt one, would be *even better*. There was always something new to discover.

Just as Daniel's mind was once again in need of reprieve, the bus stopped in front of the trailer court. As much as he didn't want it, he needed reality. Real life always grounded the best stories, a chestnut he'd learned from Stan Lee. Mobile homes laid here and there, sold as a "private community," but Daniel knew it was little more than low-income housing, a refuge of the elderly on a budget. Slumping in his seat, he tried to ignore the kids getting off the bus, hiding from the bullies. From his slumped position, he could still see up to the top of the hill. There rested most of the trailers, and the bulk of Daniel's work.

As the school bus lumbered from its stopped position, an impatient station wagon sputtered by. The wagon's horn a long continuous groan as it struggled past the rust encrusted bus.

"Sonofah!" exclaimed the white and wrinkled bus driver, pounding hard on the horn. Mr. Pan always yelled. Yelled at cars, yelled at pedestrians, yelled at the kids, but not at Daniel. He never once yelled at Daniel. Daniel was a good kid, if not a good one, he was at least a quiet one. It didn't hurt that Daniel's mom always baked Christmas cookies for him to give to Mr. Pan.

The driver of the station wagon returned the favor by continuing to blare his own horn, extending his left hand out the window, offering a thick, ink-smudged middle finger in full salute. The station wagon driver put the pedal to the floor and a short distance ahead, without stopping, turned right at the intersection, zipping across a bridge. Beneath the bridge rested rickety, seldom-used railroad tracks. Once the key to the local economy, the circulatory system to the countless coal mines in the area, now the mines were all gone. Boarded up, blocked over, completely closed. Walled over shells sat throughout the countryside like the unexplored dungeons in *The Legend of Zelda*. People either commuted to the city for work, or they didn't work at all. Nobody needed those rusty old tracks anymore.

With a puff of black smoke, the station wagon stopped just on the other side of the bridge, at the base of a driveway. The driveway extended, up and up lost into the woods. The curmudgeonly middle-aged man went to the rear hatch of the wagon. Opening it, he grabbed one of several bundles of newspapers. After a weak toss of the bundle, the man peeled out of the driveway, spraying gravel in his wake.

Daniel involuntarily lurched forward as the bus took the

corner a little too fast before stopping on the other side of the bridge. Stepping off the bus, he could still see the station wagon and its distinct plume of black smoke. The black smog of death, or as Daniel referred to it: the fart of a dying dragon. He was always grateful when the bus was late. It meant he didn't have to deal with the driver of the station wagon or breathe in the fart smog. Upon fixing the peeled-out gravel with his well-worn Nike high-top, Daniel coughed, consumed by the thought of that black smoke. Daniel adjusted the rolled cuffs of his black "dress" jeans and undid the top few buttons of his plaid button-up. "Picture day requires perfection," or so his mom had said. Daniel didn't agree, but he didn't care to argue. Besides, he loved his mom, so he let her put gel in his normally wavy poof of hair.

Halfway up the driveway Daniel began to run, rejuvenated by the rays of sun that broke through the trees just as it drove the rain away, and with the fart smog fading away into distant memory, the fresh air filled his lungs. His work still lay ahead of him, but now he was ready to attack it. Like Superman, ready to take flight, he opened his shirt. He didn't notice, but he even popped off a button and he'd never notice as later that evening his mom would sew it as she did laundry.

Daniel burst through his door into his room, shuffling off his school clothes like a crusty husk. Across the room, Daniel's perfect mutt of a dog roused from sleep on his bed. Perking his ears and raising a long, rounded snout, Mac opened its eyes and sniffed the air, returning to sleep after recognizing him. Neatly folded on the bed beside it, Daniel's post-school clothes were ready and waiting.

School clothes, particularly on picture day, should *never* be worn on the paper route. His mom simply wouldn't allow it. It didn't really matter to Daniel either way, but he was happy to slip into something more comfortable. Mom called them his "play clothes," an expression he loathed to his core. No, for him these clothes were his uniform, like Spider-Man's red and blue tights, Superman and his cape, Batman and his cowl.

Okay, so maybe not as iconic or heroic or adventurous, but they're at least like the mailman or the UPS guy.

The very nature of Daniel's room was at conflict with itself. On the one hand, it looked like he was still a kid needing his mommy to wash his "play clothes," a childishness that was eternally evident in the proliferation of toys on the shelves, posters for science fiction movies on the walls and, of course, the ubiquitous comic books. These ranged from the big guys — Marvel and DC — all the way down to Dark Horse and Image. Most of all, however, Daniel liked Main Title Comics, specifically *because* they weren't as popular as the others. They were the underdogs, and upstarts, and because fewer people knew about them, it was like he was a member of a secret club. It made him feel smart. *Special.*

Then there was the other elements of his room, the movie posters for *Bridge on the River Kwai, One Flew Over the Cuckoo's Nest, The Godfather* (Part II, of course), and *Patton.* These were peppered along with several posters for The Doors, The Who, Led Zeppelin, Pink Floyd, and so on. Granted, most of them had broken up or had core members die off well before Daniel was even born. He didn't care. They were still cool.

After Daniel jammed his discarded clothing into a corner — the "laundry area," so his mom would know what clothes to wash — he reached a hand behind the pile and retrieved a lone duck boot. Tan, brown, and ugly, the rubber boot was made exclusively for hunting and fishing, but also fell into the category of play clothes. His blue jeans had a hole in the right knee, complimenting a deep fade and wear to the left knee, preparing to be breached in the coming weeks. His dull green sweatshirt was soft, but ripe with fine fuzz from over washing.

Daniel put on his Walkman (okay, his dad's Walkman, but he never used it anyway) and dialed the volume up. The soundtrack to today's adventure? *Tom Sawyer* by Rush. He grinned, letting the sound waves wash over him.

Duck boots haphazardly laced, Daniel grabbed his paper bag, the final item on the bed. Mac groaned and rolled over, facing the wall with no small amount of disinterest. Daniel pet him behind the ears, then raised the strap of the bag up over his head. Lowering the bag onto his green sweatshirt, he felt a renewed sense of power and pride as he adjusted it to the side like a bandolier, mimicking Chewbacca's iconic uniform. Bright white letters emblazoned on the side of his navy-blue newspaper bag read "Valley Bugle," the paper of choice for the Allegheny Valley.

Star Wars and *Patton* aside, Daniel knew nothing of war. But he knew of battles. He understood what it meant to fight for a cause, a concept he had identified with in his comic books. He'd happily preach the gospel of Main Title Comics to anyone within earshot, which typically amounted to his slightly annoyed mother and his best and only friend. Jimmy. One time his older brother pretended to listen, but Daniel didn't count that.

In meticulous, painstakingly ranked order from 10 to 1, Daniel mentally reviewed his top ten Main Title characters. The very best Main Title stories coming in the anthology book, *The Borough*, where all of his favorites, and most despised came together for epic monthly crossover stories. (Note: while he also loved Young Zombie, that and its characters existed outside of Main Title's continuity, so he couldn't in good conscience count it on his list.)

10. **Vigilance**: John Scott witnessed his mother murdered by his estranged assassin father, forever vowing to avenge her.

9. **Fireball**: Geno Strelnikov, a.k.a. **Fireball**, was not yet a hero, struggling to accept the reality that a fire he started had ended up killing his beloved brother.

8. **Merkanary**: The ultimate antihero (as it said on the

cover), an angry machine-man, memory wiped clear. A past fraught with nothing but pain, he nearly sacrificed his soul, a reprieve arriving in the most unlikely of allies, **The Ultimate Rejects**.

7. **The Ultimate Rejects**: While he normally preferred to rank team members individually, but, with the exception of **Merkanary**, Daniel felt he couldn't break apart the Rejects. Oddballs and misfits, loathed because of their bizarre powers, choosing to band together rather than endure the shame and scorn alone.

6. **Tri-Burner & Brainbend**: Another pair he couldn't separate up, once again breaking his own arbitrary rules. Father and son displaced from an alternate future where **Tri-Burner** was not yet manipulated by the sinister **Dr. Spazum** to sacrifice his son.

5. **Hero**: The utterly invincible **Hero**, an infant sent to the past, narrowly escaping the obliteration of the future.

4. **The Extremist**: The very accident that gave him his uncanny abilities also obliterated all physical and emotional sensation! A tortured character if ever there was one!

3. **Valor Vendetta**: Nikko Sanchez, a Spanish explorer lost in the Netherworld, made a deal with **Sken** to return to earth hundreds of years after crossing through the portal, only to find his body zombified.

2. **The Proctor**: Race car driver Rod Stebel became **The Proctor** when he was imbued with the heart of the dying alien peacekeeper, **Amlon**.

Number one. *Oh, number one…*

Whenever he was asked to rank his top ten, Daniel struggled mightily with the order, numbers 10 through 2 fluctuating wilding, constantly changing it and rearranging the list, adding and removing characters (today, the Illuminator and the Star Spangled Soldier fell just out of the top ten) but not with number one. Never with Number One. Although Daniel realized that every one of their origins were tragic on some level, one always stood out above them all. Tragedy unparalleled, pain unprecedented, no suffering could compare to that of Glen Graboyes, the strongman of the **Fabulous Thunder Family**.

The Grim.

A brother's vain ambition, an interstellar flight, copious amounts of lunar radiation, one brother turning good, the other hopelessly evil. One benevolent, one malevolent. One the Grim, one the Ghoul. **The Fabulous Thunder Family** welcomed Glen into their superhero family, all with great powers, but none other at the expense of their humanity. Glen — kind and compassionate and ever-loving Glen — forever anguished as the heart of his humanity remained hidden beneath the visage of a monster.

"It's supposed to rain."

The voice from downstairs was firm but compassionate.

"And don't forget to take an umbrella!" his mom added.

Daniel, lost in his revery of **The Grim** and the music of Rush, didn't hear a word.

He dashed out of the bedroom, expertly sliding on his butt down the spiral staircase and blazing through the kitchen, barely pausing to retrieve the jumbo sandwich that lay waiting for him on the counter.

CHAPTER 2
THE PAPER ROUTE

Crossing the yard as he headed down the tree enveloped driveway, Daniel scarfed down the sandwich with abandon. In his mind, the tunnel of restless trees rotated and shifted to open a portal to another dimension ahead, beckoning his arrival. He grinned.

At the base of the driveway Daniel popped the plastic tie binding the newspapers with a satisfying thud. He heaved them into his bag and soldiered on, eagerly to enter an alternate existence. Beyond the driveway Daniel truly felt as if he'd walked into a different reality. If not a different dimension, then most certainly a starkly different world other than the one kept and curated by his mom. He needed no imagination, here it just felt different. He felt... free.

Walking across the bridge, Daniel took in the details of the rusted metal half-wall beside him. Dark shades of red covered it entirely, and he ran his finger over the rough, rusted metal. On the other side of the bridge, he carefully navigated the dead four-way intersection to reach Popeye's Gas Station. Although there were obviously no cars and Daniel could clearly see that without stopping, he was nonetheless cautious by nature and circumstance. Above him a broken sign read *Texaco*, but this hadn't been a Texaco since before Daniel winked into existence.

Daniel's gaze followed the road next to the gas station as it stretched up an incline, practically disappearing into the bent trees and dark clouds. The world beyond it was bizarre to him, simply strange. He had never ventured down that road. Not that he was afraid or anything, but there just seemed to be nothing in that direction, at least nothing good.

Ignoring the road, Daniel passed the regulars sitting in the gas station's open repair garage. The disparity of what he saw always made him chuckle. Each man sat on a different chair, but not a single man nor chair matched the others. Daniel didn't know their actual names, so he'd made up nicknames early on. First there was Belly, a sloppy bear of a man with the swollen belly of a woman eight months pregnant. Across from him stood Stander. Tall, skinny with leathery skin. Well-groomed, and unlike what he'd observed with the other men, he's never once seen Stander sitting down. His namesake was admittedly lazy, but remained a highlight in Daniels's mind.

Then there was Popeye. Apparently Popeye's real name *was* Popeye, at least that's what the other two called him. Daniel liked Popeye the most.

"Howdy, Skip," Popeye piped up, his egg-like frame giggling in his dirty rolling office chair. Popeye christened Daniel "Skip" his very first day on the paper route. Daniel wanted to correct him, but he kinda of didn't mind having a 1950s style nickname. It was cool.

"Hi," squeaked Daniel, almost inaudible as he passed them entering the gas station shop.

Inside, Daniel perused the drinks with hungry eyes. He considered a grape Fruitopia and an uninspired cherry pop before eventually settling on a double blast Choco-Shocko. Hat, the man behind the counter who always wore the same faded red trucker cap and matching plaid work shirt tucked neatly into his Wrangles, counted out Daniel's change with painful patience.

"Ninety-seven...

ninety-eight...

ninety-nine...

...and a dollar." The Hat paused, pulling in a breath, and for a second Daniel was afraid the man had had a heart attack from the strain. In his head, he'd felt himself age a thousand centuries as the Hat had counted. "Have a good day," Hat drawled, "Hope it don't rain on ya too much." He snickered awkwardly, and Daniel tried not to stare at him.

After a few seconds Daniel twitched, mentally shaking off his imaginary Steven Spielberg director's beard. He forced a smile and almost, but not quite, mouthed a "thank you."

Newspaper bag bouncing on his hip with every step, Daniel passed the local fire station. At least, it was called the fire station, although everyone knew it was more like a meeting hall, a place to hold expensive birthday parties (with two beers on tap!), cheap wedding receptions and frequent gun shows, as the current marquee attested.

Just down a gently sloped hill from the fire station resided the trailer park. The sign read, "Trailer Court," but Daniel knew better. Like slapping lipstick on a pig, a trailer park with a fancy name is still a trailer park full of trailer park people. They weren't bad, he knew, just... different. And they certainly weren't anything like the Knights of the Round Table as "Trailer Court" suggested.

Going door to door, Daniel opened screen doors and plopped his papers inside, sometimes simply dropping them on the porch. The papers were always bound in a gum band — the insider's colloquial term for a rubber band — and today had turned out to be windy after all. He needed to make sure the customers didn't open their doors to find an escaping funnel cloud of newspaper shrapnel. Those dropped on the porches were covered in a plastic bag and tied off at the top, ensuring the news stayed crisp and dry and ready for easy reading, just like those neon green sugar-loaded coated Teenage Mutant Ninja Turtles pie pastries at Popeye's.

At the last trailer on the first row sat a fidgety old man. Frankly, Daniel thought referring to him as "old" was being pretty dang generous. The man looked more like a pale prune than a person, save for his tan shorts, flowered shirt and matching hat. In all honestly, Daniel thought he kind of looked more like an oversized, dehydrated baby.

He knew him as Old Man Mumbles, because he didn't really speak so much as mumble word salad that Daniel interpreted as utter and complete nonsense. Next to Old Man Mumbles stood a Valley Bugle box attached to a pole. The box matched Daniel's newspaper bag perfectly, bold white letters against a denim blue.

"Here ya go," said Daniel, inserting a paper firmly inside the box. The instant he removed his hand the old man leapt up with surprising speed. Daniel yelped and flinched back, watching the man retreat to his chair, ignoring him as he sat back down with audible snaps, crackles, and pops. Quickly scanning through the pages, Old Man Mumbles mumbled to the world around him, a sly smile forming on his face.

What the heck was that about...

Daniel made his way to the main road next to two small man-made ponds and stopped, reaching into one of five rectangular plastic newspaper boxes. Unlike the Valley Bugle box, these were substantially larger, sturdier and bright, fire engine red. You couldn't ignore them if you tried. On the side, the words "USA Gazette" practically screamed, "I'm a big deal! Pay attention to me!" Removing the much larger national newspaper, Daniel stuffed it in his back alongside his Choco-Shocko.

Above the boxes stood a sign, overly ornate, unnecessarily opulent and completely out of place. It read "VALETTO LANE" in firm capital letters. Moments later, at the end of

Valetto Lane, Daniel was preparing to drop a newspaper when he suddenly sensed someone beside him. He squeaked and stumbled backwards, losing his footing and sitting awkwardly on the pavement.

Looking up, all five feet of Mrs. Valetto now hovered over him. "Oh! Dear! You scared me!" she croaked.

Daniel hid his skepticism. It took a heck of a lot more than him to scare that old bird. She didn't bother helping him to his feet, but fixed her wig and wrinkled her face, pouting her lips and flexing her cheeks, testing the layers upon layers of caked on makeup.

Truthfully, he had fallen less because he was surprised and more because he was freaked out. Afraid. Afraid of *her*. He couldn't explain why, exactly, but he thought it might have something to do with the utter artifice with which she existed. She was alive, for sure, but it was as if she somehow wasn't really *real*.

Propping himself back to his feet, newspaper in hand, Daniel extended it to her as if warding off a specter with a fiery torch. "Here you go," he said, forcing a smile. "Have a nice day, Miss Valetto."

"*Miss!*" she beamed as she took the paper from his hand. "Ooohhh, I like that! You, too! Take 'er easy!" He words came out as gruffly and abruptly as she turned and walked away from him.

Regrouping at the top of the hill in the center of the trailer park, Daniel shook off his anxiety over his Valetto experience. On the porch of a particularly neglected trailer sat a garbage bag with a hastily written note taped to it. He picked up the note and instantly recognized Peggy Hart's handwriting. He frowned. Why did such an awful person get the gift of such a cool 80s pop-star last name? Was she even related to Corey? He doubted she even owned a pair of sunglasses.

"'*This is how I find it all over my yard! I want a refund.*'"

Daniel read aloud. He snickered. "She spelled 'refund' wrong."

"Oh, did I?"

Daniel jolted, nearly dropping the note as his eyes shot up to the door.

"Sorry I'm not as smart as a *paperboy*," said a corpulent greasy woman standing at the door, brushing back her femullet.

"I... I didn't mean..."

"Got today's paper." It wasn't a question. She reached over and yanked the note out of Daniel's shaking hand.

"I'm real sorry about yesterday's paper," he said. "The screen door was locked." His mind scrambled to come up with a believable excuse. "The gum band musta snapped or something..."

Peggy ignored his apology. "S'posed to be something about my sweet little baby boy today," she said, holding out her hand impatiently. Daniel dug out a newspaper and started to hand it to here when she snatched it away from him. "Come on, already! Don't wanna be standing on the porch with the *paperboy* all day."

"I think it's on the front..." Daniel mumbled sheepishly.

"The front cover! Oh my! And the news men from channels Four and Eleven are comin' later! I'm gonna need to go to the beauty parlor." She frowned. "I think that Joann woman has a little shop in her house now." She absently brushed back her femullet.

"Have a good day, Mrs. Hart," Daniel said, backing away from the porch.

"*Miss* Hart," she corrected. "Don't you forget my refund, or I'll call and report your poor service n'at. I swear to *God* I will."

"O-okay..."

"The Better Business Bureau will know your name!"

Daniel had no idea what she was talking about, but it

frightened him as he briskly walked away, eyes wide and on the brink of tears. A few doors down and with Miss Hart and her trailer behind him, he finally breathed a sigh of relief.

"Miss Hart, Miss Hart," he repeated to himself.

A yapping terror's barking interrupted his self-correction. The mini grey Scottish terrier paced and woofed behind a white picket fence while an older man sat behind him on the porch, shirtless. The Smoking Man smiled at Daniel as he adjusted his oxygen mask to take a drag from his cigarette.

"Hey, Cosmo," Daniel said to the dog. He didn't know the man's name, so The Smoking Man had stuck early on.

Snuggly folding the newspaper, Daniel reached over the fence and gingerly placed it in the dog's mouth. Wagging its tail proudly, the Cosmo delivered the newspaper to the Smoking Man's open hand. The Smoking Man haphazardly removed the now-wet-and-partially-shredded newspaper from the Cosmo's tiny-but-firmly-clenched jaws.

Waving good-bye, Daniel plodded along to the doublewide, the largest, least appealing of all the trailers in the park. The yard, as abused and neglected as the house, remained littered with secondhand children's toys. Three young kids — Vera with pigtails and a dirty round face; Chucky with a buzzed head and green Power Rangers t-shirt barely covering his tighty-whities; and Burt, with massive, framed-taped glasses that were obviously the wrong prescription — ran around the yard in a frantic state of play. The chaos of it all always overwhelmed Daniel, so much so that he experienced a tightness in his chest as he passed them and stepped up to the the front porch.

Burt stopped, glaring at Daniel for a moment before returning to his siblings. Chucky smashed one of Vera's toys with a rock, the sound of splintering plastic mingling with her shrill wailing. Moments later they were chasing each other around the yard, Vera seeking vengeance for the broken toy.

Daniel felt bad for the kids, but he honestly kind of felt worse for the toy.

"What a waste," he muttered, looking back at the graveyard of broken toys.

"What's a waste?"

Daniel blinked and looked up to see Sheila standing next to him. He'd been completely oblivious to her arrival, and made a mental note to stop talking to himself and *especially* to cut back on making audible action noises.

Sheila was borderline cute, despite her bad teeth, and Daniel found her downright adorable, just shy of hot. She was thin but not awkwardly skinny. A tad taller than him, and had short, shoulder-length strawberry-blonde hair. She smiled at him, bad teeth front and center in their full glory.

"Nothing," he said, blushing.

"Nothing?" she asked.

"I meant… well… I was talking about the *toys*," Daniel gestured back to the apocalyptic technicolor wasteland.

"They break *everything*…" She leaned over on the porch railing, then locked her eyes on his. "…Paper Boy."

The pause held.

Daniel broke it. "Hi."

"I like your sweatshirt," she mused.

He looked down and examined his chest. *What was she talking about?* His shirt wasn't impressive. It was *old*. "Oh thanks," he said casually. "It was… my brother's."

"Burt! Chucky! Vera!" Sheila shouted past him. One by one, the kids stopped moving as they heard their names called. "Cut it out! And clean up that mess!" She gestured with a pointed finger across the yard.

"So, what can I do for you, Daniel? Or did you just come up here so you could talk to me?" She smiled, and he instinctively looked away from those unfortunate teeth.

Digging into his bag, Daniel pulled out his collection

booklet and held it up like a badge. "I'm here to collect," he announced.

He wasn't. He just thought it would make him seem somewhat more important at the time. The regret was instant, as he realized it had been the exact wrong thing to say.

The color drained out of Sheila's face. "Oh. Hang on. I'll ask my mom."

After she disappeared inside the house, Daniel watched the kids lazily clean up the mess around them, complaining to each other incessantly. Ignoring them, he turned around, propped himself up on his toes a few inches and peeked into the house. Inside, Sheila argued with a woman he assumed was her mother. Chubby with bad posture, the frumpy woman with a mushroom shaped haircut flailed her hands in exasperation and fled deeper into the house. Sheila sighed and returned to the doorway, defeated. She leaned into it and pouted at him.

"Sorry," she said. "Mom's not home."

Daniel smiled, ignoring the lie. He didn't know why, but he accepted the blatantly obvious lie as truth. "That's okay."

"Come back in two weeks and we'll have the money. I swear to God." Her eyes softened. "Will you do that? Come back to see me in two weeks?"

"Ah, yeah. That's cool," he stammered.

"Thanks. You're a sweetheart, Daniel." She raised her arm as if to squeeze his shoulder before quickly pulling her hand back in embarrassment. "My birthday's coming up," she blurted.

"Congratulations," he blurted in return.

"I'm going to have a party," she didn't say it, but her eyes and her broad smile offered an invitation.

He nodded as he felt his face flush and started walking down the steps to the sidewalk. Daniel expertly pushed down any and all feelings as he exited the yard, giving Sheila a final wave before continuing his route.

A minute later Daniel found himself standing next to a man he could have sworn was at least two hundred years old. The Ancient Man, as Daniel thought of him, with a trailer and yard that were equally immaculate. The Ancient Man rolled his dip around his mouth and spat out a large wad of black bile onto the pavement between them.

"Good boy!" The Ancient Man chortled in a heavy Russian accent. "Bring my USA paper?"

Daniel extended an arm, weighted down heavily by the massive national paper as he glanced down at the spit wad. Examining its murky, gooey surface, he envisioned it as a treacherous alien world. "Here it is," he said, extending his arm. "An' it's heavy today!"

"Good boy! Good boy! Always you bring me USA paper!" As he spoke, The Ancient Man pulled out a crisp one-dollar bill along with four shiny new quarters and traded them with Daniel for the paper. "Out of dollar bills. Only quarters today. Good for the machine arcade, yes!"

"Yeah, *Street Fighter*!"

"No!" The Ancient Man snapped, placing a rigid hand on Daniel's shoulder. "No, no. Go *inside* arcade, no fighting in street. As child I fight in street, many scar." He gestured up to his face, but Daniel saw no scars.

Bewildered, he continued on his way a few steps before suddenly stopping. "Almost forgot your Valley," he said, handing him the small local paper.

"Good boy! Never you forget! Never no fighting!" He meant it. He obviously didn't feel confident in his English, so Daniel quickly gathered the man only said things he really and truly meant.

Daniel nodded and backed away until he turned and continued walking around the bend, stepping carefully along the edge of the road. His oversized boots crushed into the crumbling edge of pavement, turning it to gravel and blending into the dirt. Down below the bend the trees nestled around the houses encasing the road and the trailers with dark shadows.

At the point where the curved road reconnected to the main road sat the second oldest and ugliest trailer in the park. The once opulent indigo trailer now resembled little more than a debris covered, oversized gray coffin. The yard, littered with overgrowth, car and motorcycle parts, hadn't been cut down or tended to in years. This is how Cowboy lived.

A big brown delivery truck rushed past Daniel, and he yelped at how close it was. Brakes squealed to a stop a few feet in front of him and Bill — or as Daniel named him, Big Bill — hopped out of the truck. Daniel looked at Big Bill and blinked. He didn't mean to stare, but, well, Bill was *really* big, and black. In fact, he was the only black person Daniel actually knew in his white bread community.

Bill didn't like being stared at, but he resigned himself to the reality of it after a while. He was also somewhat sympathetic to a kid weaving his way through a complicated world. The man effortlessly heaved a massive box out of the back of the truck and Daniel slowed to a crawl, not so much interested in Big Bill as he was the mystery of the box. Daniel himself rarely got mail, so mail was kind of a big deal to him, particularly the a package was big enough that Big Bill's big guns were needed to deliver it.

A flicker of motion in the yard ahead of Daniel, followed by an car hood thumping closed. Behind the car stood, Cowboy. Burly, greasy and balding, tattooed arm to ear, and always smiling beneath a horseshoe mustache. A good two feet shorter than Big Bill, Cowboy appeared to be just as strong as he as he approached the man, easily taking the wide, oversized box as Bill handed it over.

"Thanks, man," he said, maintaining his smile. Ignoring Big Bill, Cowboy tore into the massive box, ripping the card board asunder, revealing the unmistakable markings of a ping pong table. Daniel was fascinated, yet found himself surprisingly disappointed.

Big Bill coughed and tapped his clipboard. "I'll need ya to sign. Right here." He pointed to the line, and Cowboy obliged.

Heading back to his truck, Bill spotted Daniel and grinned. "Hey, Daniel! Haven't seen you in a long time."

Daniel shrugged. "Yeah, my mom doesn't let me order as many comics and…" He stopped himself as he realized he was about to say the word *toys*. "..stuff." He added.

Bill saw right through him, but he didn't judge. "That's too bad. Keep workin' hard," he said, leaping into his still running truck. "Tell your folks I said hello, yeah?"

Daniel nodded. He watched as the truck growled into gear and lumbered up the hill.

"You got an extra?"

Cowboy stood a few feet away on the other side of the fence, interrupting Daniel's drifting thoughts.

"Sorry, mister…"

The man lifted his hand, palm out, displaying a feather headdress tattooed in the center of his palm. "Call me Cowboy." He said it with inexplicable self-confidence, especially for a man who looked to be the antithesis of a genuine Cowboy.

"I-I don't have any extras," Daniel stammered. "Sorry, sir." He couldn't bring himself to say Cowboy. It just seemed weird and felt a bit offensive.

Cowboy shook his head and smiled. "No problem, brother."

"You could subscribe," Daniel offered, now acting like a halfhearted pitch man. "Have one every day."

"Nah. Can only afford the free ones," the man said, and to Daniel it sounded like genuine sadness in his voice. "Enjoy your walkin'."

Daniel nodded and started walking away.

"You like ping-pong?"

Cowboy's words sounded strange, forcing Daniel to stop and turn around. He eyed the gigantic box Bill had dropped off, easily worth a buttload of newspapers.

"Nope, I think it's kind of dumb," Daniel admitted, perhaps a little too honestly. Lost in his music and mind, Daniel failed to see the grimace on Cowboy's face as he turned and walked away.

At the neighboring trailer, a glowing white trailer with a pop of red trim, Daniel stepped onto the porch. Larger than most others in the park, it had a large, covered seating area. There sat the woman Daniel knew as The Sweetest Old Lady Ever. In her late sixties, she sat there, knitting in peace, surrounded by at least five cats. Each one remained permanently attached to the porch by way of string tied to their collars.

"Would you like something to drink?" she offered.

"Oh," Daniel said as he dug out a newspaper, surrounding him, the cats, watching him with curious eyes. "No, thank you."

"Milk?"

Daniel petted the nearest cat, "No, thank you. I'm good." "Hi," he added, petting the next nearest cat.

"Ginger ale," she said.

Daniel frowned. Wow, but this lady was persistent. "I'm good, thanks."

"No," she said, grinning. "That's her name. Ginger Ale."

"Oh! That's… unusual. I like it."

"But I *do* have ice cold ginger ale," she sang.

"Not today, thank you," Daniel said, making a hasty retreat from her porch. "Enjoy your paper." He avoided looking back, knowing he'd disappointed her by turning down her invitations. He felt a sense of dread and shame, as if he'd somehow be punished by the universe for not spending more time with her.

I like this job. Thought Daniel. He knew that eventually, he'd need a higher paying job to by the truly valuable comic books. But if he could, he'd have been content to be a paperboy forever, at least until he turned 30. You only work an hour a day, give or take, depending how fast you walk, and you get to meet dogs. Not a bad gig. However, somewhere deep in the bowels of his soul, Daniel knew that could never be. Financial realities of buying *Amazing Fantasy* number 15 aside, he had a sense that somehow, someway, one of these people would change his life forever.

CHAPTER 3
THE WOODS

Dragging himself up the steep incline of the hill, Daniel slipped in the wet grass and almost sprawled onto his back. Turns out duck boots kept feet plenty dry but weren't built for hiking up hills. The fine mist of a rain had slowly transitioned into a burgeoning deluge with every passing second. Cresting the hill, at the absolute steepest part made up of a virtual wall of weeds, Daniel climbed the ancient concrete block steps. Some of the blocks shifted underfoot, but most of them held firm in the softening ground.

Atop the hill, he celebrated his victorious climb with a good shake of his Choco-Shocko. The rain intensified as if in response, but the moment of celebratory bliss soon turned to one of fear as Daniel spotted movement down the hill.

"Aw, crap," he whispered.

Walking up the street were the duo of dumb punks. Trailer park bullies, local hoodlums from Daniel's class. The first one a chub of evil in a too-tight Metallica shirt. Daniel's nickname? Porkins. Like the unfortunately-named X-Wing pilot who couldn't help Luke destroy the Death Star. And beside Porkins, his crony, if you will — Glasses. Glasses was a slightly taller and skinnier version of Porkins, and today wore a motocross shirt. Of course, he had never said these nicknames aloud to anyone *ever*, and vowed he never would. It would be the Death of Daniel, and he knew it.

Oblivious to him, the bullies heaved large hunks of rock and concrete into a large puddle formed from the now vacant foundation where a trailer once resided. Trying to sink down lower among the weeds, Daniel failed in his attempt to avoid them. He'd never wanted to be Ant-Man more than ever before in his life. What he would've have given to get a hold of some Pym particles...

"Paper booooy... Come out to plaaayyy," taunted Glasses, inadvertently referencing a movie he probably hadn't even seen. Porkins stomped up to where Daniel stood as Glasses continued his taunts. "You shouldn't take the steps. Them steps are for people who live in the trailer—"

"Court only!" screamed Porkins, now just a few feet from Daniel.

Daniel smirked, a laugh squeaking out.

"What are you laughing for?" Porkins shoved Daniel.

"At," corrected Daniel, regaining his footing.

"Huh?"

"At. What am I laughing at."

"Well?" asked Porkins. Another shove. Harder.

"It's cute," Daniel said, regretting it instantly.

If he could be likened to any bug-based superhero, it certainly wasn't Ant-Man, or even one of the Micronauts. No, it'd be Spider-Man, not because of his super abilities, but because of his sarcasm. And he was technically an arachnid-based hero, so—

"We ain't cute!" growled Porkins.

"Why you laughin'?" snapped Glasses.

"Because you finish each other's sentences. That's kind of the definition of a cute couple." Despite himself, Daniel found himself locked into full-on Spider-Man mouth mode.

The bullies looked at each other first with disgust, and

then a contempt that bordered on hate. Peter Parker, Hank Pym, even Scott Lang, and every other bug-related superhero be damned. Daniel now wished he had the power set of Sue Storm, The Invisible Woman.

Porkins huffed and started circling Daniel, like a feral animal pacing before an oncoming attack. He kicked the ground at his feet, a few rocks danced with him. Bending down in gleeful rage, he scooped up a handful of rocks, young plumber's crack in full glory. Joining him, Glasses knelt and retrieved some stones. They said nothing, but Daniel could sense unspoken sinister plans were being laid. A pair of remedial Dr. Dooms plotting world conquest.

The first rock fell harmlessly a few feet in front of Daniel, and he laughed internally. Doom's dastardly death ray done missed its target.

Porkins tossed up a smooth stone, catching it, repeating the process without a word. Glasses lobbed another, this one landing a few feet closer to Daniel, and he didn't laugh this time.

Porkins giggled. Dr. Doom would have laughed maniacally, but Daniel got the point. This wasn't good.

"Those are our steps. *Not yours*," commanded Porkins. The teasing had slowly morphed into full-fledge venom, and nothing but carnage was sure to follow.

The stones continued to come, each one landing closer and closer to where he stood. Daniel froze. Whether it was out of courage or rage or stupidity, he opened his mouth once again. "People in glass trailers shouldn't throw stones!"

Darn those Spider-Man instincts.

"Fruit factory!" yelled Glasses.

Daniel *thought* he knew what those words meant, but he concluded he actually had no idea what Glasses meant by them.

A lone stone hit Daniel's rubber boot, bouncing off and glancing off his leg. Porkins burst into hyena-like laughter.

"Duck boots!" he cackled through his laughter. "How much of a fruit are you?!"

"Fruit! Fruit boots!" blared Glasses.

"It's raining!" snapped Daniel in a practical rage. "It's muddy. The grass is wet. They keep my feet dry!" He tried and failed to tamp down his anger and fear.

"No," corrected Porkins, shaking his head, "it's 'cause you're a *fruit!*"

"Pumpkin peach!"

Daniel glanced at Glasses and frowned. He really didn't know what that one meant, but the words struck him like a punch, puncturing the inner spectrum of untethered rage. They were making him angry, and they wouldn't like him when he got angry. He hoped.

No longer showing any restraint, Porkins threw a rock at Daniel's arm. Flailing to avoid the impact, Daniel dropped his Choco-Shocko. It caught on a jagged rock, an explosion of rich brown deliciousness in every direction. He stared at it, dumbfounded, until a second stone hit against the side of his head.

Daniel looked up, stunned and wide eyed. Through the tears welling up and clouding his hazel eyes he saw Glasses, body leaning forward from the motion of his throw. A small trickle of blood began to stream down Daniel's forehead, mingling with the intensifying rain.

Porkins and Glasses and Daniel all stared at each other, equally stunned at what had just happened. None of them could believe it. A second later, bursting with Wolverine ferocity, Daniel rushed forward, charging into and through Glasses.

Glasses yelped but it was too late. Knocked off balance, he landed hard on his butt, covered in mud and soaking in the center of a huge puddle.

Daniel stood over him, eyes wild and growing wider, mouth agape. He found himself suspended in the moment, consumed by his fear but simultaneously impressed with what he'd done. He hadn't planned on that, and honestly didn't know what to do next. Roar? Scream at him in feral rage?

Instinctively, Daniel lowered his arm, unfurling his fist and extending his hand to help the bully up.

Glasses swore and spat at Daniel. He swatted at Daniel's open palm but missed. Pushing himself back to his feet, Glasses walked away and rejoined Porkins.

As if the world slowed to a standstill, Daniel now knew exactly what to do next. He hauled it out of there.

As his boots pounded the pavement and the rain poured, the enraged and embarrassed bullies pursued. Jumping from one comic book universe to the next, Daniel mentally became Quicksilver before settling on The Flash. Turning on the virtual afterburners, he headed for the cornfield behind the trailer park, the only place he stood a chance of losing those two.

Porkins and Glasses soon gave up their chase, but continued to lob rocks up the street, each one falling far short of their mark.

"Run, Forrest! Run!" shouted Porkins.

"Forrest fruit" echoed Glasses.

"Forrest fruit!"

"Go eat them pumpkin peaches!!"

The rain intensifying, Daniel pushed through the corn, wondering for the life of him what Glasses was babbling about. Pumpkin peaches weren't a thing. Were they?

Soon he found himself in an unknown section of forest, safely out of range, where he paused to rest. Darkness, the weather, and an accelerated heart rate overtook Daniel as he looked over his shoulder and took a few more steps before stumbling into a thicket.

Even in the dense and dark forest, the rainfall continued, alternating between the varied cover of trees above. He took a step forward and stopped, leg locked in place. Deep mud held Daniel's left foot back, and he nearly fell over face-first before righting himself. He tugged at his left leg, finally wrenching it free. Minus the boot.

"Awww, man..."

He gingerly took a step back into the boot, lodged his foot and resumed his efforts. After a few more seconds he felt he was going to be able to ease it out, boot and all.

"1... 2... 3!" he grunted. Both foot and boot came free, but as he took a step forward he realized all too late that his other leg was equally locked down. As he fell forward, he had the presence of mind to twist in the process, assuming it would be better to land on his back than end up with both arms and a leg stuck in the mud.

He landed with a wet splat, cold mud and water splattering his head and neck, running in thin, chilled rivulets down his shirt.

Daniel's face screwed up as the evening's frustration burst forth, and as much as he fought back the tears, they were coming, whether he liked them or not. He sucked in a large breath, preparing to scream into the heavens when he froze, eyes wide, staring up at the sky.

What... is that?

Despite the rain, his mouth suddenly felt parched, and as he swallowed it was like a cheese grater in his throat. Above him, something was swinging from side to side, twisting in the wind and rain. The light was fading, but there's was no mistaking the silhouette or the shiver that ran through Daniel's soul as his eyes locked on it.

Somebody was in the tree above him.

Hanging from the tree.

CHAPTER 4
THE BODY

Daniel scrambled backwards, pulling himself out of the mud, leaving his other boot firmly entrenched. His back pressed against the nearest tree trunk as his eyes remained locked on the tree ahead of him.

And the body.

It was a person, but small. A child?

Daniel swore quietly, shaking his head.

It was. It looked like it was a small boy! Daniel was never any good at judging ages, and he'd resigned himself years ago to the fact that he would never work at a carnival. But then again, maybe being bad at guessing ages would assure him a carnival job, if they were desperate.

Giving his best estimate, he guessed the boy to be around five years old. Six at the most. The boy's motionless body dangled at the end of the rope, making lazy circles over the ground, the logo of his sneaker dancing in the rain.

Mustering his courage, Daniel found his fascination to be irresistible. He stepped closer to the body, retrieved his water-logged boot from the mud, and gently tugged at the boy's leg. He pulling back slightly and then let go. The body swung away and returned, making a slow pirouette in the air until he faced away from Daniel. The tension of the wire around the boy's neck was heavy, and he couldn't help but wince at how it seemed to dig into the mottled skin. How long had he been here? Days? *Weeks?*

Climbing a nearby tree, Daniel positioned himself on a limb and sat across from the boy, trying to get a better look despite the rainfall. The boy's jacket caught a gust of wind, and the unmistakable, four-color world of The Fabulous Thunder Family greeted Daniel.

"No way."

Daniel slipped, clutching the tree trunk with both hands, steadying himself. It definitely wouldn't hurt to be Spider-Man right about now, more for stickiness than for sarcasm. He narrowed his eyes to get a better look. On the boy's shirt, the image of The Family were gathered around the joyous Grim, proud to be a newly accepted member of the team, a part of the family. The scene was famous! Originally published as the fourth cover to the original series, it soon became a famous poster, one which hung on Daniel's wall.

And now on the shirt of a Corpse Boy.

CRACKOW!

So bright you could almost see the sound effect written across the sky, the lightning struck and the resulting thunder rumble roared in response almost instantaneously. Daniel yelped and fell backward out of the tree, landing with a muddy *plop*! His boots plunged deep in the mud. Flinging himself backward he freed both feet, but only one boot. A newly-christened diminutive Swamp Thing, soaking wet and utterly covered in mud, Daniel retrieved his delivery bag and ran.

The eyes of the boy — the Corpse Boy — combined with the echoes of the bullies' taunts, chased after Daniel inside his head, spurring him home.

Run, Forrest! Run!

Forrest fruit!

Eat them Pumpkin Peaches!

At home, a telltale trail of mud and discarded clothing followed Daniel to his bed. The green sweatshirt, old blue jeans and remaining duck boot piled in a heap on the floor. Mac groaned as he climbed into bed, but Daniel ignored him. At least *he* would sleep well. Under the sheets Daniel curled tightly into a ball to warm himself, forcing his eyes shut, squeezing them so hard they forced themselves open from the tension.

Stop it, Stop it, Stop it! Shut already!

Unable to keep his eyes shut, Daniel threw the sheet off and stared at the ceiling, eventually allowing his eyes to explore the room. He took in his toys arranged on shelves, next to his array of posters. His blood ran cold when he came across the massive poster reprint — The Fabulous Thunder Family #4.

Crap…

Letting his eyes drop, he looked at his beloved officially licensed Nintendo toy chest. All sides were adorned with Nintendo characters. On top, it featured Super Mario Bros., the back Metroid, the sides, The Legend of Zelda, and the top all of the characters in one epic mini-crossover. However, tonight he couldn't see the epicness of that crossover.

Tonight, atop the chest sat The Corpse Boy.

Daniel swallowed, his throat burning with bile. Closing his eyes gently, careful not to squeeze them so tight they'd open, Daniel wished the boy away in his mind. After fifteen seconds, he opened one and stared across the room.

The Corpse Boy remained, aloof and silent, only eye remained closed, swell shut and occasionally twitching. The other glared at Daniel.

CHAPTER 5

ME & MY SHADOW

The sunlight cascaded through yawning trees, the trunks groaning with the wind. Amber brilliance exploded through the windows of the bus, pummeling the faces of the sleepy students on board, as their droopy eyes, yawns and collective moans sounded off in response. Sitting silently by himself, Daniel admired trees. The forest normally offered him reprieve, the distraction of imagination, a.k.a. the strongest force in the universe, but today he was struggling. Even adding audible sound effects and narration didn't work. For the first time in recorded history, his vivid imagination lost to reality, as the Corpse Boy sat next to Daniel, very dead and yet very real.

The boy looked out the window with him. And smiled. Daniel had to admit, for a ghost nobody else seemed to see, he was a rather pleasant boy. Creepy, what with the one large eye, but pleasant nonetheless.

Once Daniel arrived in homeroom, where his fellow students silently lumbered in, he dragged his feet to the back of the room. The Corpse Boy followed along every step of the way, even when Daniel took his seat. He stood next to him, looking bored and unsure of himself. Daniel's eyes avoided him, darting about the rest of the room, seeking someone, *anyone* else but the undead friend beside him.

"Danimal!"

The voice could have come from a baby monkey, it was so squeaky and high. He didn't need to look up to know that baby monkey had a name, and that name was Jimmy. Jimmy had been Daniel's best friend pretty much since they were babies, as their dads were buddies who played football together in high school. It was like they were destined disappoint their dad's and hang out.

Jimmy hurried back to Daniel, occupying the exact spot where Corpse Boy had previously stood. Flabbergasted, Daniel searched the room, glancing from corner to corner and finally under his desk.

Gone.

Corpse Boy was finally gone!

Jimmy, already prepared to give a speech he'd undoubtedly rehearsed on the bus, didn't notice his friend spastically searching the area.

"Okay," Jimmy said excitedly, "I'll give you the Pete Pham autographed Merkanary card, but I want all your *Vigilance: Night Journal* and *Vigilance: Night Watch* comics. And I want to look through your issues of *Valor Vendetta* again."

Daniel didn't hear a word, still scanning the room.

"But I don't want that crappy Wild CATs hologram cover. The corner's bent."

Jimmy stopped and waited for a response. Eyes narrowed as he watched his friend's head swivel from left to right like he was having a slow motion seizure.

"Danimal?" he asked.

No response.

"*Daniel!*"

Daniel looked up at him for the first time since he'd begun talking. He glanced at Jimmy's flailing hands and noticed a crumpled paper with chicken scratch notes. "Did you write a speech?" he asked.

"Dude. Did you hear a word I just said?"

"Uhhhh…"

"The Valor comics?"

Daniel glared at Jimmy. "What?"

Jimmy tried again. "The Spawn comics?"

"Oh. No, no, no," Daniel said firmly, returning to his normal self, now that Corpse Boy was gone. "No Spawn and none of the Valor comics. And I didn't bend the corner, by the way, *you* did!"

Jimmy snarled. "But—"

"That's why I want you to take the stupid thing."

Holding up his hands in mock innocence, Jimmy attempted a more diplomatic approach. "I didn't do it! I didn't! It was my stupid brother."

"Your brother?"

"Yeah!"

Daniel frowned. "Look, when I let you borrow my stuff, I'm trusting you to take care of it!"

"I know, I know…"

"So I don't care if your brother bent it or your dog barfed on it or someone sneezed on it. It was your fault. Period."

"Fine!" Jimmy conceded at least a small element of defeat. "I'll take it."

"Yes, you will."

"But… you didn't mean that, did you?" Jimmy asked. "About the whole dog barf thing? That'd be pretty gross, and I think even you would—"

"Yeah, okay," Daniel admitted. "I got a little carried away there. But no *Valor*," he added. He had long been aware of Jimmy's looming scheme to get them. "And definitely *not* Spawn."

Jimmy moaned in despair.

"But I'll give you all my *Main Title Classics* doubles."

"Volume one and two?" negotiated Jimmy, one eyebrow raised in hopeful expectation.

"Only one."

"Deal!" He extended his hand. Daniel ignored it.

"Hey," Daniel said, "After school, can you come over? Help on my paper route?"

"No can do. Dentist appointment," Jimmy said, pointing to his mouth. "Maybe tomorrow?"

"I guess," Daniel said, visibly upset.

The late bell rang and Jimmy abruptly stopped talking, turned and rushed out of the room. Just before he disappeared, he turned and held up his hand, mimicking a phone next to his ear.

Daniel mouthed, *yeah, I'll call,* and Jimmy was gone.

Looking to his left, his heart skipped a beat when Corpse Boy once again occupied the spot next to Daniel's.

"Geez!" he squeaked, then fell silent when a few other students turned around in their desks to stare at him. He swept a hand across the desk's corner, shaking his head. "Thought I saw a spider," he lied. "Like from *Arachnophobia*."

It worked. They turned around and ignored him again as his eyes widened and he fixed them on the floor ahead of him, trying to figure out how to get through the rest of the day like this. As young as he was, having Corpse Boy creeping him out was going to get really old, really fast.

Later after lunch, Daniel concentrated on walking as normally as possible, not rushing around as if he were some kid being haunted by a zombie Casper nobody else could see. Stride for stride, the Corpse Boy walked alongside him. Daniel's gait was understandably subdued, concerned and somewhat afraid. In stark contrast, The Corpse Boy looked surprisingly chipper and upbeat. At least, for a dead kid.

Sudden movement from his left made Daniel flinch. "I

need to copy your English homework!" Jimmy shouted urgently.

Daniel froze.

He was aware that Jimmy had said something, but that wasn't his focus. No, he was keenly aware that Corpse Boy had instantly vanished once again.

Inside Daniel's head he could almost hear a gear crank against another, generating a bolt of lightning epiphany directly into his brain matter. His eyes lit up, powered by a hopeful hamster in a wheel. Daniel had no clue what Jimmy had said, but he now knew he had to keep Jimmy around. Jimmy meant no Corpse Boy!

"Hey Corsair," said Jimmy, waving a hand in front of Daniel's face in an attempt to disengage the distraction. "Stop piloting the Starjammer already and get back to Earth with your children of the atom."

"Yeah, yeah. Sorry." Daniel smirked. "Havok and Cyclops. I did the assignment."

"No. Cyclops first, *then* Havok," corrected an uppity Jimmy.

Daniel returned a cold hard stare. "The word chart, right?"

"Yeah, can I borrow it?"

"Sure. Hang on," said Daniel digging deep down into his bag. Finding it, he handed the wrinkled page to Jimmy. "Here."

"Thanks! Oh! And your colored pencils," remembered Jimmy.

Sinking his forearm deep into his bag, Daniel sighed in mock exasperation and dug out a bent and battered metal case. "Why don't you buy your own?" he asked as he handed it over.

"Because I don't have *paper boy* money," taunted Jimmy.

"You have money," Daniel said. "You just spend it all on comics."

"*So do you!*" Jimmy protested loudly.

"Yeah… I do!" Daniel smiled; Jimmy had oh-so-foolishly walked right into his trap. "Correction: you spend all your *mom's* money on comics."

"Jerk," muttered Jimmy.

"I'm not a jerk. I'm a truth-teller…" Suddenly Daniel stiffened. "I need your math!"

"Rob's got it," Jimmy said, shaking his head. "you can have it after him."

"What? Rob's not even our friend!" shouted Daniel.

"He is today. Well, my friend, at least." Jimmy turned and darted down the hall. "Thanks again!" he said, waving the paper in the air.

"Don't let your brother bend it!" joked Daniel, watching as Jimmy's tight grip was already marring the page. "And it's Havok *then* Cyclops! At least in terms of not sucking. I mean, Havok is cooler… he's not the one who sucks in this whole scenario."

Jimmy turned and flipped Daniel off, zipping backwards down the hall, middle finger stiff at full salute.

The Corpse Boy materialized on Daniel's right, fading into view. Daniel didn't flinch as violently this time. He'd finally begun to figure this thing out. Kind of a shame Daniel only had Jimmy as his one friend.

"Jimmy!" he squealed as he sprinted after him. "Wait! Wait up!"

Ahead of him, Jimmy stopped and waited for Daniel to catch up, back turned, middle finger still high over his head.

"Jimmy Pendergatz!" a voice roared down the hall. "What are you doing!?"

Daniel and Jimmy both jolted upright as Mr. McCormick approached the two of them. He was a massive, portly man, and one students rarely saw in the hallway. Both boys knew they were in for it.

"Stop goofing around and get to class," Mr. McCormick said before jiggling off, not unlike a slightly more mobile Jabba the Hutt.

The exchange with Mr. McCormick seemed to ground Jimmy and make Daniel's panic contagious. "What's wrong? You didn't finish the assignment?" Jimmy squeaked, eyebrows involuntarily scrunching up in worry.

"No, I did it. I just—"

"Then stop wasting my time!" Jimmy snapped. "I gotta copy this ASAP. Priorities!" Before Daniel could say another word he dashed down the hall and disappeared around the corner.

Daniel sighed. He turned his head to look at the Corpse Boy. The boy grinned at him, his wonky eye staring blankly at Daniel's forehead, like a miniature Joker, minus the purple suit and green hair. It was exponentially awkward, but Daniel tried to force a smile, not knowing if the boy would even care.

▭

IT ENDED up being a long and frustrating day of his failed attempts at not being alone. Daniel stood next to his mom in the kitchen, saying nothing.

"Daniel…" she asked, raising an eyebrow, "Is there a particular reason you're standing so close to me?"

"Because I love you," he mumbled through a mouthful of turkey sandwich.

"Nice try." She smiled, but it wasn't the friendly kind of smile. More like a sneaky taunt. "I'm not taking you."

"It might rain." He glanced outside the window, where it was all sunshine and butterflies, an unseasonably wonderful day. Daniel's shoulders sank.

"It's not going to rain, *Daniel.*"

"A sudden downpour? A flash flood?"

Daniel felt desperate, so he surrendered to his desperation. "If that happens and I drown, you'll think of this conversation and regret it! You will! You don't want a dead son, do you?"

Mom tensed up.

Daniel's face fell, and he stared at his feet, shocked wat what he'd just said. "I'm sorry," he said. He meant it, but he also wanted her to take him on his paper route. Glancing around, he saw no sign of the Corpse Boy, but he was determined to stretch this conversation out as long as possible.

"I am not taking you," she repeated, repressing her pain and returning to some superficial form of herself.

"Then I'll wait for Dad to get home," he insisted, knowing it was a hollow, empty threat. Even as he said the words, they echoed in his own head, like bouncing around an empty cavern.

"Daniel. Get going," she commanded. "I don't want to be getting calls from people asking where their paper is. Yes, it's terrible what happened to that Peggy Hart woman, but I don't need her yelling at me because a gum band broke."

Peggy Hart? Daniel looked around; aside from his mother, he was still alone. He decided to change course, knowing it was far too late to work. "I'm not really feeling good."

"Uh-huh. Sounds more like you're feeling *lazy.*"

"Can you make me another sandwich?" Daniel blinked his eyes, showing off the eyelashes his mother long fawned over.

"I can, but I won't."

Who is this tough woman and what did she do with my mother?

"A Philly cheese steak?" he prodded, genuinely wanting one but utterly unaware of the effort it took to make a peanut butter and jelly sandwich, let alone a Philly cheese steak.

"Daniel!" Her exasperation was palpable.

"Fine!" He gave up, shifting from subdued frustration to outright anger. "You'll have blood on your hands."

"Excuse me?" she snapped.

Daniel stopped. His mouth felt like it was soaked in battery acid. He wanted to apologize, to make things right.

He didn't.

His mother said nothing. She set down the dish she was scrubbing, turned and left the room.

Daniel watched her leave, thinking of the words to say and saying nothing. He looked to his right. The day truly *was* beautiful outside. Could the Corpse Boy feel the sun on his mottled skin? Or was that sensation reserved only for the living?

Corpse Boy appeared between him and the window, ruining his view. Sighing, Daniel lifted a hand and waved sheepish. "Okay, then," he muttered quietly. "Let's go."

A few minutes later they had crossed the bridge and walked past the empty chairs at the gas station. Daniel scowled, looking around him. *Where the heck was everybody?* When he didn't want to be bothered the guys were all over him, peppering him with nonstop questions. But *nooooo*, on the one day he's followed by Sir Dead Kid Pop Eye they're nowhere to be found!

Surely The Hat would be inside, he thought. He wasn't. From the back of the gas station shop emanated the unpleasant sound of a disagreeable bowel movement. Daniel laughed. How could he *not* laugh? Poop was the funniest thing ever at his age, even better when it was accompanied by loud farts.

At the cooler he grabbed himself a Choco-Shocko. Shooting a sideways look to The Corpse Boy, he gestured to the drinks in the case. "My treat."

The Corpse Boy didn't respond.

He shrugged. "Your loss."

On his way out, Daniel stopped by the counter and carefully counted out the exact amount next to the cash register. Another, more pronounced groan came from the nearby bathroom.

"Come on," he said to Corpse Boy. "We really don't want

to be here when that door opens." He paused, catching himself, and tilted his head sideways. "But I guess you wouldn't be around anyway if that happened, would you?"

Corpse Boy stared back at him blankly with his one eye, which somehow seemed larger and more swollen than Daniel had remembered. He shuddered and turned away.

When Daniel grabbed the USA Gazette, Corpse Boy stood with him. Walking near the ponds, no Old Man Mumbles. Just a Corpse Boy. At Cosmo's trailer there was no smoking man in sight. Only a yapping dog… and Corpse Boy.

"Huh. Guess your voodoo doesn't apply to dogs."

The Corpse Boy shrugged, open eye widening just a tad.

Daniel stopped and smiled at him. He wasn't 100% sure, but he was pretty convinced the kid had just made a joke. He liked that.

At the USA Gazette Guy's house, nobody was home. With Corpse Boy watching, Daniel bundled the local paper with the thick national newspaper and placed them in the box.

Struggling up the hill and around the bend, Daniel and the Corpse Boy plodded along side by side in silence. When Daniel walked with care around the bend's edge, so did Corpse Boy, hovering a few feet behind him. Passing Cowboy's trailer, Daniel alone. Walking a bit more around the bend he came upon the trailer of The Sweetest Old Lady Ever. There she sat, knitting on her porch. Daniel smiled out of relief.

"I apologize for asking," Daniel began, "But do you have any more ginger ale?"

She put a hand up to her ear. "Come again?"

"Ginger ale," he said, a little louder.

The Sweetest Old Lady smiles. "Oh, she's around here somewhere," she said, waving her hand about her.

Daniel took a step closer, widening his smile. "No, I mean, could I have a glass of ginger ale today?"

She paused, a smile creeping up on her face. "You say you want some ginger ale? You want a drink?"

He nodded. "Please."

The Sweetest Old Lady popped up out of her seat faster than he ever imagined possible. She walked to him, grabbed hold of his hand and pulled him toward the house.

CHAPTER 6
HISTORY, OR A VERSION OF IT

The trailer was sweet little old lady heaven. She had truly earned the secret nickname Daniel had given her, even thought he'd never said aloud to anyone and never would. But had he said it aloud? She would have most definitely thanked him because that's just who she was.

Porcelain figures and pictures of grandkids filled virtually every available porcelain figure and picture-appropriate nook and cranny. The furniture practically appeared new in terms of wear and tear, but couldn't have been newer than the mid-seventies. Exposed, darkly-stained and heavily varnished wood armrests and plaid cushions felt like burlap sackcloth. It was all a surreal walk through ancient history, from Daniel's limited historical perspective.

Over, under, and around the furniture was a smattering of cats in every size and shape imaginable. The most exertion they offered was flicker of a tail or two in curiosity or annoyance or both. Daniel found it freaky when they actually moved on their own four feet. But he found it equally freaky when they *didn't* move. Maybe even a bit extra freaky, the way they all just stared at him like he was a circus freak and the center of the show. He guessed that wasn't too far off from the truth, based on their perspectives.

Seated at a tiny dining table, Daniel and The Sweetest Old Lady Ever conversed. An ice-cold glass of ginger ale appeared in front of him, the glass itself oozing with condensation, moistening the tablecloth beneath it. Daniel, still fixated on his fear of the returning Corpse Boy, constantly looked around the room for him.

The Corpse Boy wasn't present, but now Daniel wondered if it was the extra human presence or the cats. He'd never seen Corpse Boy around a cat before, so maybe there was something to that. The thought crossed his mind that maybe some of the cats were ghosts themselves, and only Daniel could see them now. He felt his brain matter wither a few inches at the possibility of that.

To be fair, it *had* been a rather insane 24 hours. He envisioned himself twenty years from now, toothless and smoking as he worked a dunk tank somewhere in the Midwest. He'd cackle and cough, taking long and deep drags from from the cigarette. Daniel frowned in disapproval, already ashamed of his future self for smoking. Such a nasty habit. He sighed heavily, attempting to find some relief. By pure dumb luck he fixed his gaze across the room on a picture of three children. The youngest appeared to be roughly the same age as Corpse Boy, at least by Daniel's totally uneducated guess. He felt like a carnival worker with a booming voice, shouting "Step on up an' I'll guess yer age!"

"Oh! My grandchildren," cooed The Sweetest Old Lady Ever, breaking him out of his reverie.

Daniel forced a smile. He wanted to care, but he just didn't. He was a kid, and he really didn't feel like talking about other kids just then. Especially young ones.

"They live in Bradenton, in Florida," she continued, swelling with pride. "With their mother. Their father — my son Lawrence — lives in Erie." Daniel noticed her pride subsided somewhat with the mention of Lawrence's name. "You live up on the hill?" she asked, distracting herself from her own thoughts.

"Mmm-hmmm," Daniel muttered through a swig of fizzling ginger ale glory. He flinched as a cat leapt from a basket up onto the couch. Other cats stirred, but didn't move, simply staring at him as he drank. Pulsing fur did imply breathing, didn't it? Where they actually breathing, or was just part of his imagination? Filling in the blanks with what he *wanted* to see.

Daniel couldn't be sure. Maybe those were the ghosts? Or would the ones frozen in place be the ghosts? Where they all ghost cats? Was he destined to be surrounded by ghosts everywhere he went in life?!

"You know there used to be a school up there." Happier times hid behind her eyes, and it was exactly the distraction Daniel needed.

"Yeah," he said, "my Pap went there."

"I know, I went to primary school with your Grandpap."

"You did?"

She nodded in self-satisfaction, as thought she'd impressed him with her revelation.

In truth, Daniel didn't care. He didn't, but he honestly wanted to, so he forced himself to act like other humans would in this context.

"Really?"

It was a stupid-sounding question, but the best he could come up with. Daniel was perfectly capable of being an Grade A jerk when he wanted to, especially with Jimmy, but he always did his best to be polite and respectful to his elders. Which pretty much included everyone he encountered each day, not counting the one currently haunting him.

"I used to walk to school and my mother would watch me cross over, before the train came." She paused, recalling her own personal history.

"Cross over?" Daniel asked. "I don't understand."

"Back then it was connected, you see. There was no bridge. They dug out the hill for the train. At first it was a tunnel!"

"*A tunnel?*"

Daniel did a spit take, spraying the question and the ginger ale into the air with a fine mist. His interest was piqued. A cat popped up behind the family picture, and then quickly laid back down. She'd hooked him with that last bit. *Now* he cared.

The Sweetest Old Lady Ever nodded and continued. "I would walk across and wave a hankie to my mother when I got to the school door, so she knew I was okay."

"You could see that far?" Daniel furrowed his brow. "What about all the trees?"

She shook her head and smiled. "Oh, there were no trees then."

Daniel didn't believe it. He couldn't even imagine it. For him it was *ancient history's* ancient history.

"Well, there were a few. But not like now," she admitted after seeing Daniel's incredulous look. She continued, hoping she would impress him again. "In those days, this whole trailer park was a farm. My family's farm." She stopped momentarily, swallowing a sadness from her memories. "Then after the war in Korea, there was a drought."

"It didn't rain?" Daniel asked, then felt his face flush. So *stupid! Everybody knows it doesn't rain in a drought! That's what makes it a <u>drought</u>. Duh!*

The Sweetest Old Lady Ever, true to her name, chose to ignore his stupidity. "Everything was so brown then. Now it's all so green."

Two more mystery cats slowly meandered from a partially closed bedroom door. Slender and grey, they arched their backs and stretched in unison, like they were some kind of synchronized simulation. It was both mesmerizing and deeply disturbing. Breaking his gaze from the cats (and his mind from the question of their possible ghoulish nature), Daniel cocked his head and asked, "There were no woods?"

She smiled. She clearly enjoyed talking and having an attentive guest in the house. "There were, it was just…different. It was all different then." The sadness returned, but she wouldn't let it spoil the joy of a conversation. "The Valetto's bought it and tore down the farm and put up these trailers. They sold off some of the land, kept some where they still grow corn there, but I can't imagine why. I lived in the city until my first husband, Richard…" She finally brightened at a happy memory, before her face resumed its sad state. "He passed. But you know what they say, 'a life well lived is always ripe with both joy and sadness.' You can't have one without the other, now, can you?"

Daniel nodded, even though he didn't understand what she meant. "He passed?" asked Daniel, once more trying to sound like he thought an adult would in this situation.

"He died."

"Oh." He felt horrible and only slightly stupider than he had before. He honestly thought she meant he had just missed out on something, like the time Daniel and his brother missed meeting Spider-Man at the Fisher Big-Wheel next to Foodland in Natrona Heights. They arrived just at the end to saw Spider-Man, still in full costume, getting into a banged-up and beaten down Toyota Corolla. It was a punch to the gut, much like how Daniel felt now. "I'm… sorry," he whispered.

She nodded and smiled at him. Despite the words vomiting from his mouth, she still seemed to enjoy talking to him. "It was a long time ago, so very long ago. Richard used to tell me that you always end up back where you are. I never much liked the city. I do like to visit town to go shopping, but I don't care to live there, primarily because of all the city people." She paused and gave him a pointed look.

Daniel squirmed at the comment. The sweetness she exuded didn't totally disappear, but it did diminish. He told himself that's just how things used to be and tried to ignore it.

"They were all born here, you know!" she exclaimed, returning to the previous version of the Sweetest Old Lady Ever.

"In the trailer?" shouted Daniel. He quietly winced inside as how loud his voice was. *What is wrong with me?*

"Oh, heavens no," she laughed kindly. "At North Hills Passavant."

"That's where I was born." Daniel was somewhat surprised he even knew that.

"I was born in the farmhouse." The bigotry was gone, but the sadness returned. "It's gone, but I'm still here," she finished with a defiant flourish.

"Where was the farmhouse?" asked Daniel. He watched as another cat emerged from the bedroom, walking up behind the two grey ones. Jet black, it pushed over and through them and sat, statuesque and serene, staring at him. If this one was a ghost, it was undoubtedly the grim reaper of cats.

"Right behind the ponds." She pointed out past her living room, through her wall, over the hill and down to the ponds. "There weren't two ponds then, just one big one. The Valetto's changed *that*, too." She sounded bitter. Daniel thought she was incapable of such emotions, but at least she wasn't being a bigot right now.

"Mrs. Valetto lives in your old house?" he inquired, trying to sound sympathetic.

"Heavens, no. They tore that rickety old thing down." She looked at his can. "More ginger ale?"

Daniel wiggled the can, liquid sloshing around. "Nope, there's some left

She nodded.

"When did you move back here?"

"1977."

The Holy year. The moment, long, long ago, when history-according-to-Daniel began. "The year *Star Wars* came out!"

"What's *Star Wars*, dear?" She seemed sincere, but she had to be joking. Who didn't at least *know* about *Star Wars*?

She was kidding, right?

"You're kidding right?"

She smiled an honest smile, and Daniel's faded.

She really didn't know.

"I'm sorry dear, I really don't know what you're talking about."

Daniel wanted to grab her by the shoulders, shake her vigorously and scream, "Watch it now!" Instead, he decided to play nice and keep calm, in line with that darn respect your elders stuff he'd always been taught.

"Oh, it's a movie," he said. "You should ask your grandkids about it next time they come to visit. The boys, not the girls. Ask the girls about 90210 or something. Better yet, ask them who's cuter, Zack Morris or A.C. Slater." Daniel was reaching. He clearly knew nothing about girls.

BANG!

A gunshot rang out in the distance, out in the cornfield. A cat hopped down from behind the blinds in a hasty retreat from the sound.

"Darn neighbor," she muttered.

Despite himself, Daniel giggled at darn.

"He always goes winging crows out in the cornfield." Her lips drew tighter. "Not even his corn."

"Or his *crows*," replied Daniel. He didn't intend it to be humorous, but when he heard the words he found it funny.

A crow squawked, followed by a louder, closer *bang*! Then silence.

"Have you seen *The Crow*?" asked Daniel, breaking the silence, fully knowing she hadn't.

"I don't much care for crows," she responded, eyes towards the window.

"It's a movie."

"Like *Star Wars*?"

Again, Daniel wanted to grab her by the shoulders, shake her and scream, "Watch it now!"

"No, I mean it's a movie, yeah, but kind of a scary one." Daniel began his speech. "*Star Wars* is a fun one, even though Yoda is a little creepy when he says, 'you will be.' Maybe you'd prefer Gary in *Young Zombie*."

She appeared profoundly disinterested.

"He's a friendly zombie," said Daniel. "It's a comic book."

She turned up her nose a bit.

"Frank's also in *Young Zombie*," he said, attempting to justify his zombie love. "He not a zombie, he's a ghost, but he slowly rots away throughout the story. It's gross, but comically gross, it's a funny comic."

"Is *The Crow* a drama?" she asked breaking the momentary silence.

"It is…dramatic," Daniel admitted. "You see, he's dead, but back in his dead body, an' he kills everybody who killed him and his wife. The real actor was Brandon Lee, Bruce Lee's son. He actually died before they finished the movie, but they finished it anyway."

"Oh my. It sounds absolutely dreadful!" She wasn't judging him, but she obviously didn't have much appreciation for dramatic dead people. "I only watch the news, and my stories. *Guiding Light* is my favorite, but I also like the ones on channel eleven."

Guiding Light! A renewed connection. "I watch that with my mom. Well, in the summer. During the school year I can't, obviously," lamented Daniel. "I have to deliver the papers."

She glanced up at a shelf. The elaborate glass dome clock spun and rotated. "You could watch Guiding Light now, but I'm rather enjoying our conversation." She sighed heavily, dramatically. "It's so quiet most of the time. I'm all alone you know."

Daniel fought back tears. Not for her, though. Sure, he felt bad for her, but not enough to actually cry about it. No, his own fear of being alone with Corpse Boy again was enough to make his eyes well up.

"I'm *never* alone anymore," he admitted, unsure if he sounded crazy or not. He probably *was* crazy, even if he wasn't, which he was pretty sure he totally was. Maybe even *carnival* crazy.

Across the room a small all gray cat with white paws hoped up onto a plastic cover armchair. The cat loafed, staring at Daniel its tail flipping about. Upon it's otherwise gray face, a spot of white beneath its left eye.

Emboldened by her genuine love and kindness, Daniel continued. "I mean, I *feel* like I'm never alone." Daniel wanted to say more, but a cat bumped his leg and distracted him, nudging him for attention. He obliged with a soft pat to its head.

"When I'm alone I like to keep the TV on," she said as a tear escaped one eye. "Makes it feel like people are around, like the kids are still here. Sometimes..." She paused. "Sometimes I'll even put on the children's programs on QED."

Daniel scooped the cat off the ground and placed it in his lap where it made itself comfortable. It was very solid and very much not a ghost. A zombie? Maybe.

"Like Sesame Street or Mr. Rogers?" he asked.

"And Lamb Chop!" she threw in, as though she were singing the lyrics to a song only she heard.

Daniel scooted upward in his chair prompting the cat to leap away. "I'm not sure that'll work for me, turning on the TV. I just want to *feel* like I'm alone. For real."

"You want to feel alone?"

He looked down at the table, realizing how offensive it must have sounded to her. "Uh... yeah?"

"You don't have any friends?"

He lifted his can and retreated behind the shield of his now empty ginger ale.

She sighed. "Is it the boys in the trailer court?"

He shrugged. "Sort of."

"You're such a nice boy," she said, sounding super-ultra-mega-grandmotherly. "I'm sure you can make friends with anybody if you just try."

He watched the cat that had lept from his lap enter the kitchen, seeking a snack. He wished it hadn't left. "I don't know," he said, watching closely. If it started eating another cat's brains, he'd know for sure it was a zombie. Maybe it was for the best that it had left.

"You just find something you both like. Maybe they like *Guiding Light*?"

He snickered at the thought.

"You know, I hear it even works that way with girls."

Daniel blushed and retreated, looking back to the kitchen for the cat, even if it *was* a zombie. He was willing to risk zombification for the comfort it briefly provided. Daniel suddenly wanted to shrink down and hide.

"There *are* a few cute ones around here," she added, raising one eyebrow.

A crow squawked. Daniel jerked.

Another gunshot. He flinched again, eyes wide.

Smiles disappeared. The boogeyman was back at the door, unwelcome and uninvited.

"Poor crows." She fixed her eyes on his. "Would you care for more ginger ale?"

The smiles returned. Daniel looked around them. No Corpse Boy, but Daniel knew he'd be back. Later on, when he was alone, the ghost *would* return.

"No, thank you," he sighed, staring back at the kitchen and beyond the window. "I think it's time I get going again."

A crow squeaked, the gun fired, the ginger ale fizzed in his glass. Daniel wondered where the Corpse Boy was.

CHAPTER 7

MAKING A NEW FRIEND

Corpse Boy was back.

After returning from his paper route, Daniel slept. Or more accurately, he *attempted* to sleep. This was a possible Ghostbusters situation, after all. Seriously, how could he be expected to sleep with the ghost of a Corpse Boy sitting on his toy box, staring at him? Mac, perpetually asleep at the foot of his bed, didn't seem to mind or notice the boy. Who was he gonna call? *Nobody.* That's who.

Daniel sat up, maneuvering to the edge of the bed. Mac stretched but didn't get up. He searched his shelves around the room. Not a single Ghostbuster in sight, not even any action figures, even though every single year at Christmas he'd circle the Ghostbusters car in the Sears Catalog. *Every single year.*

He never got that car. Or action figures or *anything.* So how could he expect to get their phone number and call for help? It was hopeless.

Frustrated from the haunting and lack of sleep, Daniel crossed his bedroom and turned on his TV. Years earlier lightning struck the house, actually the old house, and kind of sort of fried the television and much of the roof, part of why it was now the old house. It worked, but not well. Now you turned it on and waited for the image to warm up. It took about 45 minutes for it to achieve full brightness.

Mac groaned and moved a few inches. Along with Corpse Boy's, the eyes watched Daniel across the room with subdued interest.

The TV fuzzed to a dim half-life. He quickly turned it off and on again, several times, until slowly the screen brightened. Daniel liked zombies, but he wasn't thrilled to own the zombie equivalent of a television. It was old, pretty much dead, but like Bub in *Day of the Dead*, with some coaxing it could at least be somewhat functional. On the television Daniel's go to channel, CAM, or Classic American Movies, played *The Last Man on Earth*, starring Vincent Price.

Daniel turned his head over his shoulder and looked at Corpse Boy.

D'oh.

The boy had been sitting, twirling his feet in sheer boredom. Now his feet stopped dead, his gaze fixed on the television as Vincent Price fled from the zombie-vampire people around him.

"You like that?" Daniel asked.

The Corpse Boy nodded.

"Affirmative," confirmed Daniel, mimicking Newt from *Aliens*.

From a thoroughly disorganized stack of VHS tapes near the TV, Daniel pulled out the 1970s remake, *The Omega Man*. He held it up, a grimacing, scarf-wearing Charlton Heston emblazoned the cover. "You should watch this one. It's a remake. It's awesome." Daniel paused. He wondered if death was a touchy subject for a ghost. "Um, dead people come back as vampires. Well, sort of vampires." He swallowed. "You're not a vampire…are you?"

Corpse Boy shrugged. Apparently he didn't think so.

"Or a zombie, maybe?"

Corpse Boy again shrugged. Daniel wondered if maybe he didn't know what a zombie was.

"You're *clearly* not a zombie," he continued, "and you're certainly not a vampire. Are you a crow? Not the bird, like this." Daniel held up a copy of James O'Barr's *The Crow*. The stark absence of color on the cover felt in contrast to the apparent reality of the Corpse Boy. "Never mind. I don't even think the dead people who come back in that are *called* crows. I don't know why I asked."

Daniel dug out *Dawn of the Dead*. Its iconic sunrise cover shone in the black and white glow of the TV. "They filmed this one at our mall! Have you ever been to the mall? Not Ross Park, Monroeville. It's kind of far. You have to take the turnpike to get there. You know, the big fancy toll road? Did... your mom ever take you there?"

Corpse Boy shrugged. He didn't remember.

"Either way, don't suck my blood. Okay? That's what vampires do. You know that, right?" Daniel wobbled the case and gestured at it. Corpse Boy emphatically shook his head, nodding. A part of Daniel felt like a professional wrestler revealing kayfabe to a mark. Did that make him a carnie? He wanted the answer to be yes. As to the Corpse Boy and the answers to the universe's grand questions, Daniel didn't have much to offer.

He decided to educate the boy. The fact that he was already dead and would probably be stuck as a ghost-kid forever informed his decision. Daniel began to feel as if he were giving an address to the module UN he signed up for just to get the free Gator Aid bottle, but had no desire to actually be there. "Flesh may be tempting to a zombie, but as it's really essential for my human survival. So don't eat my flesh. That's what zombies do. And for sure don't eat my brains! Not all, but some zombies do that." Daniel scoffed at himself again. "Who am I kidding? You're not a zombie *or* a vampire. You're...some kinda kid ghost." Daniel laughed the fakest forced laugh he could. He had a knack for making things weird.

Corpse Boy smiled. His smile was pleasant and inviting. It warmed a cold room, like restoring color to an old black and white movie. It was as bright as the colors on his shirt, and Daniel needed to see that smile at that moment.

"I like your shirt," he said, gesturing with a tepid hand.

Corpse Boy opened his jacket slightly, examining his own shirt. He'd apparently forgotten what he was wearing when he died. Daniel wondered if he didn't really want to remember.

"Did you see my poster?" He pointed to the massive Fabulous Thunder Family poster adorning the wall opposite the TV. Corpse Boy looked up at it. "You like them?" Daniel instinctively reached out to touch his shoulder, then hesitated. He didn't know if he even could, and was unsure if he should.

"Um…"

He hesitated, assuming being dead was a touchy subject, Also, Corpse Boy needed to get out of the way.

"You'll need to get out of the way. You're sitting on my toy chest."

Corpse Boy glanced down, got up and turned around in a fluid movement as though he floated on the air. Still careful not to touch him, Daniel opened the toy chest. Bright colors of the treasures within sparkled like diamonds and gold. This treasure chest, however, wasn't filled with gems or rubies or wealthy coins, but with superheroes and villains from the farthest reaches of all comic book universes. Including, of course, Main Title.

Daniel dug through the collection, looking for a very specific toy. Corpse Boy's smile widened as he apparently recognized hero after hero. Each one became his favorite, until he spied the next one and the one after that.

"Finally!" Daniel said, pulling out the Grim action figure.

The real strong man from the Fabulous Thunder Family, not the imposter the Ghoul. "This is one of my favorites," he whispered, holding it up for his new friend.

The Corpse Boy sat cross-legged on the floor a few feet away, transfixed by what he saw.

Daniel beamed. He began taking out figures, one after the other, regaling his apprentice with his extensive knowledge and insight to the comic world.

Outside the trees danced at the wind's urging and the stars raced through the sky. Asleep on his bed, Daniel's chest inflated and deflated in sync with his dog's.

Corpse Boy sat on the carpet, fixated on the conclusion of *The Omega Man*. As Charlton Heston overacted and yet somehow nailed the performance, the boy felt a sense of solidarity with the character. First, the obvious fact of being dead at the end, but also in being unlike anyone else in your world. Charlton's character lived and eventually died as the only person in the world not affected by the vampire in a rogue plague. Sure, he had some friends, like the woman with the afro, but he remained alone.

The Corpse Boy related to this existence.

Curled at the bottom of the bed, Mac slept. Likewise, curled at the top of the bed, Daniel slept, hugging a mangled bulge of blanket. In the center of the room sat the Corpse Boy, television glowing a few feet in front of him. Had Daniel been awake, he would have pointed out how this scene was eerily similar to the iconic one in *Poltergeist*. The exception being the semicircle of superhero toys encasing Corpse Boy, all his favorites.

CHAPTER 8
WHEN THE MORNING COMES

Snapped awake from his deep sleep, Daniel's eyes shot open. His vision blurred with the weariness of a late night and an early morning. The world seemed to vibrate and rattle, and he couldn't focus.

Wait, no. The world wasn't shaking. Daniel was.

Someone was shaking him.

"Get up, Daniel!" shouted the blurred image, slowly resolving to become his moderately agitated mother. She stood directly over him.

Reluctantly sitting up, Daniel rubbed his eyes. *Where did she come from?*

"Where'd you come from?" he mumbled.

"The bus comes in fifteen minutes!" She thrust an outfit into his hands. Unlike a typical day, this one actually matched. Color coordination was a science Daniel hadn't yet mastered. "Why did I even buy you an alarm clock if I have to wake you up every day?" railed Mom, looking for and not finding the alarm clock. "Where is the alarm clock?!"

A reluctant Daniel wearily pointed to a heap on the opposite side of the room.

"You threw it across the room?!"

"I didn't know how to shut it off!" he protested. It was a lie. He knew how to shut it off, but he hated that alarm clock; it had belonged to his brother.

Her back still turned to him, his mother smiled. She hated that alarm clock; it had belonged to her oldest son. She scowled at the collection of toys littering the floor. "I see somebody had a late night."

"Mac?" asked Daniel, looking over at his dog, still asleep beside him.

"Daniel. I don't think the dog opened the toy chest, played with these dolls…"

"*Action figures.*"

"…and pulled all these videos off the shelf." She pulled him to his feet and stared to make his bed.

"You'd be surprised at what goes on here at night," said Daniel, fully aware how extremely clever he was with his word play, yet also fully aware his mother would think he was being a smart aleck. He felt it was worth the risk.

Mom gave a gentle kick to the Grim action figure. "I thought you grew out of this…" She paused, seeking the right word, eventually finding it. "This *phase.*"

His brother had done the exact same thing. Played with toys until he was fifteen and was bullied mercilessly. He'd turned to weightlifting and football. She secretly prayed Daniel wouldn't.

Mom cleared her throat, almost as an apology, then snapped back into full-force Mother Mode. "You have to let the dog out before you go."

Daniel and Mac shared a look. He was pretty sure that Mac could see the Corpse Boy, and that he'd never say a word, being a dog and all. Mac lay his head back down and groaned.

"Will do," Daniel said nodding. "Sorry."

"You can be sorry later," she said. "For now just get dressed and go-go-GO!"

. . .

THE SCHOOL BUS rolled and bounced down the street, and Daniel rolled and bounced along with it. He wasn't entirely sure what a hangover was, but was pretty confident he had one. He looked to his right. Directly beside him rode the Corpse Boy, who seemed to be thrilled to be on a bonafide school bus. Digging into his backpack, Daniel pulled out the Grim action figure.

Corpse Boy beamed.

Daniel returned the smile, and for a split second, he felt he was sitting next to an angel, instead of a creepy ghost kid.

Fifteen minutes later in homeroom, he sat in his normal seat, eyes closed, yawning and struggling to stay awake as the Corpse Boy stood ever observant by his side. Suddenly Jimmy leaped in front of Daniel, Corpse Boy vanishing without a word.

"Dude!" shouted Jimmy. "Wake up! We're at school!"

Daniel moaned, opening his eyes and rolling them up into his head, very nearly rolling himself out of his chair.

"Today's the day!" Jimmy continued, a flair of his arms and a flourish in his voice. "The day we make the trade of trades, on the day of days. The great hereafter of trading stuff and—"

"What trade?" Daniel was annoyed and had genuinely forgotten what day it was. Being haunted by a dead kid tends to change your priorities. Trading comics and cards may have been utterly important yesterday, but today was a super weird new day, and he wasn't in the mood.

"For the Vigilance comics!" reminded Jimmy. "And the Spawn comics," he said under his breath.

Daniel's nostrils flared. "*Not* the Spawn comics!"

"Dude, your nostrils are flaring." Jimmy sat at the desk next to him, acting as contrite as possible. "Geez, fine. We'll negotiate later. You know, when you're more desperate and

I have more power. How about I ride your bus home today?"

"Let's do it another day. Tomorrow? Or what about next week?"

"Stop trying to hold onto those Spawn comics!" snapped Jimmy.

"Okay, fine, ride my bus today," Daniel snapped back. He'd just have to get Jimmy and his nonsense out of the way.

"You do your History map?" asked Jimmy. Without waiting for a response, he plunged a hand into Daniel's Jansport backpack. Daniel half-heartedly tried to stop him, but his sleep deprivation won out.

Jimmy spotted the Grim toy — the very reason Daniel wanted to stop him. *Darn sleepiness.* He partially pulled it out of the bag, potentially exposing it to all of Daniel's classmates — including bullies and, perhaps more importantly, cute girls.

"Do you like being weird?" asked Jimmy, feigning worry. "Asking as a friend."

"Just put it back," Daniel sighed, too weary to fight.

Jimmy dropped the toy back into the bag. Daniel leaned over and pushed it down to the bottom, safely out of sight.

"Or is it that you like being beaten up?" asked Jimmy. Granted, neither of them had ever actually *been* beaten up. Although, once on the stairs Jimmy was punched in the stomach by the senior who worked at the video store. Although the administration mostly kept middle school and high school kids separated in the hallways, every day after lunch the middle schoolers had to go up the stairs as the high schoolers came down them.

And so, every day the kid from the video store punched Daniel in the stomach at the halfway point of the stairs. His brother eventually went to the video store and settled things when he found out, but his brother wasn't here anymore, so Daniel would either have to fight his own battles or avoid them entirely.

"You're going to get eviscerated today, you know that?" Daniel glared at him. He was pretty sure Jimmy didn't even know the definition of the word eviscerated. "I was going to trade it," he lied.

"Trade the Grim!!" Jimmy shouted.

For a split second everyone in the room stopped talking and gawked at him, but with attention spans shrunk to split-seconds, nobody really cared so they just as quickly looked away. Jimmy continued, not bothering to lower his voice. "You would never trade *the* Grim!"

"Well, I was going to," Daniel sighed dramatically, adding in a bit of manipulation, "but now I'm not." He paused. "And it's the green paint variant."

Jimmy's eyes widened and he groaned. He wanted that toy. He's always wanted *that version* of *that toy*, but right now he needed to get his homework done more than he needed another toy, no matter how cool or rare it was. "Did you do the map or not?"

"No." Daniel zoned out, looking around the room.

"Earth to Danimal? Dude?" Jimmy was now actually really kind of sort of worried. "You in there?"

The bell rang.

"I'll see you on my bus?" Daniel asked.

"So no map."

Daniel shook his head and shrugged. He really hadn't done it. And it had been Daniel's turn to do the work so Jimmy could copy. Every other time they'd switch — that was the deal. Jimmy walked away, confusion and disappointment spreading across his face. Now he needed to find someone who had *actually done the map*, as he only had first period to copy it. Maybe Rob would be his friend again today.

THAT AFTERNOON the bus ride was mostly in silence, other than a brief conversation about the map and Daniel's responsibility to do his work so Jimmy could copy it.

"Be a better friend," insisted Jimmy.

Daniel shrugged and looked out the window.

When they got home they didn't say much, going through the motions as they completed the paper route. Constantly on the cusp of saying something, Jimmy would snap his mouth shut and hold his words. Daniel wondered if he felt guilty. *Be a better friend? What was he thinking? Who says that?*

A police car pulled up to a stop beside them, lights bouncing off the white of an adjacent trailer. The boys slowed down a few steps, staring at the car for a second before continuing down the sidewalk. Daniel subconsciously bobbed his head to the rhythm of the lights. Music played in his head along with a dramatic narration. The epic dance party ended, and the dread came as they approached Peggy Hart's trailer.

"What's going on?" Jimmy asked, emboldened by curiosity.

Daniel shrugged in rhythm with the lights.

"Wait here," he said, blocking his friend with an open hand. "I have to issue Miss Hart..." *Mrs. Hart?* Daniel caught himself. He couldn't make that mistake when talking to her again. *Is she Mrs. Hart, or Miss? Which is it?* "I have to issue a refund." At this point, Daniel really had no idea if it was Miss or Mrs.

Ignoring Jimmy's perplexed look, he approached the door and knocked twice. The screen door clanged on impact and the inside door flung open behind it. Peggy Hart filled the door. Behind her, a well-below-average-looking but fit-and-trim, thirty-something police officer nervously scratched the back of his head.

"Whadaya want?" snarled Peggy.

"I..." Daniel bumbled in fear. "I have your refund."

Peggy pushed forward and opened the door, revealing more of the childless mess of a home. "Oh, good! My money!" She sounded genuinely happy. He was about to issue a refund of a total of thirty-five cents, and this was all it took to make her happy. Like really, truly happy.

"I was about to report you to the officer," Peggy snarled, throwing the officer a flirty look and a toss of her mullet. The officer burped, but Daniel was pretty sure that wouldn't do much to discourage Miss Hart's advances.

Peggy flattened her hand in front of Daniel, palm up, ready for riches. Daniel dropped a quarter into it. "Twenty-five," he said, then dropped a dime. "And thirty-five."

That was it.

Thirty-five stinkin' cents and Peggy squealed in elation.

She raised her open palm up to her face, like a jeweler examining the exquisite cut of a diamond, ogling the money. Noting the year on the quarter, she glanced back at the officer, "1973," she announced. "The year I was born."

Nobody believed her. Peggy's eyes locked on the officer and flickered. This time he straight up belched. Daniel turned and made his escape, grabbing Jimmy's arm and pulling him onward, away from the creepy scene.

"But you didn't give her today's paper," Jimmy observed, glancing back.

"I know. Keep walking."

Jimmy's eyes stayed on Peggy's trailer as he walked, watching the door shut. The flashing police lights and officer inside were way more interesting than delivering the next newspaper. He grabbed Daniel by the arm and pulled him back, hovering behind the fence at the edge of the year, just within earshot.

"Jimmy…" Daniel protested.

"Shhh!"

The boys heard the police officer talking inside. The dude was loud, but he wasn't exactly shouting. The shouting happened a few seconds later. Like a foghorn on the fritz, Peggy Hart chewed out the officer and the entire police force. The distance made it difficult to make out the words, but phrases like "he had to be in on it" and "how can you release him?" were clear enough as she roared.

"Come on," Daniel said, turning away. "We got papers to deliver."

"Did you hear that?" Jimmy said excitedly, falling in behind him. "That was awesome!"

"That was eavesdropping."

"Yeah! And it was awesome!"

"Well, I'm glad you got a kick out of it," Daniel said, "But we have papers to deliver so…" He fell silent as his eyes narrowed, staring ahead of them. "Oh, crap."

"Oh, crap?" Jimmy asked, confused. "What's oh crap?"

Daniel reached over and placed a hand on Jimmy's chest. He gently pushed his friend behind him, repositioning the newspaper bag as if it were some kind of bulletproof vest.

Jimmy swung his head around, peeking past Daniel.

Porkins and Glasses paced up ahead on the street.

Porkins's arm was extended, and as Jimmy's eyes followed the arm down he saw a tightened chain and a shaggy, over-sized and auburn-haired mutant taking a monster poop on a neighbor's lawn. A spiked metal collar around the demon's neck featured a skull and crossbones tag, the name *HETFIELD* etched beneath it.

Daniel loved dogs, but Hetfield was no dog. He was, and always would be, a *monster*. And Daniel had no love for monsters.

Although he was surprisingly cool with ghosts.

A blur of brown fur erupted from under the nearest trailer. Daniel's eyes widened as the foolish rabbit darted across the road, just within the slack of the chain.

"No…"

Hetfield abandoned his dog duty mid-squat and sprang forward. With a sickening yelp, the rabbit was plucked out of the air and pinned to the ground. Hetfield flipped it into the air playfully, snatched it and started shaking it violently in its gnashing jaws. The bunny went limp, a lifeless puppet in the mouth of a monster.

"Did that dog just murder a rabbit?" Jimmy stammered, naïve innocence quaking in his voice.

The sound of Jimmy's voice was like a thunderclap. Hetfield's head snapped toward them. He dropped the rabbit's lifeless body into the dust and jolted forward, leash taut as he lunged in their direction, a guttural bark erupting from his bloody throat. Daniel winced and turned away, bracing himself as he half expected the sonic boom to peel the roofs off the trailers behind them.

The only thing it blew was their eardrums.

"Look at that," said Porkins. "It's a Rice-A-Roni pair."

"Is that an insult?" asked Jimmy.

"From these guys, yeah," muttered Daniel.

"A couple'a San Francisco fruits!" shouted Glasses.

"It's the San Francisco treat!" corrected Daniel.

"Shut up, pumpkin peach!" returned Glasses.

"Should I let Hetfield go?" Porkins whispered to Glasses.

Glasses said nothing, but held his hand out ahead of him, watching Daniel and Jimmy squirm up the street.

The leash snapped taut, nearly yanking Porkins off his feet. Hetfield lunged forward, a guttural roar erupting from its throat, drool splattering the pavement, massive black paws churning the ground.

Jimmy disappeared behind Daniel, his body trembling. Daniel felt somewhat emboldened by facing a ghost the night before, but still found his new sense of bravado wavering. Corpse Boy was real enough, but Hetfield... well... he was exceptionally real, and very, very terrifying.

Porkins, sweating and visibly straining to retain control, fumbled with the leash. Finally, with what appeared to Daniel to be a practiced stumble, he "accidentally" dropped the leash. Unsure of its newfound freedom, Hetfield took two tentative steps forward, a low growl rumbling in his chest, somehow far more menacing than the earlier ear-splitting onslaught.

Daniel clenched his fists, his breath coming in shallow gasps, preparing for the worst. No question — this was *far* scarier than any ghost.

"Call that dog off!" a firm, authoritative voice yelled from behind them.

Thank you, Jesus.

For Daniel it was akin to hearing the voice of God Himself.

Porkins glanced over to the police officer on the porch and blew a hard, powerful whistle between his two fingers. The beast's menacing façade instantly vanished. A hellish-nether-creature no more, it sniffed the air, walking away from Daniel and Jimmy.

"Come, Hetfield." The dog glanced at Porkins and lowered its head, continuing its slow, sniff-filled walk, making his way to the bullies.

"Fruit loops callin' the cops!" shouted Glasses irrationally. Daniel wondered if he honestly believed they somehow called the cops.

"Shut up, idiot!" squealed Porkins. "The cop's comin' this way you four-eyed freak."

"You boys okay?" asked the officer, stopping next to Daniel and Jimmy but glaring at the dog.

"Yes, sir," Daniel and Jimmy said in unison.

The officer cracked his knuckles and clenched his jaw. He was utterly calm and thoroughly intense, but kept his voice under control, like that wrestler, Jake "the Snake" Roberts in a police uniform. "Keep that mutt on a leash, and muzzle your-selves while you're at it."

"Screw you, cop!" shouted Glasses.

Daniel and Jimmy both sucked in a breath, shocked at what was happening. Were they about to witness the two dorks getting snapped in two? Their internal magic 8-balls said *Yes, Definitely*.

The calculated rage of Jake the Snake simmered, invisible venom spewing from his fangs with each word he said next. "You're adorable," he hissed. "You're also why I don't have kids, you little goblins. You're done here. Walk away, and do it fast."

Tails tucked firmly between their legs, the three dogs turned and retreated down the street.

"Thanks," Daniel said to the officer.

"Here to serve," he said, nodding as he watched the three shadows disappearing in the sun's silhouette. "You two best wrap up your deliveries and get on home, though. Just to be safe."

DANIEL AND JIMMY didn't speak as word as they finished their route, a thick tension wafting about them. If tension had a smell, they could smell it. If it had a taste, they could both taste it. Daniel didn't like it. He absolutely loathed any kind of conflict, but he couldn't talk about things. How do you explain to someone you have a new friend and he's dead? At least, how do you do it without sounding batcrap crazy?

Parting the gas station a few minutes later, they each left with a Choco-Shocko in hand. Daniel paid for them both, even though he didn't feel like it. Honestly, he just wanted to get through the afternoon and be done with Jimmy.

Daniel tucked his Choco into his bag as Jimmy gently shook his, attempting to get that glorious fudge off the bottom and spread it about. The usual crew greeted them, Popeye, Belly, and Stander.

"Palin' around today, Skip?" asked Popeye, sounding like he actually cared, though he didn't. He was just a perpetual businessman.

"Who bought the drinks?" inquired Belly, clearly setting up some previously scheduled bad joke.

"I did," Daniel said. He wanted to make sure everyone knew it, *especially* Jimmy.

"You wanna buy me one, too?" giggled Belly. The glorious Christmas bulb of a belly jiggled above his waist. "Pops, you should give 'em free drinks," he said with a laugh, but genuinely hoping he'd say yes and therefore maybe score a free drink himself.

"Nope," said Pop Eye firmly. "Not good for business." He cracked a smile and added a halfhearted, "Sorry fellas." Yep, a non-stop businessman, through and through.

A little farther on, just past the gas station and before the bridge, Daniel kept his stride but broke his gaze. As he passed through, he looked back up the twisted and windy road. His mind became tangled itself, lost off the road and in the brush, near where he found the Corpse Boy.

Where he knew the body remained. Alone.

"You ever go up there, Dan?" asked an intuitive Jimmy. He looked worried, almost scared.

Daniel stumbled, dragging his feet on the uneven payment. His mind lurched back to the intersection, to the moment in front of him. "No."

It was easy to lie. The lie kept him safe.

"Anything up there?" It was a stupid question, considering what Daniel had just said, but Jimmy was apparently trying to make conversation.

"How would I know?!" Daniel snapped. "I've never been. I just said that I've never been up there." His misery swelled. Having a secret and then having to hide it from his nebby friend just sucked.

"Jesus, man! It was just a question!"

Jimmy was angry, now. Like, for *real* angry. Daniel couldn't remember the last time he saw him so ticked off.

As they reached the driveway, Daniel strode several feet

ahead while Jimmy dragged his feet through the crinkling, semi-moist gravel behind him. The loose, ashy bits clinging to his shoes and the cuff of his jeans.

Daniel stopped and looked back. His eyes would have shot lasers had he been that evil Superman from Superman III.

"Hurry up, Jimmy!" he scolded. He was the boss of this paper route. If Jimmy wanted to tag along, he'd have to pull his weight. "Or we won't have time to trade," he added.

"What?!"

Jimmy's voice popped like an exploding helium balloon. "All of a sudden you want to make the trade?" It was the angriest question a twelve-year-old could ask.

"No!" Daniel was incredulous. "I just want to go home."

Jimmy doubled down on being a jerk kid and a bad friend. "Oh yeah? Well, I don't even *want* to make the stupid trade."

"Yeah, you do!"

Jimmy knew it to be true, but said nothing.

"You get the Pete Pham card," Daniel added.

The Pete Pham autographed card was the most valuable item in the isolated world of Daniel and Jimmy.

Before Jimmy had a chance to goat in his screwed trading card victory, Daniel asked, "What time is your mom coming?" It was a low blow, the lowest of low blows. A blow so low, even Lobo wouldn't have taken it.

"You want me to call her? Want me to leave?" Mewled Jimmy.

Daniel hated being such a jerk, and could see himself in college having the same basic conversation with a girlfriend. He'd know better then, too, but he'd have to be at least in his mid-twenties before he grew up. He sighed. Just like twenty-six-year-old Daniel likely would, fourteen-year-old Daniel tried to patch the fracture he'd created. "I was just wondering about it," he said. It wasn't much of an effort.

"The trade is *off!*" Jimmy announced.

Daniel frowned. What just happened? Did they just break up as friends? Did Jimmy dump him? Was their friendship over? Kaput? He only wanted his best friend to remain his best friend, but he was fourteen, and again, even at twenty-six he wouldn't fare much better. "What?"

"Off! Done!" Jimmy spat. "Over! *No trade!*"

Every word was a kick to the stomach.

"Just… come on." Daniel resolved to fix it, or at least make Jimmy be less annoying about it all. "We'll make the trade, then you can call your mom and—"

"No!" Jimmy protested. "I don't want to make the trade anymore. And it's Cyclops, *then* Havok! Cyclops is always first. He's older! He was born first! Cy means one!"

"What? No! That's because he has *one eye!*" bellowed Daniel. He knew he had hurt his friend, had wronged him in trying to push him away, but still, he knew he had to keep him away from the truth. He put his hands up in surrender. "I'll give you the Spawn comics," he said.

Jimmy looked at him and crossed his arms, understandably skeptical.

Daniel swallowed his pride, trading it for a friendship he could control, at the distance he would choose. "All of them."

Jimmy smiled.

CHAPTER 9

I ONLY NEED ONE FRIEND, AN IMAGINARY ONE

Mac slept on the bed, a typically-twitchy, whimper-filled coma. Comic books and trading cards were scattered around the room, spiraling in a circle to the dead center of the floor where Daniel sat next to the Corpse Boy.

This time he stayed nearer than before, nearly close enough to touch him. He didn't. After all, was he a ghost, or did he exist in another dimension? If Daniel actually made contact with him, would the universe collapse on itself? He was pretty sure that was a possibility, based on some of the movies he'd seen recently. Either way, Daniel had no intention of finding out, but he was cool with showing him his new prize.

The LIMITED-EDITION PETE PHAM AUTOGRAPHED CARD.

Daniel held the card to the light, illuminating the shallow canyons of the official embossed stamp. He dared not voice it aloud, but inside he *knew* Jimmy was acting like a fool about the trade. Leaning over, he showed the card to the Corpse Boy. "Check it out."

Corpse Boy leaned in and Daniel subtly leaned back to avoid contact, awkwardly stretching his neck away from his body, his arms remaining in front of the Corpse Boy. It would be foolishness to risk destroying all time and space just to show the card to Corpse Boy. As awesome as it was, it wasn't *that* awesome. Nothing was *that* awesome.

"Look here." Daniel pointed to his open binder on the ground. "Pretty cool, huh?" he asked, tapping the second card on the first page of the trading card thick binder. "There it is without the autograph, and even *that* version is worth ten bucks. Ten bucks!" At least, that's what Daniel assumed the value to be. He had little sense for real world value, and probably never would.

Corpse Boy's one good eye looked at the card in the binder, leaning down and nearly hitting Daniel's outstretched arms. *Could he even make physical contact?* Daniel didn't want to find out.

"Do you like Merkanary?" Daniel asked, in part to physically draw the Corpse Boy back, but also because he wanted to climb onto a soap box.

The Corpse Boy nodded a slow, dead nod. Exactly the kind of nod Daniel would expect of a dead kid. They said dead men — or kids, in this case — told no tales, but they were certainly good listeners. At least Corpse Boy was.

Daniel liked that. More and more lately it seemed like nobody listened to him. His mom didn't listen. His dad *definitely* didn't listen, but then again, Jimmy didn't really listen to him a whole lot.

His brother had. And if he were being honest, Daniel missed that. He missed moments like this, but reversed, where he was the one learning all this stuff. Being the expert kind of made Daniel uncomfortable.

"Everybody likes Merkanary," he continued with a sassy shake of his head. "I think I like Paunch better than him, and Brainbend's my favorite, even though nobody else likes Brainbend. They say he's just Tri-Burner's lame son from the future, but he's not!"

Corpse Boy looked at him, saying nothing.

"Well, okay," Daniel said, "He *is* his son, and he *is* from the future, but he's *not* lame. I promise! He's way more powerful than Tri-Burner. Jimmy says Tri-Burner is more powerful, but it's not true. He isn't." Daniel's eyes darted from the page of cards over to the door.

Deep in the confines of his mind, Daniel imagined Merkanary coming alive, heaving a large proton cannon and lunging up and out of the confines of his card. He charged, firing the weapon at the massive villain in the middle card of the page. Tyrel the Terrible. Tyrel swatted Merkanary away.

The portly but super-strong Paunch caught him in his card. Finally, Tri-Burner and Brainbend battled each other from their card frames on opposite sides of the page, on opposite sides of the divide between good and evil.

Then it all stopped.

They were static images again, nothing more than thin cardboard in a binder.

"Their powers cancel each other out anyway, like Cyclops and Havok." Daniel paused to ruminate on that point. "Maybe they stole it from Marvel?" He looked again at the door. "Jimmy's kind of an idiot, actually." He said it rather loudly. Dangerously loud.

When no response came from beyond the door, he continued. "Who's your favorite?"

Corpse Boy moved slowly, like a stereotypical ghost would. Daniel assumed he was a ghost, but maybe it was just an alternate dimension thing. Something like that might cause a temporal dilation that results in a slowdown of some sort. Maybe he was just a slow kid, in life and death? Finally, the Corpse Boy landed on Merkanary, affirming it with a firm nod and a smile.

"Merkanary," confirmed Daniel.

Corpse Boy nodded slowly, silently.

"He's pretty cool. My third favorite. Well, he's my seventh

overall, but my third favorite Ultimate Reject." Daniel decided to deepen the education of his new dead friend.

"Here, let me show you something else." He flipped through the card heavy plastic pages of the binder. "You'll like this one." Daniel stopped several pages in. He pointed to a rather unique card. "Do you know Wolverine?"

Daniel didn't even bother to look at Corpse Boy to see the answer. *Of course* he knew Wolverine. *Everybody* knew Wolverine. Daniel heard the theme song to the X-Men cartoon in his head and he began to hum it aloud. The card depicted Wolverine, but without his normal yellow costume, nor the brown and tan one that Daniel preferred; instead, he wore a black costume and an eye patch. "Bet you've never seen Wolverine like *that* before," Daniel said triumphantly. "You know, with a patch and just one eye…"

He paused to stare awkwardly at Corpse Boy's one swollen eye. "Oh…" he said. "Uhhh…"

Corpse Boy didn't sense the awkwardness of the situation. He looked at the illustration and shook his head. Nope. It was new to him. At five and dead, most things were new to him.

If *that* was a surprise, Daniel was about to blow his mind, he flipped a few more pages. "They call him Patch," said Daniel, somewhat more comfortable in the role of the expert. "He hung around with the Hulk for a few issues. But he wasn't called 'The Hulk' then, but Joe Fixit."

Corpse Boy was either exceptionally interested or perpetually bored. Daniel had a hard time reading that one eye.

"Never mind," he said. "That's not important. But let me show you more Merkanary," said Daniel as he flipped through the heavy plastic UltraPro pages.

"There!" he said with a burst of emphasis. The character on the page kind of sort of looked like Merkanary, but different. Younger, lighter, happier, free of the terror and trauma that would define his future. "That's Merkanary as Range."

Corpse Boy gasped and Daniel almost shrieked in

response. The boy's face slowly turned to Daniel, his grin forming a soundless squeal.

"Yeah! I know!"

Daniel felt fatherly, like a teacher, but more like a father or teacher who actually listens. The kind Daniel wanted, but never had. The kind he resolved one day to become. "Freaking awesome," he concluded in a whisper.

A toilet flushed, dissolving Daniel's perfect moment into minuscule chunks. A moment later, after the sound of a not-nearly-long-enough-washing of the hands, the bathroom door opened and Jimmy entered just after Corpse Boy disappeared.

"I just took a crap that looked like a *hydra* monster," said Jimmy, a freshly squeezed and proud turd-father. "I swear, Jack Kirby could've drawn that power poop as a Fantastic Four villain, it was so massive."

Daniel could not have been more disgusted. More than that, he was annoyed. The wrong friend was in the room with him now, and he wasn't happy. Ignoring him, Daniel moved about some of the cards in silence.

Unfazed, but fully aware he was being slighted, Jimmy prattled on. "I think if I were on death row, I'd choose to eat a last meal that allowed me to take a really good, monster-sized last crap!"

"Nobody cares about you your turds, Jimmy," blurted Daniel. Jimmy glared at him. "Is my mom here yet?"

"I hope so."

Even from Daniel's peripheral vision he could tell Jimmy's face turned red. What he didn't know was it wasn't out of rage as much as it was Jimmy doing everything in his power not to cry. His fingers curled into a tight fist. He shook it at Daniel in unfocused, wounded rage. After self-control won over, he turned to the door and just as abruptly back to Daniel. He raised his fist between them and cranked his other hand on an imaginary gear, slowly raising his middle finger until it was fully erect. He held it in place for a few extended seconds to ensure Daniel receive the message, then scooped up his loot from the trade, carrying an arm full of comics books and a broken friendship with him. "I'm gonna wait downstairs!" he announced.

Upon Jimmy's parting, Corpse Boy instantly returned. Daniel smiled, despite the dissipating tension. "I forget what we were talking about," he said. "Oh! Right. Cards." He scratched his greasy head. "Oh well. Want to watch some T-*VEEEE*?" Why he extended the "V" in TV, he had no idea, but it seemed right at the time.

The Corpse Boy shook not just his head, but his entire body with an exuberant yes.

"Yeah?" Daniel said, grinning. "The Simpsons are on at six and six thirty..." He started changing channels but stopped when he saw the news flashing across the screen and Peggy Hart, front and center. Her hair stood taller, with more poof and make-up covered and caked her face.

"Hey!" Daniel exclaimed. "I deliver her papers!"

Below her, the words "Peggy Hart, Mother of Missing Boy," accompanied by a recent photo of a young boy who looked all-too-familiar to Daniel.

"Oh, crap..." he whispered. Looking from the photo to Corpse Boy, Daniel's eyes widened in recognition. If a ghost could have become even paler than he already was, Corpse Boy would have disappeared into transparency.

"That's... that's you?" Daniel asked, even though he knew it was.

The Corpse Boy nodded, inching closer to the screen.

Daniel looked back at the screen and listened. They thought he was only missing. Had no idea he was *dead*. The reporter mentioned a neighbor being arrested in Michigan on a drug charge before being transported back to Pennsylvania. There was speculation on his potential connection to the case, as he left town around the same time Corpse Boy originally disappeared.

Suddenly Daniel understood what Peggy Hart had screamed at the cop about. She wanted to find her boy, even if her fury and frustration wasn't aimed at the right person.

On the screen Peggy brushed back her hair, obviously enjoying the attention. It was a bit crass, but Daniel understood on some level. Tragedy or not, it *was* pretty cool to be on TV, even when it was about your missing son . Corpse Boy pointed emphatically to his ear, and Daniel nodded.

"Oh! Right! Sorry..."

He reached over and turned up the volume knob. Peggy's voice filled the room. "I just want my boy to come home. He's my baby! My baby boy!" She brushed her hair back again and the news cut to another story.

The Corpse Boy's head dropped and his bubble-up eye stared at the carpet. Daniel wondered if a ghost could cry. It didn't look like it, from the likes of it.

"You miss your mom?" he asked , hoping to offer some kind of comfort.

Head still hung low, he nodded.

"You know you can't go back, right?"

Corpse Boy's eyes were deep wells of water. He didn't respond.

"I'm serious. It's not like I can just take you home or something. Nobody else can even see you! And I can't just go cut the wire and bring down your..." He cut himself off, blinking rapidly as the gears of his mind started churning.

Daniel clicked off the TV, the old tube fizzing out and slowly fading to black, taking several seconds to fully power down. Glancing out the window, he watched Jimmy get in his mom's car. He knew he should feel something, some kind of remorse or regret, but he felt nothing but contempt at the moment.

Noticing the sun setting behind the trees, Daniel sighed.

"Look, it's almost time for dinner. Sometimes my mom lets me take my food to my room, but dad's getting home early tonight, so I think I'll have to eat with him. He comes home early on Fridays. We used to all go to my brother's football games, but–" Daniel sucked in a breath. "He still tries to take me to a few football games up at the high school. I used to have to go, back when my brother played."

Daniel looked at his dead friend. "Anyhow, I guess you'll have to go for a while. While we eat." He stopped, shaking his head. "Where exactly do you go when… you go?"

Corpse Boy shrugged.

"You don't know?"

Another shrug.

"Yeah," Daniel mused. "There's a lotta things I don't know these days either." His eyes drifted over to the blank TV screen, replaying the images, words and every summer blockbuster he'd ever seen. All of which he'd seen with his dad and his brother, until last summer. Then it was just Daniel and his dad. He hated sitting next to his dad in the movies and hated sitting next to him at the dinner table even more.

His dad awaited him at the table.

CHAPTER 10
MY FATHER'S SON

The kitchen itself was large, with cabinet after cabinet snaking around the walls. Still, it felt small to Daniel whenever his dad was home. It wasn't out of fear or intimidation or anything. He was a kind man, a loving father, but he was just so incredibly *different* than Daniel. Even the kitchen – the only space they usually shared – felt crowded with both of them in it.

When Daniel's brother had been there it strangely felt larger, even though it was filled with more people. He wasn't sure why, but it just didn't feel right anymore. It felt...wrong.

Dad sat at the head of the table, the area near him a mess of papers and work junk. Daniel was puzzled at a construction worker having so much paper, but he never questioned it. It just was. Next to him sat Mom — when Dad was home, she stayed close to him. They needed each other.

Did they know that? No.

Would they admit that if they did? Probably not.

"Anything exciting happen at school today?" Dad asked. He didn't really care about school, but he did really care about Daniel. Not that he had a clue how to express it.

Thus, the king of sarcasm made his entrance. "It's school."

Daniel tried to be nice, but he really didn't want to be there. Hence, the sarcasm, both as a shield and a crutch.

Daniel took the seat opposite his father, oddly, where normally his mom sat, and dug into the overcooked chicken breast set before him.

"How about the paper route?"

The old man stabbed his chicken. Raising it to his mouth, he ate it directly from his knife. Daniel had to admire that, but the king of sarcasm would not give up his throne that easily.

"It's my paper route," he said with a shrug.

In his head Daniel saw himself as Batman and sarcasm as Bane. He envisioned the crucial moment that Bane broke Batman's back and took over Gotham City. Daniel attempted to saw through the dry rubbery chicken with a butter knife, before simply mashing it down and pulling it apart with his fork.

He reasoned he needed an even more intense version of himself as Batman to battle the darkness of Gotham City, though. Bruce Wayne wasn't going to cut it. He needed to be Jean-Paul Valley, when he became the *new* Batman. Jean-Paul was willing to do whatever it took to protect the city. Or in Daniel's case, anything to hide his feelings. Daniel also really wanted to re-read the Knightfall comics. Maybe he could show them to the Corpse Boy later. This thought momentarily brightened Daniel's disposition.

Daniel looked up and caught his father's eyes, the eyes of a man about to give up on his son. Maybe he should have told him about Knightfall? Dad didn't like comics, but he *did* like action movies and that comic would make an awesome action movie. He wasn't about to mention the comics, but he tried to be present in the moment. To be like his brother. "Nothing exciting ever happens on my paper route."

Sensing the tension between one generation to the next, Mom gave more context. "Jimmy went with him." It was a safe, fun fact. No cause for conflict.

"See?" his dad said, "that right there is exciting." Even as he said it they all silent knew it wasn't remotely exciting, but they couldn't blame a guy for trying. Thinking about it, Dad found something he knew Daniel would bite on, like the chicken he wasn't so sure he'd be able to swallow.

He threw out a line with his best, most expensive bait. "Did you get him to give you the card you wanted?" For a moment he forgot which card. Daniel knew he'd forgotten the card. He *wanted* to remember, but just didn't care about that stuff.

"Merkanary," informed Mom.

Daniel didn't answer. He looked off into a boring empty corner of the room, pushing the food around on his mostly-full plate. He wasn't chewing the chicken, and he was gobbling up Dad's bait.

"Deer Lakes is playing Hampton tonight," continued Dad, hoping Daniel would volunteer to join him at the game while knowing full-well he wouldn't. Mom hated how he still wanted to go to the games, almost as much as Daniel.

"I'm really full," Daniel announced to his mom, totally ignoring his father. "Can I go back up to my room?"

"To your room...?" Mom asked, speaking at a bizarrely drawn out pace. She gave Daniel's dad a seething look. Dad squirmed in his chair, reaching over and pouring a ridiculous amount of salt on his chicken.

"Needs a bit more salt." He wasn't sure if he was joking or not.

"A bit?" Mom was definitely not joking.

Daniel stood to his feet. He wasn't going to eat what Mom was calling chicken anyway, so he stopped waiting for permission and granted it to himself. "I'll be in my room." "With the door closed?" Mom raised an eyebrow.

Dad added more salt to the chicken.

"Uh, yeah?" Daniel took a few steps away from the table.

"Up in your room. With your door closed." Mom looked to Dad. "Maybe, I should let you boys have a talk."

"A talk?" asked Daniel innocently, sounding an awful lot like Peter Brady.

"A talk!" squeaked his dad, as much as he had the potential to squeak.

She left the table and the kitchen so quickly Daniel wondered if he'd missed the Nightcrawler-like smell of brimstone and *bamf!* X-Men sound effect. From his dad's perspective, she streaked down center ice faster than Mario Lemieux on a breakaway at the Civic Arena. "So...Danny," croaked Dad.

Oh, Lord.

He only called him Danny when he was trying to soften him up for something terrible to follow.

Dad took a deep breath and continued. "What do you do up in your room..." He paused, catching another breath, wheezing a little. "...with the door closed?"

Daniel was relieved. They were about to have THE talk – the one every father and son dread with equal despair. With utter clarity, he realized he still needed to avoid the conversation at all costs.

Daniel's response was tactically casual, refusing to go down that road until it was absolutely unavoidable. "Watch movies, read comics..." He stopped. He couldn't stop there! He needed to throw in some good stuff before he revealed too much. "And...do homework. I do my homework. Really, like, at least two hours a day." Crap. Daniel realized he'd oversold it. Time to reel it back in. "I take a break to watch *The Simpsons*, then right back to work." *Not bad*, thought Daniel. A pretty bold lie, but believable to a dad. *Right?*

"Uh-huh. Anything else goes on in there?" It was like he completely ignored most of what Daniel had just rambled about.

"Nope. Nothing."

Dad scooted his chair closer to his son, then decided to stand and take a football coach stance, kneeling at Daniel's side. "Anything that you don't like to talk to anybody else about?"

He asked his question as indirectly as possible, yet it was nearly impossible to ask. Dad put his hand on Daniel's shoulder, and Daniel tried not to flinch. Daniel liked his dad, but he also didn't like to be touched by anybody – even his dad.

"Anything, Daniel." Tears welled in his eyes. This really meant a lot to him. "I'm your father, you can tell me. You trust me, don't you?"

Oh, sweet Jesus, he knew! His dad knew there was a freaking ghost in his bedroom!

Or was it in his head? Or floating near him? Worse yet, did he know Daniel still played with toys?

His body and mind became comatose, frozen in place, determined to reveal nothing that could incriminate him.

"Well, do you?" pressed Dad.

Daniel turned to his father, "Yeah. Of course. You're my dad. Kids tend to trust their dads."

"Alright. Then is there anything you want to tell me?"

"I don't want to talk about Miah."

It was a bold gambit, but one Daniel had to take. He knew the mention of his name would stop Dad dead (for lack of a better word) in his tracks.

"I'm not talking about..."

He couldn't even say his name. His eyes welled with tears, and after a few seconds he swallowed his pain and moved on, repeating his question. "Is there anything you want to tell me?"

Daniel had to once again be bold, but in another direction. "No," he said. "Never. Not today, not tomorrow, not next week, or next month or next year." Daniel took a breath and continued. "Look, whatever conversation you think is going to happen, or Mom wants us to have, we're not going to have it. Never, never ever."

His dad nodded quietly, swallowing as he gathered his thoughts. When he spoke again, his voice popped with a childish terrified squeak. "You know what? That's okay, Dan. Perfectly okay. I'll tell your mother that we talked all about it, but I'm sure they cover it at school, so..."

"Great."

They both hurriedly vacated the table. Moments later, Mom rematerialized, spotting the half-eaten dry chicken left in their wake. With a disappointed sigh she gathered up their dirty dishes.

Upstairs Daniel entered his room abruptly, shutting the door behind himself and leaning heavily against it. Glancing around the room, Daniel panicked.

Corpse Boy was not there.

In the hallway outside, his dad stood at the bedroom door. He raised his hand, readying it to knock, but stopped just short of tapping the door. Shaking his head, he walked away from Daniel's room. He walked away from Daniel. In his mind he justified it by reminding himself that Daniel was a good kid. He'd find his way, with or without his dad.

Inside, Daniel's eyes darted around the room, panicked and bulging in his head. "Are...you here?" he whispered.

When Corpse Boy appeared he felt an unexpected sense of relief.

"You had me worried for a second," said Daniel, acting overly casual, attempting to sound like he didn't mean it. He totally did.

Daniel leaned against the door and slid down to the floor, the coarse hollow wood bunching his shirt behind him. "I think my dad knows I still play with toys! He almost asked me about it at dinner." He caught his breath to calm himself down. "I mean, I *know* my mom knows, but now my dad!

Geez!" The idea of playing with toys forced a smile to his face. "So, you wanna play? We could assemble the Vindicators, and then do an epic crossover with the Avengers!"

Corpse Boy smiled back. Apparently that was a good idea.

On one side of the room, the Vindicators stood assembled in a row of brightly-colored plastic characters with cloth capes. Their leader in red and white with a bright blue cape, the Star-Spangled Soldier. On the opposite side of the room stood The Avengers, headed by the far more original, but equally patriotic, Captain America. Cap wore a similar red, white and blue outfit, but in place of that blue cape, he had that indestructible shield. Assorted villains from the rogue galleries of both The Avengers and The Vindicators occupied various surfaces of the room. They had been defeated by the unbearably awesome team up of these unbeatable super teams.

"Next time we'll include the Justice League," Daniel said with a tinge of regret as he realized he'd missed an opportunity. He considered mentioning the X-Men, but thought that might be overkill.

Standing over the toy chest, Corpse Boy sought out members of the Justice League. Failing to find Batman or Hawkman, another musclebound character caught his eye. He pointed out the figure, sporting long bleach blonde hair, face paint, and neon tights, and tassels, gesturing for Daniel to see.

"Oh, no," said Daniel, "He's not part of the Justice League. That's Mr. Gorgeous, he's just some stupid wrestler. He's a kind of a jerk. Wrestling's dumb — my brother gave him to me."

Corpse Boy pouted and shook his head. He obviously didn't agree and pointed with an angry emphasis.

"Wait. You like wrestling?" asked Daniel, removing his foot from his mouth.

The Corpse Boy's eyes shouted joy, emphatic with excitement.

"Alright. Uhhh... I think I have some of my brother's old tapes."

Later, the boys sat in front of the television. A cynical Daniel had been proved wrong. He just assumed wrestling was stupid because it just looked so ridiculous with those insane costumes. As he watched Mr. Gorgeous roll through the Doom Warriors with the help of the Butcher Brothers, he was sold. The man ran and leapt, punched and grabbed, and it was amazing.

Thoroughly impressed, Daniel turned to his dead friend. "I guess it's like a ballet of real-life superheroes." He meant it. He never in his life thought he'd say anything that ridiculous without absolutely and utterly believing it.

Daniel watched the Corpse Boy. He saw himself and didn't want to. Today Daniel was less a boy and more a man, but what does a man do?

CHAPTER 11

KRISTOFF'S VIDEO MAGIC

Another day, another dollar, thought Daniel as he walked up the road. *Actually pennies on the dollar. We're talking about a local small rural town's newspapers, after all* . Regardless, another newspaper delivered another few pennies on the dollar in Daniel's pocket.

He drifted happily from trailer to trailer with his sidekick, The Corpse Boy. Daniel strode like a superhero, patrolling his city after a big mob takedown. Today, however, Gotham gave him no crime to fight, and he enjoyed the satisfaction of an imaginary victory.

If Daniel were honest, he would have told himself he needed a break. He wasn't ready to be a ghost parent or para-normal pal, or *whatever* he was these days. And he *certainly* wasn't ready to be a vampire. The lifestyle of being up all night was not nearly as glamorous as Bela Legosi made it out to be. What was worse, he had quite literally run out of ways to entertain the Corpse Boy. The real predicament he found himself in was simply what to do when they got home. But mainly he just really wanted some decent sleep.

"What do you want to do?" blurted a desperate Daniel.

As usual, Corpse Boy only shrugged.

Daniel seriously wondered if his lack of talking was a ghost-thing or a little-kid-thing. But he was pretty sure it was a ghost thing.

Remembering those neon tights from the night before; inspiration struck upon Daniel. "We can go to the video store," he said and smiled. "I think they have *Wrestlemania 3*."

THE SCHOOL DAY had been another slog of a day. Daniel had ignored his teachers, ignored his friends — well, his *one* friend. At this time and place, his one friend just happened to no longer be a vibrant living kid named Jimmy, but a dead one named...

Wait, what *was* his name?

Daniel felt bad. He only had one friend and he didn't even know his name. Daniel had read it in the newspaper when Corpse Boy first went missing, he just couldn't remember it.

The normal ebb and flow of the paper route took them up and over the hill. Once they were out of the trailer park on the main throughway sat a nondescript, once white, now more a weathered, gray building. The building had a single door, one window and no other features of note, save a sign that read "Kristoff's Video Magic." However, the implications of those words were spot on. For Daniel, there was no more magical place in the world than this video store. Nothing else in life could ever captivate him in the same way. It was *magical*, and it literally told you so.

"Are you ready?" Daniel asked his tiny, dead friend.

Corpse Boy's eyes shimmered and glowed. Daniel wasn't sure if it was a ghost thing or just something exclusive to Corpse Boy— meaning his eyes would have been just as amazing were he alive. Regardless, he was ready to go inside.

"Here we go!"

With a grand sweeping flourish of his arm, Daniel pushed

the door open. However, like a disappointing smokeless version of Nighcrawler, Corpse Boy *bamfed* away.

The Clerk noticed Daniel.

Oh, God, not him.

Kristoff's Video Magic was a small, family-run business. Ninety-nine percent of the time the mom, Liz, greeted patrons with a cordial smile and a poof of true Yinzer hair. Daniel liked Liz; she was nice. The scumbag clerk of a son, Daniel definitely did not like. Heck, he didn't even know the jerk's name. However, it occurred to him that calling the clerk Scumbag insulted Liz, whom we've already established he liked.

Still, in Daniel's mind? That dude was Scumbag.

Scumbag glared. It's possible he didn't mean to glare, but he couldn't help *but* glare, it was so integral to his DNA. Glaring had been such an ingrained expression that he didn't know how to turn it off anymore, an automatically triggered response whenever someone came inside.

Scumbag had always hated Daniel. He probably did the math and figured out he worked an hour and got more money than he did working in a week, a month, a year, at the video store. His mother had once said, "It's a family business. You want to get paid? You can also start paying rent, paying for your food, doing your own laundry..." Her list was actually a few items longer, but Scumbag always stormed off right at the mention of laundry, as he apparently had to do his own laundry anyway.

Daniel hated Scumbag Clerk. In 1970, they combined East and West Deer into one school district. The two Deer's academic marriage resulted in Deer Lakes, and it also resulted in the closure of West Deer Middle School. The merger resulted in the middle school kids living in fear of the high school kids, due to the post lunch crossover.

And so, Scumbag despised Daniel the little dip-wad whenever he came into the video store. He always wandered the aisles for an hour, and only spent 50 cents on some old movie that nobody else would ever rent. Ever.

He never spent big money on the new releases. It made him want to punch the dumb kid right in the stomach and scream, "Stop renting that stupid Flash Gordon movie serial!" Therefore, whenever he'd see Daniel on the steps at the lunch crossover, he'd be sure to punch him in the stomach, which he knew he couldn't do in the store. There was a security camera, after all. Granted, he didn't hit him as hard as he could've, but just hard enough to let the kid know he needed to spend more money at the store. Message delivered.

Daniel, on the other hand, had no Earthly or Multiversal idea why the holy hell that video store bully targeted him, and remained terrified that he'd one day decide to pummel him right there in the store. Logically, he knew that wouldn't happen. Daniel no longer feared Scumbag, though, not since the day they passed on the steps and he didn't use his fist to purge Daniel of the jumbo sandwich on Jewish rye bread he'd just ate.

Turns out Daniel the little dweeb's brother was a linebacker on the football team. One day, that linebacker invited Scumbag Clerk to settle matters at The Clearing in the woods behind the school. The Clearing became a ritualistic fighting pit, and a few years later Daniel himself learned of its existence when Jimmy would find himself in a hair pulling battle for teenage life and death.

Scumbag didn't take a single shot to the face, but rather a series of shoulder tackles and body blows which left him in bed and out of school for three whole days. On the fourth day, he walked by Daniel without even looking at him. Now the linebacker was dead and the dweeb was alone in the video store. Scumbag glanced at Daniel.

Daniel caught his eye, unblinking.

"I'm sorry about your brother," blurted Scumbag. Daniel blinked. "What?"

"Your brother," Scumbag The Clerk repeated. "Sorry to hear what happened."

"Oh, it's fine," babbled Daniel. "Thanks."

The Clerk blinked rapidly in response before darting into the small office behind the counter.

Corpse Boy returned to Daniel's side. Daniel guided his friend through the store. "Were you ever here when you were not dead?" he whispered.

The Corpse Boy shrugged.

"The wrestling videos are in the sports section," said Daniel as they approached the area. "There's actually a really funny video called 'Baseball Funny Side Up.' See." Daniel held up the video cassette, featuring a baseball cracked like an egg. "It's a joke."

The Corpse Boy blinked his open bubble eye.

"I'm guessing you like your eggs scrambled," said Daniel. The Corpse Boy pointed to a wrestling video. The cover instantly captivated him. It featured two giant men, the yellow clad and tan Hulk Hogan and the even more giant black clad and pasty white Andre the Giant. "That's a good one! *Wrestlemania 3*, where Hulk bodyslams Andre the Giant. It's amazing." Daniel grabbed the small circular paper tag on a nail directly in front of it the video. A handwritten number, some indecipherable code, led to the proper VHS somewhere behind the counter.

The boys shuffled over to the sci-fi and fantasy section. Daniel grabbed *The Dark Crystal*. "Dude! They have it today! I haven't seen it here in a while!"

The Corpse Boy winced.

"It's not *that* scary." Daniel paused. "Well, a little scary."

The Corpse Boy pointed to a copy of *Follow that Bird*.

"I assure you that's just as scary as this." Daniel held the empty VHS sleeve in front of his face and tapped both sides in a bit of a dance. Something on the shelf caught his eye, he lowered the VHS sleeve. "Have you seen Blade Runner?"

The Corpse Boy shrugged.

"All you ever do is shrug," observed Daniel.

The Corpse Boy dropped his soulful eye.

"I'm just teasing you," Daniel smiled."It's what friends do."

The Corpse Boy smiled and then shrugged.

Daniel laughed, then added, "But seriously, we should rent Blade Runner." He searched for the video and the right words. "It's not about ghosts. More about what it means to be human."

Daniel noticed the Corpse Boy's eye, more swollen, more purple, more puss. The sliver of blue beneath the bulbous eyelid was mostly gone.

"You're like the Illuminator," stated Daniel.

The Corpse Boy shook his head, he didn't know.

"He has powers, but he's sick," he stopped momentarily, briefly unsure if he'd continue. "The more he used his power, the closer it took him to death… but he wasn't a ghost."

The Clerk returned to the counter and The Corpse Boy faded into the 'nothing.' Daniel and the Clerk exchanged no words, only VHS tags and video cassettes. The Clerk might've been a bit surprised at how many movies the kid was renting, particularly on a school night, but was overall glad to see him actually spend some money for once. Transaction complete, there was an awkward pause before The Clerk blurted out. "Do you want to buy some pogs?"

Thirty-five minutes later at home, with a stack of plastic encased video tapes and a pocket full of pogs – and two pretty rad slammers – Daniel successfully avoided dinner with the family so the wrestling and movie marathon could ensue.

Reaching into his pocket Daniel found a 5 dollar bill. The same 5 dollars bill he brought to pay for the movies they rented. He realized the Clerk didn't charge him for the movies.

CHAPTER 12

THE STRANGER, YOU KNOW?

Yesterday school went by quickly, mainly due to the fact that the upperclassmen had an assembly in the morning and the middle school kids got to watch a movie, a LaserDisc in Mr. McCormick's class. Daniel was awed at the sight of the disc reflecting the harsh fluorescent light of the science classroom. Before then he'd only seen the massive record-like sleeves at Suncoast in Ross Park Mall.

The movie was a science film, but it was a computer-generated narrated guide through the Milky Way with classic music. It was kind of like *2001: A Space Odyssey*, but even *more* boring, at least to the other students.

To Daniel it was simply magnificent.

That night Daniel educated Corpse Boy all about science fiction. They watched *The Explorers*, *The Last Starfighter* and most of *Star Wars*. The next night Daniel wanted to finish the *Star Wars* Trilogy and show Corpse Boy *The Flight of the Navigator*. Most of all, however, Daniel wanted to show him *Enemy Mine*. He wondered if Corpse Boy would start to call him Uncle? If he ever started to talk. Which would be creepy, now that he thought about it. Maybe he should be more careful what he was wishing for.

Dropping a paper in the door of the Sweetest Old Lady Ever's Trailer, the army of cats meandered around the boys. One of the cats stopped and flat-out stared at Corpse Boy, its icy gray eyes locked on him. Another cat, a significantly friendlier one, circled around him. It inched closer, stretching near the boy, ready to rub against his legs, but stopped short and continued its circle.

"Cats can see you?" puzzled Daniel.

The Corpse Boy only offered his stereotypical "beats me" shoulder slump.

"There are even more inside," said Daniel as he pointed to the nearest cat. "At least twenty! Maybe more, I lost count." In the window, the all gray cat with white paws and a white spot under its left eyes observed the boys.

Going in reverse of his normal order, Daniel took The Corpse Boy down over the bend of the road. They neared Cowboy's trailer, walking closer through dying grass and patches of dirt, through an endless arrangement of discarded car, motorcycle and other identifiable mechanical components. In the middle of the micro-junkyard Daniel discovered a cleared space, edged by walls of junk, erected out of parts and garbage pushed to make way for a ping-pong table.

It was weird.

What is this Cowboy guys deal?

Daniel noticed the balls and paddles laying on the ground near some other junk, pristine and unopened.

The Corpse Boy lingered near the table. His eyes darted at the junk around him, the table, up to the sky, but never to the trailer or the cornfield behind the house nor the woods beyond the cornfield. Inside the trailer blared a cacophony of discordant noise, music, television, and Lord-only-knew what else.

Approaching the door, the noise only grew louder and more jarring. Daniel frowned. What was he hearing? A table saw? The buzz continued, worn metal teeth loudly biting into wood. Daniel knocked, pounding as hard as he could, praying Cowboy wouldn't answer the door.

He counted to ten and knocked again.

Thanking his maker, nobody came.

Daniel turned to go just as Cowboy opened the door.

Daniel stood there, staring at the man. He felt like he couldn't breathe, and suddenly had no idea why he'd knocked in the first place. He assumed it had something to do with money, but no amount of money could be worth dealing with this weirdo.

Other than the insane amount of noise surrounding him in the trailer, there was an eerie silence. Sniffing and sniffling, Cowboy remained behind the screen door as the loudest silence Daniel had ever conceived of smothered the life out of the space between them. Finally Cowboy spoke, his voice barely audible over the noise.

"Hey, it's my paperboy."

Looking for an out, Daniel glanced over to the ping-pong table. His sidekick had vanished. The noise screamed from within the trailer, but now he could distinguish some of the noises. A few TVs, of course, mostly on the news, some on fuzz, one on *Star Trek,* a handful of radios, some talkshows, some music, each one lacking a finely-tuned signal, creating all kinds of static. *It's maddening,* Daniel thought.

"It's really loud!" he blurted.

Cowboy reached behind the door and Daniel flinched in fear. A surge protector popped with a zap of sparks out of the wall. Behind Cowboy, silence and darkness.

"Sorry. I was sleepin'," croaked Cowboy, sniffling and snorting as he stood in the door.

SLEEPING?!

Daniel struggled to remember why he'd even knocked on the door. After more silence, millions of years' worth of waiting or maybe a few seconds, Daniel finally spoke. "I have a thing for you. A form." He cringed, hearing how his voice sounded like Mickey Mouse, except without Mickey's natural endearing cockiness.

Daniel dug into his bag and pulled out a folded form. Granted, he had never actually read it himself, but it was some kind of promotion to get you free newspapers for three months. Pretty good deal. Normally that'd cost like fifty bucks, or something like that. Daniel wasn't very good at math.

"What form?" asked a suddenly lucid Cowboy. "A petition?"

"Uhhh..."

"Already told everybody when I moved into the neighborhood."

Daniel hadn't the slightest clue what Cowboy was talking about, but he knew one thing: Cowboy was lying. Even a 14-year-old newspaper carrier could tell that.

"I know my rights," Cowboy continued. He, like Daniel, hadn't a clue about any petition.

More silence as Cowboy glared at Daniel.

"Oh, no, Mr. Harrison," said Daniel, stopping and blushing. *Mr. Harrison.* He suddenly wished he were speaking to Indiana Jones, or that Indiana Jones would drive by in a motorcycle with a sidecar so he could jump in and escape. However, his own logic bothered him, as Indiana Jones was kind of an old guy back in World War II. By now, if he wasn't dead he'd at least be super old.

The thought of an old Indiana Jones depressed Daniel. In another ten years it would be more than just a depressing thought and a depressing reality. He tried to correct course.

"I mean, Mr. Cowboy." *Do'h!*

Daniel smacked himself on his forehead in his mind. "Mr. Cowboy."

Cowboy bared his sharp, yellowed teeth. He didn't smile. "None of that mister bullcrap. Just Cowboy" He pounded a fist against his chest. "That ain't my real name, anyway."

Daniel had no idea where this was going, but he wanted an escape, any escape, even an elderly Indiana Jones. He decided he would try to escape the way his mom and Mr. Rogers had taught him, by being nice.

"I'm sorry sir." He was, but he wasn't. "It's not a petition. It's a form for the newspaper. You can get three months free." Daniel glanced at the form, "Oh. Sorry. Six months free. Wow, that is a good deal." He raised the form closer to Cowboy, looking for the life of him like a caged beast behind the metal slats mesh and grating of his screen door. "I'm supposed to give them out to people, but I always forget."

After wiping a whole lot of snot and a little blood with his forearm, Cowboy opened the screen door and Daniel stumbled backward to give him room. Now exposed to the open air and afternoon light, Cowboy was exactly as scary as he had appeared to be behind the door.

"I won't have to pay at the end?" he said with a sideways glance to the street. "Cause there has to be some kinda catch. Nothing's free. *Ever*. Learned that the extra hard way."

"Nope," Daniel said, turning to look at whatever Cowboy was fixated on in the street. When there was nothing, he turned back to face him. "I'll stop it personally after six months, or just give you a new form. They give me a bunch and they tell me to give them out, but I never do." "You tellin' me you're gonna still be doin' this in six months?"

Daniel shrugged. "What else would I be doing?"

"Don't know, I just got a lotta expenses..." Cowboy paused to inhale phlegm. "...don't want another one." He stole another glance at the street over Daniel's shoulder.

Daniel looked behind him again, annoying when it was still empty. *Did this guy have some kind of lazy eye or what was going on, here?* "You just fill out the form, no charge," he said as he faced him again, trying not to scowl. He tried to sound as assuring as possible, like an adult would, but he still felt he sounded more Mickey Mouselike than ever. Again without that confident cockiness and general moxie.

Eyes back on the street, Cowboy reached out for the form without looking at Daniel. "I gotta get back to my things," he muttered as he crinkled the form in his sweaty hands. His eyes never left the street as he backed into the house, grabbed the inside door with his free hand and swung the door shut in Daniel's face. Inside the noise resumed almost instantly, and Corpse Boy returned by his side as he walked back from the house to the street. Daniel smiled, this one genuine. "I guess it's nap time again."

CORPSE BOY SHRUGGED, never saying a word.

"So can you hear the conversations I have when you, uh..." Daniel stopped talking, struggling to find a word he liked, one he felt acted as an appropriate descriptor for Corpse Boy's disappearing act. He really wanted to say "bamf'ed," but that wasn't right. He never disappeared in a puff of smoke, like Nightcrawler. He just...vanished. Was it that easy? Sure. He went with the simple and probably most accurate choice. "When you vanish?"

The Corpse Boy shook his head. Nope.

"Too bad," Daniel said. "Because you're missing out on a lot. That guy makes me call him Cowboy. Can you believe that?"

The Corpse Boy shuddered.

"Yeah. Tell me about it."

The boys continued their walk back up and around the bend. At the intersection, where the bend part of the bend began to bend, a police cruiser was parked. Daniel looked at the officer inside, ready to wave a friendly hello as he passed, but the cop's eyes were fixed at a point over his shoulder. *What was with everyone staring over his shoulder today?* Daniel wondered. It was like everyone else got the memo to play a practical joke on his or something. Then he followed the officer's line of sight and understood.

They were fixed on Cowboy's trailer.

Irrational as ever, Daniel feared being arrested, so he waved anyway. The officer seemed to snap out of his trance and waved back with a sincere but forced smile. *He probably knows my dad,* thought Daniel. But the officer's smile disappeared just as quickly when he returned his gaze to Cowboy's mini junkyard. Then Daniel understood what was going on. Cowboy's junk was everywhere, and he realized there was probably something illegal about it after all. The cop was just doing his job, noting the situation so he could have the right citation written up later. Made perfect sense.

He stood adjacent to the intersection, just outside of The USA Gazette Guy's trailer. In that exact moment Daniel realized that he referred to him as the USA Gazette Guy because he had no idea what his name even was. He did that a lot, and it came naturally to him. Maybe when he grew up he'd get a job just naming people. *Was that even a thing?* Daniel hoped it was a thing, or maybe he'd try to make it a thing someday. Someone somewhere should make that a thing people could get paid to do. That'd be cool.

In the driveway idled a big, brown, boxy delivery truck. Wearing shorts and a jacket, Big Bill strolled from the front porch to his truck. "Hey Big Dan!" Bill said cheerily. "You following me?"

Daniel looked at him, confused and oblivious. He was still rattled by his encounter with Cowboy, and felt almost as if he were being accused of something. "Oh, no! I wasn't! I was just coming from down around the bend–"

"Have a good one!" Bill bellowed in response as he passed him. He leapt up into his truck, swung it into gear and backed out, miraculously all in one motion, the gravel crunching loudly as Bill pulled away.

With the truck gone Daniel, had a direct sightline to the

porch where the USA Gazette Guy was. USA Gazette Guy stood at attention, holding a hat-sized box and glaring at the police car, now visible in his line of sight thanks to Bill's departed truck. USA Gazette Guy didn't even notice Daniel. His eyes screamed rage, grimy teeth grinding between his dark brown gums.

When USA Gazette Guy eventually noticed Daniel standing there, his demeanor instantly changed, his rage substantially subsiding as his care for his paperboy overtook him. For whatever reason, Daniel knew he genuinely cared about him, as if he thought he were in danger or something. Corpse Boy was gone, and therefore not "listening" like Daniel had recently learned.

Through the dirtiest, chew-filled choppers the world had ever known, the USA Gazette Guy coughed up words in his thick accent. *Russian? Maybe. Probably.* Daniel wasn't sure, but it was foreign, for sure. Foreign and ancient. "Police everywhere," he growled, sounding like a rock tumbler. "No good, boy, is no good."

Not knowing what to say, Daniel didn't say anything, just stepping forward and handing him the paper.

"Watch, boy. No good here, no good. Is...is..." He ground into a prolonged pause, struggling to find the right word in English. "*Dangerous.*"

The USA Gazette Guy reached out and patted Daniel on the back. "Thank you for newspaper," he said before he turned and headed inside.

Daniel lingered in the yard, watching the police car the same way USA Gazette Guy had been. Glancing to the window of Guy's trailer, Daniel noticed him pulling an old army helmet out of a box. He wasn't sure, but the black helmet looked an awful lot like an SSh-40, a Soviet Army helmet from World War II he'd read about in school. He smiled internally – USA Gazette Guy *was* Russian.

A few minutes later and bit farther up the road, out of

sight of the police car, the sun continued to inch away, bringing with it an ever-increasing chill to the air. The boys were now approaching Peggy Hart's trailer, and Daniel slowed down, watching him closely.

The Corpse Boy didn't seem affected by it. Maybe he knew he was home or something, but he knew he couldn't go back there. He didn't belong there anymore. He didn't belong *anywhere* anymore, Daniel thought. He didn't belong to a house, or a trailer court or a country or a planet or a solar system or a universe or a multiverse, nor any plane of existence. He wondered if he really understood that.

They approached the trailer they saw a man sitting at the base of the stairs. He was grungy, Daniel noted, but handsome. Surprisingly handsome, with greasy shoulder length hair and crippling blue-grey eyes. To Daniel the man looked to be a bit of a deadbeat, so he labeled him as such. The Deadbeat took a drag from his cigarette. He shamelessly made smoking look cool, and even though he smelled like Swamp Thing's ashtray, Daniel had to admit he looked kinda savage. At his feet, the evidence of his previous smokes complimented his snakeskin boots. The dude was so effortlessly cool, aroma and all.

As Daniel and The Corpse Boy approached, he looked over to the boy and noticed his eyes had become a bluish grey, even the one under the semi-closed lid seemed to light up. The Deadbeat took a slow, heavy drag of his cigarette and looked up at him.

"It's the paperboy," the Deadbeat sang to himself.

So cool, Daniel thought.

"Yeppers," he responded. Daniel was, after all, the paperboy. *So uncool.*

"Your old man graduated in, what...?" His lips contorted, click-smacking with each year he counted backwards. "Seventy-three?"

"Seventy-four, I think," Daniel said. It was seventy-three, but for some reason he didn't want to share this with a stranger.

"He was a year ahead'a my brother, Rick."

Daniel nodded. He really didn't care about some guy named Rick his dad went to high school with. Despite the Deadbeat's, coolness, he had a job to do and didn't need to hear old dudes – even cool ones – reminiscing about the good ol' days. He attempted to reach past The Deadbeat and put the paper inside the screen door.

"No," Deadbeat said, gently grabbing Daniel's arm. "I'll take it."

Not cool.

Daniel stopped and, surprising himself, felt a wave of toughness wash over him. "You don't live here," he said, punctuating each word into the air firm and true. He may never be cool, but very occasionally he *could* be tough.

"I know that." The Deadbeat smiled, "But I know Peggy."

Daniel hesitated. "Uhhh... I don't know, man..."

"Just lemme read the thing," snapped The Deadbeat.

Definitely not cool.

Deadbeat calmed down and his smile returned a second later, although it was less of a smile and more of a smirk. Daniel surmised it was a smirk he'd worn his whole life, one that got him out of or into more trouble than he'd see in a lifetime.

"Just lemme read it," Deadbeat continued. "I'll put it in the door when I'm done. Promise. She...ah...won't let me inside, anyway. In the old days, though, she always let me in." Daniel didn't quite understand the remark, but he knew it was dirty and thoroughly uncool.

Finally he conceded and handed him the paper. The dude's relentless coolness had defeated Daniel's utter uncoolness.

"You promise to give it to her?"

The Deadbeat chuckled. "I'll do my best," he drawled as he examined the cover. His smile faded and he read the headline aloud. "Police. Intensify. Investigation."

Apparently reading wasn't his thing, as the words came out choppy and with irregular rhythm. With every passing second Daniel thought Deadbeat seemed to grow a little less cool. He wanted to feel sorry for him, and he kind of *did*, but mostly it just made him feel better about himself.

Which in turn made Daniel feel bad again.

Nonetheless, Daniel strained to understand how a grown man could struggle to read those three words. Sure, they weren't small words, but they weren't Shakespeare or anything. Not that Daniel had actually *read* Shakespeare. He assumed he would in high school, and just as quickly assumed he'd hate it.

"You know the kid?" Deadbeat held up the newspaper tapping a finger on the face of photo. The Corpse Boy.

Panicked, Daniel looked around them. *Was The Corpse Boy here? Did this guy somehow know? Did uber-coolness give people some kind of spiritual clairvoyance and divination or something?*

He swallowed and steadied himself, thinking it through. The Corpse Boy wasn't there, so there was no way Deadbeat could know anything. The dude could barely read, after all. *That was mean.* Daniel felt both good and bad about himself. He decided he would try to honestly lie. "Not really. I mean, he lives here." *Well, he did.*

Deadbeat wasn't really listening, just smirking and looking at the sky waiting for his turn to talk. "He's my son," he announced with some sort of pride.

Daniel went pale white, more ghostly than the Corpse Boy. He felt as if the ground beneath him had fallen six floors down, his stomach lurching inside him, falling into limbo.

"You got a minute?" Deadbeat asked, continuing before

Daniel even had a chance to consider how many minutes, if any, he had. "'Course you do, you're a kid All you *have* is time. Until you don't."

Puzzled and scared and maybe a little depressed, Daniel sat down on the stoop next to Deadbeat. "I have time," Daniel informed him.

"Fair enough, we're usually all in a big damn hurry I guess," he paused to smoke. "Everyone except the cops."

"Okay..."

"THE PRINCESS," Deadbeat yelled loudly, before regulating his volume again, "won't let me inside."

Uncool, Daniel thought.

Deadbeat glanced back at the trailer. "I've been out here for like, THREE HOURS!" Finding what he believed the appropriate words, Daniel cleared his throat. "Miss Hart can be... a challenge."

Deadbeat chuckled. "That, my man, is an understatement. THE understatement." He shook his head. "Miss Hart, ha!"

Daniel said nothing, waiting patiently for the conversation to run its course and be over already.

"Let me tell you kid, that woman? Peggy? She used to be..." He paused, frowning as the thought weighed him down. "Beautiful. She was *beautiful.* And kind, believe it or not. She really was. So very sweet. Those walls around her, I... I built those walls. I did. I was no good for her. Still not. She's tough, though. Strong."

Daniel was dumbfounded. He tried to process those few sentences, but couldn't fathom a proper reply. He instantly learned two significant lessons:

1) WORDS HAD INCREDIBLE POWER, and

   2) it's generally best to use them sparingly, or just shut up.

• • •

DEADBEAT CARESSED the newspaper picture of his son, The Corpse Boy.

"There was one before this one," Deadbeat mused, saving Daniel from his internal torment on how to respond.

"Another...*kid*?" Daniel asked with an innocence he was on the verge of losing.

"Sort of..." Deadbeat searched out the appropriate words. "One that...didn't make it." He looked over at Daniel, staring at him without expression. "You don't know what that means, do you?"

Revealing nothing, Daniel looked again for the Corpse Boy, knowing he wouldn't appear while wishing he would.

Deadbeat no longer wore his trademark smirk. "You ever lose someone you love? A person you love as much as it's possible to love another person?"

Daniel's eyes fell to the steps and beyond. "Yeah."

"That's a shame." A tear escaped Deadbeat's left eye, trailing down his cheek. "That's too bad, you knowing what that's like. Kid your age shouldn't know that."

"Thanks," Daniel mumbled. "I guess–"

"You know, I never even met the kid." He looked at the picture of his son on the front of the newspaper. "My own kid. I bailed before he was born. I didn't want to see him if he didn't make it, like his sister didn't."

"Oh."

"He's cute. Woulda been a real lady killer, just like his old man," said Deadbeat. Daniel regarded the picture of his young friend. "He looks like his mom though, before me." He tapped the picture firmly. "Those are my eyes. I wonder what he's like. What kind of person he became. Where he even is–"

"He's into comic characters and wrestling." Daniel blurted out without thinking.

A little perplexed, Deadbeat stared at Daniel but did so with that smirk. "What?"

"I mean, I'm sure kids like that kinda stuff. At least, *I* like that stuff. It's...good stuff to like...if you're a kid and all," Daniel rambled.

"Wrestlin'? *Everybody* likes wrestling." He sounded so strangely proud.

"He'd probably like Merkanary. I mean everybody does."

"I have no idea who that is."

"People who really know comics know who he is."

"Fair enough," returned Deadbeat. "Maybe he'd like Wolverine?"

Daniel rolled his eyes. It wasn't that he didn't like Wolverine – everybody and their dog liked Wolverine – but it was just so mainstream. He kept that to himself and hoped Deadbeat didn't see the eye roll. "I'm sure he would."

He smiled a real smile, not just his ordinary smirk. "Too bad you didn't know him; it would be nice to be sure."

"All kids like Wolverine, but the really cool ones love Merkanary." He couldn't resist adding the last part, confirming his total lack of coolness.

Deadbeat started to sing.

"Now they call you prince charming
Can't speak a word when you're full'a ludes
Say you'll be alright come tomorrow
But tomorrow night might not be here for you." Retrieving a pill bottle from his jacket, Deadbeat swiftly popped the cap and popped a pill. He swallowed it dry, then looked at the bottle. "Burns the throat a little," he said, "but it's a mild pain. Goes away soon."

"Is that a poem?" Daniel asked, trying to avoid acknowledging what just happened. He very nearly asked if it were Shakespeare.

"That's a valium," Deadbeat replied, thinking he'd asked what the pill was.

"Valium's the name of the song?" Daniel asked, genuinely wanting to know.

"What? No." Deadbeat laughed. "It ain't a poem, but it's

damn sure poetic." He snuffed out the cigarette and lit up a new one in fluid, successive movements. He made smoking look so cool, but that *smell*! "Maybe it is a poem?" he pondered aloud, speaking his thoughts to himself more than Daniel.

"That's Lynyrd freaking Skynyrd! That's poetry alright. And a reminder for me to take my medicine." Deadbeat reached back into his inner jacket pocket, grabbing the bottle and momentarily considering another pill. He regarded the bottle as he rattled it before relenting.

"Peggy used to have a pet hamster. I would crush Valium into its food. That little guy'd run super-fast all around the cage, in circles, back and forth. Then, all'a the sudden he'd go like he was movin' in slow motion."

"Wow."

"Then it died."

Daniel frowned. "You probably shouldn't take those pills." Deadbeat chuckled again. "No," he said quietly, "I shouldn't."

It was quiet, the silence lingered like Bill Murray in that old *Saturday Night Live* skit, "The Thing that Wouldn't Leave." Daniel fidgeted, he had to break the silence or he felt like he'd die, just like that hamster. "I like Lynyrd Skynyrd, but they play them on the radio too much."

Deadbeat's eyes nearly popped out of his head. "Too much!" he yelled, a little too loud. "You can never play Skynyrd enough."

"Maybe, but..." Daniel paused. "Never mind."

"What? You were gonna say something else?" The last part somehow struck Daniel as a jab. He felt called out and uncool as he normally did, but he felt extra uncool being called out by such a cool dude.

"No, no. I finished," he lied. He hadn't, but he also couldn't remember what he'd meant to say. He felt painfully uncool. As if he suddenly in an instant became honestly aware of how uncool he really was, and how uncool he would always be. It stung a little that he'd never be as cool as someone who smelled like a diarrhea-crusted ashtray.

"No, man, go ahead." Deadbeat had that smirk again. "I'm a big boy, I can take it."

Daniel gathered himself and recalled his Lynyrd Skynyrd criticism. "Well, I think they need to stop touring. Like, it's kind of unfair to the guys in the band who died in that car crash."

"Plane crash."

"Oh. Right. Plane crash."

Deadbeat closed his eyes and waited for the comfort of numbness that came with the drugs. He'd have to wait a few minutes longer. "You don't want them keepin' on?"

"No," snapped Daniel. "When something's over you should just stop."

"It is really over though? Is anything *really* over?"

"Some things, but not everything I guess." Daniel took a deep breath, mustering his strength. "But Lynard Skynard, they're done."

"Dang kid, it was his freaking *brother*. It's a family thing, keeping the band alive. Keeping his–"

"*He shouldn't have to be his dead brother,*" Daniel interrupted. "He can't..."

Deadbeat paused, nodding his head. "Fair enough."

"I think... I guess I just think some people aren't very good at letting things go."

"Tell me somethin' I don't know," he said, nodding. "But son, you're preachin' to the choir, here, trying to teach an old dog old tricks."

Daniel furrowed his brow. "I don't think that's an expression." He felt, maybe not cooler, maybe not wiser, but certainly smarter.

"I said it," Deadbeat said. "*I* expressed it, it's an expression."

"Right. But...I don't think that's what makes something an expression." In that moment Daniel grew in social stature. He accepted the reality of being uncool, and yet he was cool with it. He also embraced his intelligence, maybe to the point of being a smart aleck."Well, damn! If it ain't, it should be!" The valium hadn't kicked in yet and the kid was too smart for Deadbeat, who felt he needed to keep the conversation on his level. "What other music you like?"

"Pink Floyd. *Comfortably Numb* is my theme song, I think. Original Genesis with Peter Gabriel, but not the Can't Dance stuff with Phil Collins." Daniel stopped, but only to try to think of more detailed answers that would make him sound cool and smart, while also accurately reflecting his taste in music.

"You're a paperboy from a bygone era kid," Deadbeat said. He fished out and finally popped a second pill just as the first one started to kick in. "You were born too late, I'd say."

"I like some newer stuff," Daniel added, hoping to show he wasn't out of touch with the times.

"Play any instruments?"

"My dad does." He paused and then blurted, "My brother did." He didn't want to say it, but the words just came out. Daniel prayed he wouldn't ask about his brother.

Deadbeat snapped a bit. "I didn't ask if your dad or brother played any instruments, I asked if *you* did." He reached over and poked Daniel in the forehead when he said the word *you*.

Daniel suddenly became a bit sad. "Dad didn't want to teach me, I guess. Besides, it seems too hard." He felt weird, justifying it, but thought maybe part of what he was saying was true.

"Eh, I can't play crap myself." Swaying a bit with the

rhythm of the cars over the hill, Deadbeat added, "Personally, I think music is for listenin', not for playin'. Then again... *somebody* needs to play it." He widened his eyes, as if he blew his own mind with that profound statement. "What else you like? Old stuff?"

"I like The Doors," Daniel said. "There's this really cool girl at school who's way into Jim Morrison."

"She sounds cool." He paused, assessing the smart nerdy kid with an elderly soul. "She pretty?"

"Of course."

Deadbeat sniffed. He was more interested in talking about music than 14-year-old girls. "You like The Doors, huh? Kids grow up too fast these days..."

Daniel was pretty sure that was the valium talking, but Deadbeat appeared to be just coherent enough to be understood. He knew what that meant, and yes, he was growing up fast. But he was also a good kid and wanted to someday be a decent, gentlemanly adult, so he went down another road. "I still play with toys," he said. Again, the words just popped out. He didn't think he'd go down that road, but at least he didn't mention his brother again.

"Good! That helps, I guess. Grounds you." The second you grow up is the second you realize there ain't no value in this world."

Deadbeat paused for a long time. Daniel wanted to get up and leave, but he felt bad for the guy, and wondered if the guy felt bad for Daniel.

"You just keep on playin' with them toys," the man added. "You keep right on. Maybe you can play with your brother..."

Daniel scowled at him, but Deadbeat was dead beat at that point and proceeded to pass out on the porch. For a second he wondered if he was dead, but then he saw he was still breathing and decided he was ready to move on.

The remainder of the paper route was a hazy stroll. Daniel actually had two papers still left in his bag, and at first he assumed they'd sent him too many. He used to count every day at the start, but the longer he did the job, the less he cared, so he didn't count anymore. He was lucky that the houses he missed were the nice people who always gave him tomato plants in the spring. He had no clue why. He hated tomatoes. But it was cool of them, and his dad had a garden anyway.

In his bedroom, he tossed the paper bag on his bed where it hit Mac on his backside. The animal groaned a bit at the slight impact of two remaining newspapers, but didn't budge. It sniffed the bag, groaned again with a profound stretch and went back to sleep, ensuring he hit his daily goal of 20 hours before midnight.

The Corpse Boy sat himself on the toy chest, smiling and obviously ready to play. Daniel paused. "I have to pee."

In the bathroom, Daniel peed for a good minute. All the earlier shenanigans on the paper route delayed his regularly scheduled peeing by nearly thirty minutes. He leaned his head back, rolling his head across his right shoulder. The muscles moaned from the agony of a heavy paper bag.

It occurred to him that even in death the Corpse Boy was polite enough to leave Daniel alone in the bathroom. He wondered why? Was it all in his head? Or did ghosts just respect your privacy?

Returning to the bedroom, Daniel opened the door. There the Corpse Boy sat, watching the short lived *Young Zombie* cartoon Daniel had recorded on VHS. In the show Frank the Ghost hid in a bush as his friend Gary the Zombie went on a date with Gwen the werewolf. *How am I the only one who liked this show?* Thought Daniel, *it's awesome!*

In the cartoon, Frank the ghost leapt out to confront his friend for dating his crush. *Maybe kids didn't like the zombie romance aspect?* When Frank landed cartoon blood splattered all over and his eyeball fall out. *That's probably why it didn't catch on.*

The Corpse Boy looked at Daniel, his eye was that much more swollen. He seemed more blue gray, the ruddiness in his checks gone. Puss burst from his eye, Daniel flinched. He whipped his shirt, there was no puss on him, but it oozed out of the Corpse Boys swollen eye, next to it, the good eyes stared at him.

CHAPTER 13
EPIC DOG BATTLE ...AND ALSO THE COPS

The previous evening, following night, next day at school and anything in between all seemed to merge and drift around Daniel. It felt as if he stood still the entire time and the world moved him.

He hated the feeling.

Numb and yet a raw, an overexposed nerve feeling everything, everywhere, all at once. And what was even more disturbing is how in the chaos and noise and ensuing quiet, he thought he heard a voice. His brother's voice.

Plodding along down the street, Daniel and the Corpse Boy went through the motions of the paper route. Nearly getting smashed by the passing grill of a Cadillac SeVille, the boys stopped abruptly, narrowing avoiding death. Or, death again, in the Corpse Boy's case. Although Daniel doubted he could die twice.

"Hey!" Daniel yelled.

Peeling past them, a very big car with a very small woman inside it, peeking over the wheel. The Queen of the Court zoomed by, oblivious to their presence. Rarely if ever did she drive her boat of a car up here, and now Daniel could see why. It took up a huge chunk of the road!

"We could have both been ghosts!" he exclaimed, believing he narrowly escaped death.

The Corpse Boy tightened his brow and pouted angrily. The message was clear: *Not funny.*

"Sorry." Daniel legitimately felt bad. He always thought of things he should say after the fact, and just as often said stupid things he shouldn't have. Things that got him in trouble. Things he knew to be hurtful, and sometimes things he said because they were hurtful.

Once he caused all kinds of havoc when he told kids at school his grandma had once been in a mental institution. He didn't think anything of it. He loved his grandma, but she was *clearly* crazy. Daniel mentioned it to one of the "cool" kids at school, thinking he'd impress him. Unfortunately that "cool" kid happened to be buddies with Daniel's cousin. A cousin who, of course, just *had* to go and ask grandma if Daniel was right about her.

In all honesty, Daniel didn't understand why he was in trouble about it all. The family talked about it *all the time*, so he thought it was…cool. Conversely, Daniel's dad, the crazy lady's son, had been *very* uncool about it all when he found out. Daniel cried in his bed that night, but later fell asleep laughing with his older brother as they imagined their grandmother in the looney bin. It was also the night Daniel watched *One Flew Over the Cuckoo's Nest* with his brother, after which they had some pretty great conversations, no matter how sad, or weird, or interesting, or funny they were.

"I shouldn't joke about that," Daniel said, walking back up the street with Corpse Boy beside him. "It's not fair, but I guess I've been stressed out lately." It was true. He *had* been very stressed, and he wasn't sure having regular conversations with a ghost was helping much.

The Corpse Boy shrugged what he interpreted to be a gesture of forgiveness. Daniel looked him in the wonky eye and smiled, nodding his appreciation. He was a good kid, even if he was dead and decomposing

At Peggy Hart's trailer the Corpse Boy stopped and stayed at the edge of the driveway. Daniel delivered the paper and returned to his friend. On the walk from the door to the end of the driveway he rolled over several options on what to say to him, something to comfort him, or maybe make him feel loved.

It all sucked.

On the side of the road he finally spoke. "I'm sorry...and not just about the ghost joke." Daniel found himself derailed by his own spongy brain. He was about to continue his heartfelt speech when a whomping bark, flush with aggression and angst, caused the Corpse Boy to *bamf* away. Daniel's preferred, albeit somewhat inaccurate way of describing it.

Hetfield, the auburn-haired mutant that Porkins called a "good dog," didn't so much bark as he vomited dog-ish sounds. For a split-second Daniel wished *his* dog were here, and then remembered what his dog looked like and how little his dog cared about...well...just about anything. Still, he could use a friend, even a lazy disinterested one like Mac.

Alone, Daniel faced the single dog in the known universe he actually feared. It was the one stupid-jerk awful dog which *had* to live in the freaking trailer park he delivered papers to. And it just *had* to be owned by the two weirdos who arbitrarily decided Daniel was their mortal enemy. Next to Porkins and Hetfield, Glasses guffawed loudly. All Daniel could think was how stupid he looked while he laughed, but he was also wary of the dog. Lack of allies be damned, Daniel knew he was about to do or say something stupid. Something he knew he shouldn't, something intentionally hurtful and frankly not even remotely clever, but he was pissed.

"You look stupid!" he bellowed up the street.

"Kill 'im boy!" yelled Porkins.

The dog tried to oblige, yanking his owner violently forward a few feet, damp gravel dancing about them.

"If he lets go, paperboy..." Glasses said.

"...you'll be dead!" Porkins finished.

"I'll be careful," responded Daniel instinctively, referencing a movie he'd seen dozens of times.

"What?" chortled Porkins. He shook his head in confusion. "What are you even *talking* about?"

Daniel had had enough. He didn't care what these jerks thought, or said, or if it ended with him getting eaten by a dog. It was a requirement for living that people should get that *Star Wars* reference. His normal human anger went atomic as it collided with his nerd rage, and Daniel's brain fractured. "It's from *Star Wars*, you idiots!"

Having expelled his frustration, his brain reassembled itself in his skull. Was he angry? Sure. Was he stupid? Abso-freaking-lutely. But even a riled-up nerd had his limits.

"Fruit loop!" Glasses raged. "He's just a pumpkin peach!"

Daniel shouted back at him. "What does that even mean? I don't know what that means!"

The Smoking Man watched the entire spectacle from his porch as his dog, a Norwich Terrier named Cosmo, calmly circled his legs and his oxygen tank.

On the street, Porkins snarled. "Get 'im!" He let go of the mutant mutt's leash. Glasses exploded in maniacal laughter. Under normal circumstances, Daniel would have made a joke about the laugh, but as the beast approached him, he was more concerned he'd just wet his pants. Or worse.

He didn't. (Thank God)

But it did appear he was about to be eaten by a dog, which was disconcerting.

Hetflied rumbled forward, gravel and debris following in his wake with a Looney Tunes-like cloud.

With a disappointed huff, the Smoking Man dragged his oxygen tank across the porch until the pesky left wheel got stuck in a groove. Holding the stubborn tank dolly in his left hand, with his right hand cradling a cigarette, he gingerly unlatched the porch door.

Cosmo shot out faster than Krypto chasing Bizaro with a milk bone.

Hetfield closed in on Daniel. Cosmo darted by, and although he was a smaller dog, at the moment Daniel though he was the biggest dog on the block. The debris cloud following him was much more adorable, despite the seriousness of the situation.

Upon reaching Daniel, Cosmo spun and faced Hetfield. Locking its back legs, the tiny dog claimed his ground with an impressive growl. Hetfield instantly went from top dog to finger-lickin' chicken, turned tail and ran off the road into the woods.

The bullies were aghast.

"You S-O-B!" shouted Porkins.

"Me? Or the dog?" asked a suddenly confident Daniel.

The bullies didn't hear him, however, as they were already running off into the woods. Futility shouting after the dog, their sounds soon faded with the forest. Daniel smiled, and heard the iconic song "Gonna Fly Now" from the movie Rocky in his head. He saw himself from the outside, a camera panning dramatically around him as the music played. Overwhelmed with a surge of confidence, he leapt into the sky, fist in the air...only for gravity to suck him back down into the utter silence of reality.

Daniel sighed. Reality sucked.

The Smoking Man stared at him from the porch, huffing away.

Before Daniel could relay his gratitude to Cosmo, the dog proudly trotted back to his porch and sat next to the Smoking Man, who waited patiently for his paper. Sighing, Daniel slowly walked over to the trailer. He pulled a newspaper out of his bag, snapped a rubber band around it and handed it to

Cosmo. Taking one end of the heavy paper, Cosmo's head tilted sideways at an awkward angle as he dragged it over to the Smoking Man.

"Thank you," Daniel said to the Smoking Man.

"Thank *him*," he replied with a drag from his smoke.

Daniel hesitated but relented. After all, he owed the dog that much. "Thank you, Cosmo. That is by far the best tip I've ever received." He paused and while he kept his eyes on Cosmo he raised his brow in the direction of the Smoking Man. "I still accept cash though."

"That jump was weird," droned the Smoking Man as he took the moist, mangled paper from Cosmo.

Daniel nodded. *If only you'd heard what I heard...*

As The Smoking Man smoked behind his newspaper on the porch, Daniel and The Corpse Boy walked on. "I thought it was cool," Daniel said, kind of sort of believing it." Turning to his friend, he added, "Man, you are really missing out on some crazy stuff when you disappear. A big dog wanted to eat me, but a smaller one..." he paused, deciding he wanted to spice things up a little bit. "...tried to eat *it!*"

The stunned Corpse Boy listened in complete awe, his one eye opened even wider, while the second one almost seemed to flutter open in excitement.

"I know," said Daniel as they strolled, "it was crazy."

They walked on and Daniel felt obligated to add. "well, it happened basically like that. The jump was cool, though."

Near the ponds the boys approached Old Man Mumbles and his trailer. The Corpse Boy remained stride for stride with Daniel as Old Man appeared to be sleeping. Daniel didn't realize the phenomenon until the crunch of the leaves he shuffled through woke the droopy old fella up. In an instant, the Corpse Boy disappeared. *Huh. That's new...*

Dutifully, Daniel placed the newspaper in the waiting newspaper box. "Afternoon," he said, giving a half wave.

Leaping (well, as much as it was possible for a human

being that ancient to leap) up from his sun-worn and weather-beaten folding lawn chair, he walked over and removed the paper from the box, looking down at the cover.

Daniel heard a whole bunch of mumbles and then somewhat clearly one word. "Police."

Old Man Mumbles had Daniel's full attention.

After a handful of additional mumbles came a second word. "Missing."

Well, Daniel heard "messin'," but he corrected it in his head. Regardless, the man now really had his attention. Daniel wondered about all the cops and now he might get some answers, but up until this point it hadn't occurred to him to read the very newspaper he was delivering for some answers.

Actually, it *had*, but he realized he didn't really want those answers. He didn't want to know what he had to know because knowing meant changing. Knowing that truth, figuring out what had happened to his new best friend would inevitably change all that. It would change everything, and he didn't want that. He wanted the world to stop, so he could stay in this moment, today.

Then came the final words, downright dirty words hidden amongst the inaudible mumbles of his favorite customer. "Child Predator."

Daniel wished he had shivered. That would've been normal. Instead, he dry heaved and very nearly threw up.

After the eternity it took Old Man Mumbles to climb his stairs, struggle to find his keys, and then drop them before finally opening the door and going inside, Daniel had caught his breath and began to read the paper. He read in silence, sitting in Old Man Mumbles' vacated lawn chair. The Corpse Boy stood beside him.

Daniel read and then reread the entire article, but the headline and the article's picture said it all in bold black and white. "VALLEY INVESTIGATION: CONVICTED CHILD

PREDATOR WAS MAN NEXT DOOR." The picture in the fading colors of the newspaper: Cowboy's mugshot.

Daniel jammed the paper into his bag and darted off. He hurried on, The Corpse Boy nipping at his heels.

Returning to the bend, Daniel found the cop car still parked nearby. Empty. Near Cowboy's trailer, two more police cars idled, lights flashing. At first Daniel thought he had impeccable timing, but as the scene dragged on and nothing happened, he began to have doubts. He and Corpse Boy waited and watched, keeping a far enough distance to go unnoticed.

At the trailer, the cops stood and mingled. They seemed relaxed, albeit a bit tense. One gestured in a very cop way and rhythmically bobbed his head. Although he couldn't see him, Daniel assumed Cowboy stood just inside the door. They talked and talked and talked some more, and that cop's head just kept on bobbing and nodding.

Finally, the screen door opened, and Daniel sucked in a breath. Two of the officers went in. Then, after what felt like another eternity, Cowboy stepped out of the door. His hands were not bound, but held at his back. The bobblehead cop had one hand on him and the other cop stepped in front of them.

At the police car, the second officer opened the door and guided him into the back seat. The first car, driven by the bobblehead cop, drove off. The second officer remained behind.

"Daniel."

The words were quiet, whispered from somewhere beside him. Daniel's eyes widened, he craned his neck to where The Corpse Boy stood. He was gone, but Daniel could have sworn he heard him say—

"Daniel!"

This time Daniel was able to locate the source. Up on the porch of her trailer stood the Sweetest Old Lady, waving him over. Hurrying her direction, Daniel soon joined her on the porch. "Hey," he said. "Crazy stuff, huh?"

"I've been watching! I didn't even see you!" She gathered herself a bit. "It was like watching a daytime story from my very own porch." A moment later her kindness overtook her need to gossip. "Do you want anything to drink?"

"No," Daniel said. "I'm okay."

"I've been watching for forty-five minutes!" She continued, not missing a beat. "The police have been sitting there and then talking. So exciting!"

"Did you read the paper yet?" Daniel interjected.

"I did."

Daniel wasn't convinced. "Did you see the article?"

"What article, dear?" Somehow she seemed even sweeter when she was utterly confused.

"About...uhh..."

Daniel had just read the article but had already forgotten his real name, so he went with what he knew. "About Mr. Cowboy?" He gestured toward Cowboy's trailer.

"Oh, no. No, no, no," she said, shaking her head. "Ever since that poor little Hart boy went and disappeared, I could only bring myself to read the Arts and Leisure section."

He nodded in agreement, realizing she was onto something. Avoiding the news certainly made life easier, emotionally, but you can't escape reality entirely. Still, Daniel was determined to attempt to spend most of his life trying to do just that.

"Did Mr. Harrison do something wrong?" she asked, not noticing he and his mind were clearly adrift in thought.

Mr. Harrison! He knew the name was somehow and unfortunately connected to Indiana Jones, who he really wished would show up on that motorcycle about now. "I hope not," replied Daniel. "But I'm going to find out."

"You are?" she asked, a worried look crossing her face. "How?"

"I…don't know," Daniel admitted. He thought about it for a moment. "I'm going to read."

"You're going to…read?"

"Yes! *I'm going to read!*"

He felt inexplicably proud of himself. First, it was honest and second, Daniel was recognizing he had to confront information to find the truth, kind of like homework in real life.

The Sweetest Old Lady Ever wasn't sure how to respond to such a bold statement, so she responded the only way she knew how. "Would you like some ginger ale?" she offered.

"No time," Daniel said, as heroically as he could.

She smiled at him. "You could take it with you. I have cold cans in the fridge inside."

Daniel's heroic resolve started to wane, and he smiled.

WITH A CAN of ginger ale firmly in hand, Daniel ran back past the Smoking Man's trailer. On the porch, Cosmo ran alongside him as he went, yapping behind him. Daniel offered a hasty salute. The Corpse Boy mimicked the movement perfectly, keeping pace with him the entire time. Passing the ponds, the Corpse Boy lagged for a bit as they passed Old Man Mumbles trailer.

Back in his chair, Old Man Mumbles had a habit of sleeping in his lawn chair. The boys' heads both turned as they ran past, momentarily concerned he might be dead. Daniel noticed the shallow rise and fall of his chest and kept on running. He was on a mission, a new purpose and calling, and The Corpse Boy was his loyal sidekick, at least in Daniel's mind. At the Gas Station, the usual crew had all gathered as Daniel rushed past them.

"Slow down, Skip!" shouted a concerned Pop Eye. He held up his hands. "Where's the fire?"

Daniel stopped. He turned slowly and said, "I have to go."

The Hat strode out of the shop portion of the gas station. Laughing as he spoke, he asked, "What? No drink today?"

Wielding it like a badge, Daniel held up the can of ginger ale.

Belly moaned. "Told ya, Pops! Kids are buyin' pop up 'ere at the video store."

"Ice cream too."

Everyone halted, staring at Stander. He rarely spoke. In fact, Daniel had never heard him speak. And although he wanted to stick around and soak up the moment, he didn't have time to worry about that now. He had to go! He darted off across the bridge and ran all the way home.

CHAPTER 14
INVESTIGATIVE JOURNALISM

Daniel had a bit of a peculiar habit. He would take all of one of his collections, most often his comic books, and spread them throughout his room. He covered the floor with them, save for a series of narrow pathways to navigate the massive, four-color world surrounding him. He organized based on various categories: age, character, teams and the related subsets. More often than not, they'd return to his stack of short boxes in pretty much the order they came out of, but it helped Daniel fully immerse himself in the stories and the worlds therein. On more than one such organizational occasion, Daniel's mom entered the room and commented something to the effect of, "Your room looks like a crime scene."

Tonight, Daniel's room looked not like a crime scene, but like a robust and full-blown criminal investigation. At least, it did in his mind.

He sat in the middle of the floor, surrounded not by comic books, but by newspapers from the last several weeks. Getting up, Daniel moved like a cat, pouncing on various papers from the previous weeks. Reading and rereading the articles, he was thorough and committed. He couldn't miss a single potential clue to what he assumed must be some deep-rooted criminal conspiracy in rural Western Pennsylvania.

"Oliver," he whispered.

Daniel repeated the name aloud, rolling it over his tongue. He decided that calling him The Corpse Boy had been unfair. It was kind of insulting, as if he were one of Daniel's play-things, a living toy. Well, without the living part. And that was the whole problem. He had lived and died as Oliver, a real boy. The Corpse Boy was only an identity Daniel had made up to make it easier to communicate with and identify him. Despite the bulging puss filed eye, despite the fading color of his face, he wasn't just a Corpse Boy anymore.

He was Oliver. Oliver Hart.

Daniel held the newspaper up to show Oliver, even though he knew the kid probably couldn't read. "You know you had a neighbor who bailed just before you went missing? Just got in his car and drove off one day."

Oliver sat on the bed, legs criss-crossed like a stereotypical kid his age. Hearing his name whispered by Daniel earlier had piqued his interest, but he didn't seem to fully under-stand why. He knew he had said his name not so much for Oliver's sake, but for Daniel's sake.

On the Sci-Fi channel, pretty much the only channel Daniel ever watched, played an awful late 1970s *Star Wars* knock off called *Jacob's Passage*. Oliver had been watching Jacob's Passage for about thirty minutes, so unfortunately it was still a bit dim on the older screen. None of it mattered to Oliver, who always found himself captivated by the moving images.

Not that you could really call it a film. Films were movies like *Lawrence of Arabia* or *The Godfather*. Heck, *Jacob's Passage* barely even ranked as a B-movie. But Oliver? Well, Oliver found it totally epic. In the film, Jacob battled a giant mechanical spider. The effect was terrible, and were Daniel paying attention he would have scoffed at it and suggested ways they could have done it better. Pouring over the papers, however, Daniel had no time to criticize terrible movies.

Surrounding Daniel, he frowned at the richly woven tapestry of a decades-old evil. As hard as he tried, he just couldn't make sense of it. He continued to read, until finally he felt he had a breakthrough.

"Okay, I think I've figured it out," he said with utter conviction, although wasn't half as confident as he sounded. The reality of the situation was that it was both simple and grotesque. Deep down, Daniel knew this – he just didn't want to admit it.

Oliver's ears perked up, curious to what Daniel was going to say next.

"It's all a big conspiracy," Daniel said boldly, desperately needing to believe it.

But Oliver knew the truth, even though he couldn't speak it into existence. His eyes drifted from Daniel back to the movie, Jacob scramble through a series of dimly lit tunnels.

Too engrossed in his own fiction, Daniel continued. "Mrs. Valetto stole the land all those years ago, and she has *something* going on back in those cornfields." Daniel pointed to the field on a map he'd drawn.

"Remember your neighbor? The guy who took off? He was arrested in, get this, *Anaheim, California*! That's where Disneyland is! I guess he was arrested for something else, but they questioned him about *you*."

Oliver perked up, looking at Daniel again, hopeful.

"He didn't know anything."

Oliver's head dropped down, depressed and morose.

Daniel felt bad. He's been hoping to impress him somehow. "I think it's drugs," he announced, and looked up to notice Oliver not paying attention. Sighing, he continued his tall tale, pointing to a newspaper with a completely unrelated article about a local drug bust. "She's a big drug dealer. I know the high school kids have crazy parties back there, my cousin goes sometimes.

"The drugs must be where she gets her money to buy the nice house and cars and stuff. All the jewelry, all those perms." Daniel's eyes grew wild as his imagination took over, adding to the nonsensical conspiracy. "That fatty and the jerk with the glasses are pushing her drugs. They have to be! They sell the drugs to Mr. Cowboy, but he was in prison and can't afford the drugs. Are you with me?" The conspiracy seemed to spew straight from his lips more than his head, maybe a bit from his heart. The actual truth scared the crap out of him, so he needed to believe this softer fiction.

Oliver ignored him. On the Sci-Fi Channel, Jacob stood before two openings, black circles and white light. In the light of each circle a silhouette: one of his mother, the other, his mysterious father. Jacob didn't know which way to go.

"You might want to listen, this is where you come into it," he informed his ghostly buddy.

Oliver glanced back to Daniel and then back to the television. In the movie, Jacob lamented his choice. He rambled on about what happened to his father. He questioned why his mother didn't tell him about the mysterious man? Was his father evil? Was he good? Oliver was enthralled.

"You must have seen the drugs," Daniel interrupted the film.

Without looking at Daniel, Oliver shook his head. *No.*

Daniel frowned and looked at his papers, telling him the true story. At least, the words and even the phrases could be found there, but the causality couldn't. Not a single word of what he said could be found in the newsprint surrounding him. He needed his lie, so he continued with it.

"That part I'm not sure about." He almost relented, but he didn't. "Mr. Cowboy couldn't pay the money, so Mrs. Valleto had him...you know...uh...hang you from a tree." Daniel's lips scrunched at the sound of his words. He knew they didn't sound right, didn't make sense. Of course it didn't make sense, it was actual bull crap and nonsense. It was Daniel's own bull crap and nonsense and he almost believed it. Almost.

Daniel could see the reality, sitting in the room and staring him in the face. Looking at Oliver, Daniel envisioned it all, every terrible thing the little one suffered. His mind's eye splintered; it was so ugly, so unspeakably painful to think of what Oliver suffered upon his death.

Daniel watched the screen, trying to distract himself from his painful imagination. United with his father, Jacob now cried tears of joy. The father had been deceived by the Space Lord and needed to flee the universe, entering the under dimension, but now he could be free.

"That movie sucks," Daniel announced bluntly. Oliver didn't react, so he decided to be nicer. "But I kinda like that part."

From the door came three gentle knocks, followed by his mother's voice. "Daniel? It's time to go."

"Go where?" "Sheila's birthday party."

"Oh. Right. One sec..." Gathering and stacking the newspapers, Daniel quickly cleaned up his room. He now knew very well what had happened to Oliver, however, he was too afraid to face it. The reality was too awful.

The credits rolled on Jacob's Passage.

He whispered to himself, "There's probably nothing we can do."

CHAPTER 15

JIM MORRISON AND BIRTHDAY CAKE

It was dark.

Daniel had never been to a girl's house after dark.

Actually, he'd never been to a girl's house *before* dark, either, but he'd *really* never been to one after dark. And it wasn't actually at her house, it was her Aunt Sue's house. Daniel knew Aunt Sue from up at Shop 'N Save. She was nice, at least as far as Daniel could tell from the other side of the deli counter. She never got married, never had kids and had a gigantic, house despite only working behind that deli counter at the grocery store. She also always let Sheila have her parties there. The real difference between those times and this one was the glaring fact that Daniel had never been invited. Sure, he was invited through Sheila's Aunt Sue via his mom over that same deli counter, but here he was, going to a girl's house. After dark. Everyone in the car seemed to be simmering with varying degrees of rage and contempt. On one end of the meter was his mom, coming in at moderate. On the other end of the severe spectrum sat, Jimmy, down-right seething. There were a number of outside rage-inducing factors, but the most immediate source being the fact that Daniel and Jimmy had walked to the wrong house.

They had confidently walked down the driveway, across the bridge and into the trailer court. But then they dared not knock on the door to a house that appeared to be empty, so instead they walked home and told Daniel's mom it must've been the wrong night. Consulting the invitation, the instructions clearly stated the party would be held at Aunt Sue's house. So in a fantastic flurry of embarrassment and rage, the trio hurried into the car and went on their way.

The sky darkened into a desperate blue as the trees zoomed by, the sunlight fading into it with a quiet surrender. Jimmy sat in the back seat, muttering things to himself as he looked out the window. He'd been snippy before he got into the car, once he sat in it and remained snippy the entire drive over., although he did manage to offer a pleasant hello to Daniel's mom and a thoroughly sarcastic one to Daniel.

Daniel didn't know exactly where the house was, but he knew it was in McGraw Plan and it was getting close. He had to say something before it was too late. "Jimmy and I are going to walk home."

His mom shot him a glance so severe the car seemed to swerve with it. She straightened the cautiously slow-moving Dodge Caravan. "No, you're not."

Stupid me, thought Daniel, *why did I ask permission for that?*

Jimmy looked forward, feigning ignorance. He knew the plan as they'd discussed earlier at school. Daniel's mom would do the taking to and Jimmy's mom would do the taking home. Daniel wished he'd had one of those cotton candy cocoon guns from *Killer Klowns From Outer Space*. He could just trap all these people in a giant ball of cotton candy and just stay home and watch movies.

Daniel hoped his friend would be supportive and back him on this. He took the gamble. "Fine," he said. "Jimmy's mom will take us home."

"Good," said his mom. She looked back at Jimmy.

Jimmy smiled.

He smiled at the thought of his friend being attacked by a bear in the woods. Not killed, mind you, just maimed badly so maybe he'd learn how to be a better friend.

The smile was good enough for mom. "Fine, I'll see you at home."

Aunt Sue's house sat in the middle of McGraw Plan. McGraw had been the first planned community built in the area. Prior to that it had just been a bunch of trees, now there were less trees and a bunch of houses laid out in a fairly roughshod pattern. As Daniel grew through high school and eventually went to college, similar but far-less-roughshod plans popped up. Each time they'd have more and more houses and fewer and fewer trees. The split-level house had a short walkway from the street to the front door. At the end of that walkway the mailbox sprouted a bobbing bouquet of balloons.

Daniel's mom pulled up to the curb, put the car in park and looked in the review mirror at Daniel. "Goodbye," she said, suspicion drenching her voice. Without a word , the boys exited the car, mumbling a half-hearted thank you to her as they shut the door. Halfway down the walkway Jimmy declared, "Have a good walk through the woods at night in the dark." He envisioned that bear making Daniel's arm a nub and his begging for Jimmy's forgiveness from his hospital bed.

"Thank you...," said Daniel as they stepped up to the door and rang the front doorbell.

The olive-skinned, jovial Aunt Sue answered the door, quickly stepping past them to wave Daniel's mom off. Jimmy stepped toward the door, but Aunt Sue's outstretched palm held him back, her other hand holding the door.

"Party's in the back," she said, "as all good parties should be. Go on around." She moved her hand from Jimmy's chest and pointed to the driveway that wrapped down around the side of the house. The boys leaned back, attempting to peer around, as if they'd see the party if they leaned enough. They looked at each other and then to Aunt Sue.

"Okay..." Daniel said.

"You boys get to be with the girls," she added. "adult free."

Daniel audibly gulped. "Okay..." he said again, voice quivering in unspoken terror.

Wordlessly, he and Jimmy walked to the driveway, now unified in their shared dread. Their fear subsided as they heard the murmuring noise of the party, and Daniel found himself wishing he could swap out Jimmy for Oliver. In fact, he actually attempted to wish for it, starting to pray under his breath. "God, I pray..."

"That was weird," broke in Jimmy, really trying to be friends again.

"What?" snapped Daniel.

"What do you mean 'what?'"

"'What do I mean, what?' Don't ask me–"

Daniel had gone from annoyed to confused, still annoyed, but now also confused.

Jimmy raged on. "Genesis does what Ninten-Don't!"

Daniel laughed out loud.

"It's not a joke! It's never been a joke! Nintendo isn't a joke!" Jimmy halted, but Daniel continued walking. He now stood at the lower corner of the house. At the bottom of the driveway several feet from Jimmy, he turned around.

"You've always liked weaker systems," snarled Daniel. "Even when the Genesis came out, you still played Nintendo."

"The SNES kicked Sega's obsolete rectum! You know that!"

"And PlayStation is wiping the floor with Nintendo every passing day," said Daniel. "You just can't let it go, man. Outdated hardware, inferior graphics, crappy gameplay. Not even in 3D. Get with the nineties, Jimmy. 2D is as dead as Atari. Nintendo is *over*. It's over."

"I'm going to call my mom," Jimmy huffed.

"Tell her to buy you another lame Nintendo game like that unplayable *Swamp Thing* one."

"That's a good movie!"

"I didn't say anything about the movie," Daniel replied with an eerie calm. "I happen to like both *Swamp Thing* movies, even the TV show is good, and it's a highly under-rated toy line, almost as underrated as Zen: Intergalactic Ninja."

"Zen is the second-best game on the NES!" shouted Jimmy.

"What is that? Is that like being the nicest guy in prison?" Daniel asked. "Who wants to be the best 8-bit game. 32-bits is *way* more than 8 and 16. Do the math."

"I'm *done* doing your math." Jimmy turned back and started walking up the hill. Daniel watched him walk away, fading into the darkness. He shook his head and swung around walking toward the corner of the house.

Bamf. Oliver stood next to Daniel as if he'd been there the entire time. Daniel smiled and pointed to the party now in sight.

"I'm about to go over there," said Daniel. "It's a girl-boy party, but I wanted you to see it before I go over." He paused to give Oliver a chance to respond, but he just stood there, staring at him. "That Zen: Intergalactic Ninja game is pretty awesome," Daniel blurted out.

Oliver blinked his one good eye, obviously having no idea what he was talking about.

Under the porch a string of Christmas lights glowed. The music played just loudly enough to meld indistinguishably with the cacophony of voices. Cans of pop were strewn about alongside half-eaten plates of cake. Daniel and Oliver stood close enough outside the downstairs window to see a furnished basement with shag rug, an ugly mushroom-shaped chair and a big screen TV. Beyond the TV he eyed a large bookcase, only to realize it was full of video tapes.

"Whoa..." he whispered. Daniel wanted to crawl through the window, plop down in that mushroom chair and watch every single one of those movies. Didn't matter what they were, he was entranced. Stumbling a bit in the gravel of the driveway, Daniel's gaze returned to the party. His eyes widened as the tension tightened around his neck, invisible hands grappling the breath from his lungs.

"No..."

Realization settled on his shoulders like a specter, and his fear burned at the touch. This wasn't the party he thought it was, with both girls and boys. This was a party with girls...and ONE boy.

Daniel.

Petrified, he swung around in Oliver's direction, but the boy had already vanished to the nether regions. "Oliver?" he whispered through clenched teeth.

"Daniel's here!" a voice called from somewhere behind him.

"Oh Lord..." Daniel muttered, turning around slowly, forcing a smile to his face.

A few of the girls around a resistant Sheila began pulling her forward. She held her ground under the patio. "No," she protested with a smile, a mighty big one from what Daniel saw.

Daniel heard a voice in his head and recognized it instantly. One of the great leaders of the Rebel Alliance, bravely leading the fleet against the second Death Star in *Return of the Jedi*. It came from the Captain's Chair of the Mon Calamari, from the esteemed Admiral Ackbar. *It's a trap!*

Before he'd devised a plan of escape, the girls swarmed around Daniel and pulled him forward. Lacking the willpower of Sheila, he was yanked by both arms into the center of the party. He felt a rush and wondered if there was a part of him that didn't want to resist. Maybe, just maybe, he was glad they forced him over to her. After all, if they hadn't, he'd likely have run back up the hill calling after Jimmy.

He felt as though he were floating towards her, but not exactly in a good way, more like one of those floating zombies in *Corpse Killer* on the Sega CD. Eventually, Daniel's feet landed at the base of a folding table. Next to the table: Sheila. On the table: Jim Morrison, in cake form.

Daniel was speechless. Sheila was equally silent, smiling but avoiding eye contact. The girls chatted and pointed a few feet away, forming a perimeter around Daniel and Sheila. The perimeter was completely unintentional, however, for Daniel it was unbreachable. Like the walls of Attilan, only the supersonic voice of the Inhuman leader Blackbolt could break them. He still didn't know what to say, but he was at a birthday party. He pointed to Jim Morrison. "Can I have a piece of cake?"

"No," Sheila replied.

"Oh,"Daniel said, frowning. "Okay."

Silence floated between them like a wispy fart.

"Are you sure?" He looked at Jim Morrison and licked his lips. The shirtless image of him from *The Best of the Doors* perfectly captured in the photographic icing .

"The cake was expensive."

"Oh," he said, eyebrows creased. "Was it good?"

"It was okay. The picture was the expensive part. My mom had to put money aside to save for it."

"Wow. That was nice of her," Daniel smiled. "Maybe if she paid a little more, they would've put his shirt back on."

They both smiled at each other, started giggling until they busted out laughing Daniel took a step closer to the cake, carefully-yet-awkwardly cutting around the image of Jim Morrison.

"You really like Jim Morrison," he said through his first bite.

"Not enough to *eat* him," she laughed. He glanced up and caught her eye. He could have sworn they were sparkling, but that might have been the Christmas lights. He couldn't be sure. She moved a few inches closer and closed her eyes, her lips parting slightly, almost imperceptibly.

Oh god, thought Daniel. *Does she want me to kiss her!?*

He swallowed his bite, eyes wide.

Yes, yes she did! But certainly not now with everyone watching, right? That'd be crazy!

He instantly changed the subject. "I wish I had a birthday party like this."

She opened her eyes, frowning slightly. "You could have them at your house," she said.

"I guess." He didn't want to say it aloud, but he had absolutely no desire to have people come to his house. On the other hand, he also didn't want to seem like a weirdo hermit.

"You live in a big house," she blurted.

"What? What does *that* mean?"

"Nothing, it's just that mine's a dumb trailer full of crazy little brothers," she said, with great sadness and honesty.

"My dad built my house."

"Really? I didn't know that," she said. "That's really cool. My dad couldn't hang a clock let alone build a house, let alone a big one."

"It feels empty."

He didn't mean to say it. The words just fell out of his mouth, and as they settled between them, he looked away, shocked at his unabashed honesty. "Because of your brother?"

He sighed, not out of sadness as much as relief. She'd said the on thing that he couldn't bring himself to talk about, and the floodgates were starting to open.

"The house just... it isn't the same without him." Tom Petty's *Free Fallin'* played in the background, and Daniel smiled, gesturing to the stereo. "He used to love this song," he said. "He'd play this album over and over and over again. I can hardly listen to it now."

"I can turn it off…"

"No," he said, cutting her off. "A great song is a great song. It doesn't take him away or bring him back or anything. It's just a song. A really great song, no matter what it does to me inside."

"I'm sorry he's not here." Sheila smiled and looked directly into his eyes. "But I am very happy you came to my birthday party." She paused, adding, "since I missed your last birthday and all."

"I didn't have a party," he said. "Well, Jimmy bought a Star Wars…" he stopped short of the word "toy" and awkwardly replaced it. "Gift." He blushed. "But it wasn't a real party."

"Well, since I missed your last birthday, and you never know, it could be your last birthday…" she leaned over, hugged him and said. "Happy birthday, Daniel."

Daniel wasn't sure if he'd landed at the gates of heaven or the mouth of hell. She held him for what felt like forever, and yet wasn't nearly long enough.

The music stopped briefly, and she let him go just as Lou Gramm started to sing. *I gotta take a little time*, later accompanied by the rest of Foreigner. Sheila started to sing along.

"This mountain, I must climb
Feels like a world upon my shoulders"

"I feel those words," muttered Daniel. "But I don't really see the sun through the clouds. Not yet, at least."

"It must be cold up there," she continued, almost in rhythm with the lyric. "It keeps me warm when life goes colder." She sighed, and a moment later the chorus connected them. both. *I want to know what love is, I want you to show me.*

The song went on and she silently swayed for the next few verses, eyes closed. Daniel couldn't help but take in her body as she moved, entranced by the intoxication of a girl breaking into womanhood, perhaps not gracefully, but earnestly. "I like this song," she announced, swaying in perfect sync with the rhythm.

"Do you ever feel you have a real purpose in life, but that you don't know what to do?" Daniel asked, breaking the moment. "That it's too much, too soon, and you're just not ready for it?" He immediately regretted asking, it all, the words having just spewed out of him.

She opened her eyes and mulled it over, and Daniel got the impression she was thinking he was speaking about them. Finally, she replied. "Do something, even if it's wrong."

Daniel smiled. She caught his smile and returned it. They were sly, romantic smiles, although neither of them had the slightest idea what they were doing. "The girl with a Jim Morrison cake would like this song," he said. He grinned, thinking he'd just given her the greatest praise he'd ever offered another human being.

She disagreed. "Are you making fun of me?" she snapped. "I love Foreigner, but they aren't exactly The Doors."

Puzzled and maybe a bit offended that the greatest compliment ever wasn't perceived as such, he decided to clarify. "No. I've never been further from making fun of someone. In fact–"

"Do you want to dance?"

She obviously didn't care that they remained on display like the Red Panda at the Pittsburgh Zoo.

Did he want to? Yes! *Was he physically or emotionally capable of doing so?* No. No, he was not.

Majestic by Wax Fang played next, the lyric,

"*I'd rather be dreaming of someone than living alone.*" Hung in the air, Sheila didn't seem to notice it, but Daniel did.

"Can we just talk?" he heard himself say.

Her smile grew wider. "I'd like that." For the next few hours Sheila ignored the friends she'd invited to her party as she and Daniel sat on a half wall at the edge of the patio, just talking. They talked about Jim Morrison, they talked about how the cake tasted, they talked about her brothers, they talked about the crazy characters in the trailer court. They just...talked. And it was beautiful.

While Daniel did have his fair share to say in the conversation, he did his best to just shut up and listen, and if he were being truthful, that's what *he* wanted to do. Before they knew it, 10:00p.m. came and the party had to end.

Daniel didn't get to say a proper goodbye, as the girls swarmed Sheila to get the juicy scoop on their two-hour conversation. He didn't feel like sticking around only to be pointed at, so he made his graceless exit. Besides, he had to walk all the way home and he wasn't even sure which direction to go to get there. He hurried back around the corner and up the driveway and then froze, stopping completely.

At the end of the driveway, perched on a large decorative rock, sat Jimmy.

"My mom said she'll be here at about 10 after 10," Jimmy said, not looking at him.

Daniel said nothing. He walked over and leaned against the rock bench. Jimmy slid over on it, sharing the limited space.

"Was the cake good?" inquired Jimmy.

"I wouldn't know," Daniel said. "They wouldn't let me eat Jim Morrison's torso."

Jimmy snickered. "Jerks," he whispered.

Jimmy's mom pulled up in her Ford Taurus, and both boys walked over in silence.

"That Zen game is pretty great," said Daniel.

"I know," Jimmy sighed.

Daniel smiled, but he tried not to let Jimmy see it. He couldn't after all, give him any leverage in future comic book trades.

CHAPTER 16
THE DARK OF NIGHT

The Corpse Boy sat atop the Nintendo toy chest. For the moment, he wasn't Oliver, he had to be The Corpse Boy. He could be Oliver again when he found redemption, whatever that meant. Daniel often stared at the toy box and considered painting it black, like the Rolling Stones song. While he didn't hate Nintendo, he believed it to be kids' stuff. He'd moved on from Mario to Sonic and Sega, and after last Christmas he and his brother pooled their Christmas money together to get a PlayStation, although he could never bring himself to play it.

Tossing and turning beneath his New Orleans Saints blanket, sleep eluded Daniel. He didn't care about sports, but he certainly wasn't a Saints fan. Come on, he lived less than twenty miles from Pittsburgh. His mom had bought it for him. She bought it from the after Christmas Ritter's Clearance Catalog. Like the regular Christmas Catalog, it featured page after page of clothes, sporting goods, apparently bedding and best of all toys. However, it was much smaller and bound with staples and not the fancy book style glue binding of the regular Christmas Catalog.

Every year Daniel anticipated the Clearance catalog, almost as much as he anticipated the regular catalog. The highlight of his fall was spending hours, even days, going through the toy section, carefully circling and highlighting everything he wanted. And he wanted *a lot*.

Now, he knew very well he couldn't, wouldn't and probably shouldn't get it all, but he legitimately *wanted* it all and also very much wanted to be surprised by what he got, but not so surprised that it wasn't pre-approved. He'd accept nothing "off list", so to speak. Last year he did the same, and when he'd handed her the dog-eared and marked-up Ritter's Catalog, his mom responded. "You're still doing this?"

It bothered Daniel, but he didn't say anything, and got mostly what he wanted. This year the catalog sat on his desk, unmarked, although thoroughly well read.

Sleep. That was not a thing that was going to happen for Daniel. He could not. He *would* not. He didn't deserve sleep. Once upon a time, he'd been famous for his ability to sleep. Their old house was not only adjacent to a bar, it was actually a single building with a shared wall. Late at night some commotion or another always occurred. Not every night, but certainly every weekend night. Fridays and Saturdays often ended in the police escorting someone away in handcuffs.

Once the chaos spilled into their backyard. Under the crabapple tree some white trash Jesus had beat his girlfriend up. Daniel's dad grabbed his hunting rifle and stepped outside. The drunken creep cussed him out, but fled yelling up and down Main Street until the cops finally arrested him. The poor woman then yelled at Daniel's dad for a long while before eventually coming in the house and sobbing hysterically on the couch until an ambulance showed up to take her to the hospital, with sirens and everything.

Daniel had slept through it all. He only heard about it from his brother the next morning.

Oh, how he yearned for those halcyon days. He no longer slept like a five-year-old, but this had traveled well beyond normal "I can't sleep." No, this was driven by guilt. He had to do right by his friend The Corpse Boy. By Oliver.

He popped his head up from his blankets, looked mournfully at Oliver, and smiled. He knew the time had come.

The time to say goodbye.

A jolt of energy and desire overtook Daniel. He hopped out of bed and hurriedly dressed, all the while wearing his mournful smile. Oliver's eyes followed Daniel as he went from one side of the room to the other. A sock here, a belt there, his pants back over there, a jacket under the bean bag chair. He relied himself, to the wood they would go.

He owed it to Oliver, he wasn't sure what he owed him, but after the magic of the evening with Sheila, Oliver deserved a bit of his own magic. Granted Daniel had no idea what that magic was or how to perform it.

They crept through the house. Daniel walked carefully down the metal spiral staircase, his feet covered in heavy, soft gray hunting socks. Like most of his clothes, these were hand me downs from his brother. The staircase spun down from the end of the hallway where his parents slept. He'd seen his brother sneak up and down these steps countless times and knew exactly how to navigate them. Oliver took the same delicate steps as Daniel, even though he couldn't make any noise if he tried. It was cute, and Daniel appreciated the solidarity in their sneaking about.

The world outside slept in darkness, the trees rustling quietly as the boys walked down the driveway. Crossing the bridge, only the howl of the wind accompanied them. Through the intersection, no cars. The light above Popeye's buzzed and flickered, but otherwise everything remained shut. Daniel had never seen the front garage door of Popeye's closed, and it was a strange sight. Even in the winter, the garage remained opened. The chipping and peeling mismatched white paint became intimidating shades of grey in the flickering light, the two upstairs windows black voids of eyes, watching the boys, passing silent judgment.

Daniel suddenly had two thoughts: 1) he realized there actually was a second floor, something he'd never noticed , and 2) he wondered what the heck went on upstairs from a gas station/convenience store. He felt the gas station following them as they walked, its gruesome face scowling at their backs.

Eventually they found themselves in the unknown woods. Daniel had forgot his watch, but he was pretty sure it was 3 AM and nothing good ever happened in the woods at 3 AM.

The wind howled and gusted, cutting into his thin, hooded sweatshirt. Camping would be great right about now, in particular a campfire, or at least a flashlight. Daniel gingerly led Oliver through the dimly lit forest.

The clouds covered the moon. The wind howled like a wolf. Daniel stopped. No, he had to keep going. But boy, he didn't want to. Daniel didn't like having to make grown up choices. He never would. Right about now, he wanted nothing more than to curl up with that Ritter's Catalog.

Daniel and Oliver walked, lost in the intensity of a horror movie setting, magnified tenfold. Horror was Daniel's least favorite genre, and he watched very little of it. The notable exception being George Romero's Dead series. Being a "Pittsburgh Kid" and those being Pittsburgh movies were somehow okay. At this very moment in time, however, he wished for more than just some zombie films to reference. He needed a longer list of pitfalls to avoid. The first thing to avoid, hanging out with a ghost boy, and going into the forest with him at 3 AM on a windy night, and visiting his rotting corpse, but here he was.

Inching forward, Daniel stumbled on an old tire. On his hands and knees he noticed his duck boot. He still hadn't told his mom he lost it, or his dad, it was his dad's boot after all. He tried to pull it out, but it was stuck in the now dry mud.

Regaining his feet, Daniel and Oliver marched forward to where the Corpse Boy hung.

Alone, Daniel walked over to the tree. Just ahead, he saw the body. Before it had been a scary sight, because it was just a body hanging in a tree. Now he didn't just see the body of a boy hanging in a tree. He saw his friend. He saw Oliver.

The body was rotting with every passing minute, becoming less and less of who he was, Oliver slowly becoming lost to the identity of the Corpse Boy.

Daniel stopped and looked back for Oliver, but he was gone. Steeling himself, he turned back to the tree. He reached into his sweatshirt pocket and pulled out a sheathed knife. The knife, a single piece of metal, also belonged to his dad, one of his throwing knives. Dad would often have him stand by a wall and throw the knife into the wall beside him. Daniel hated it, but his dad was good and hadn't hit him yet, so he trusted him. Most of the time. Removing it from its sheath, he held the knife in his mouth, clenched between his teeth to avoid cutting his own face up and appearing like victim of the Joker.

Fighting the wind, Daniel began climbing the tree. He was hardly a good climber, however the stump next to the larger trunk from which Oliver hung had plenty of good footing and handholds. He soon reached the branch across from Oliver's body.

The wind pushed against the body, rotating it in a slow, steady arc. Oliver and Daniel were now eye to eye, and he froze. It looked like him, like Corpse Boy, but there was no movement, no smiles or shoulder shrugs to give it life. Oliver was truly dead. More flesh had rotted off of his body, patches of his skin had dropped away while others were mottled and gray. Daniel frowned. Dead bodies weren't blue like in Romero's *Dawn of the Dead*, and they didn't walk, at least not in the body.

Taking the knife from his mouth, Daniel reached for the

wire from which Oliver hung. He began to cut, it was diffi-cult. He struggled through it, making a minuscule amount of progress. Oliver's dead eyes stared back at him, both pleading with him and scolding him for his lack of progress. Or was it a lack of resolve?

Daniel stopped.

He stared back into that one dead eye, eyes drifting down the rotting corpse of his friend. He cried.

After a few minutes, he pulled his arm back and jammed the knife into the trunk of the tree, and began to climb down.

As he walked away, Oliver reappeared and joined him. Daniel glanced at him, studying the boy's peaceful demeanor, considering the stark contrast to the corpse still hanging behind them in the forest. Tears streamed down Daniel's cheeks as he quietly cursed himself and how selfish he was, how he wasn't ready to let this go already.

Wasn't ready to let Oliver go.

CHAPTER 17
THE ORIGIN OF THE CORPSE BOY

Although he didn't look like it, the Grim was a hero. An accident in space ravaged his body and made him appear a monster, as it did his brother, the Ghoul.

Glen "Gray Hair" Graboyes, a hot shot shuttle pilot, along with his brother Reuben, a crackpot scientist; together attempted to travel around the rings of Saturn, spinning backwards and forwards through time. A cataclysmic miscalculation on Reuben's part, and overly impetuous piloting on Glen's part, resulted in the interstellar radiation that changed them. Interstellar rayons changed the identical twins into matching monsters, save for the distinct scar across Glen's face. Still, they remained two stupendously different men who happened to spring from the same chromosome. They shared only two things, their appearance and their bold, daring sense of adventure. They returned to earth, but they did not return as Glen and Reuben. Glen came back as the noble and loving Grim, however Reuben's dark heart grew only shades blacker as he became the murderous and hateful Ghoul.

When Oliver's mom presented him with the toy, the package read "THE GHOUL" in bold yellow and red letters, but he knew better. He knew it was actually the Grim. It was the hero. The Ghoul lied, cheated, stole and even killed! Oliver's mislabeled toy was that of a good man, a man befallen by tragedy who clung to his integrity, which made him a better man. His toy was *not* the Ghoul, but the Grim.

Everyday Oliver played alone in his yard, as inside the trailer his mum yelled so loud at the TV it was hard to get into the role play. It forced Oliver to gather a handful of toys and make his way to the barren front yard, where the tall dying grass became a desert savanna, a tropical rainforest, a distant alien world, anywhere other than where Oliver actually lived. His imagination was fertile and boundless, carrying him off with one consistent feature to his tall tales: a quiet, thoughtful hero subduing a loud and bombastic villain.

The toys he took would vary, with one exception – he always took the Grim. The Grim was always the hero. Oliver's hero.

The yelling happened when his mom was alone, as she was nearly all of the time. When she wasn't yelling, the television blared or the radio blasted. Sometimes she shouted about those "scummy liberals," or "those dirty Republicans." He didn't know what any of it meant, but he knew if his mom did not like them, they must be no good.

Other times when people visited, she called them her "Special Company." When "Special Company" came during the day, she never had to tell him to go outside. He already knew what to do. He hated to be a bother and he didn't want to be in the way, so he remained outside until they left. On those days, Oliver ventured as far from the house as he could go without leaving the yard.

In the yard he played. He took the Grim on adventures all around the world and into the multiverse. In his hands the Grim traveled deep into the past and far into the future.

The noise from inside often prevailed, so he would move farther out into the yard where he wouldn't be bothered. On the boldest days, he played almost on the gravel road that weaved through the trailer park, often coming close to the edge, but never stepping into the street.

Every day the paperboy would come, deliver the newspaper, appreciate Oliver's toys and be on his way. Other than the paperboy and the Special Company visiting every now and again, Oliver was alone while he was outside.

Occasionally he had company from the neighbor, a former Marine turned constant mechanic. The neighbor periodically stood over the open hood of his rusted-patch-work-primed Trans Am. On the rarest of occasions, he even got as far as taking a wrench to a valve or hose on the engine, but in the whole of Oliver's short memory no progress had been made.

It was Tuesday, and it was hot. Oliver's mom groaned somewhere inside the house in response to muffled pontificating from a talking head on the television. The noise persuaded him to the edge of the lawn where he wouldn't be bothered. He never stepped onto the road, but he did pull several bunches of pebbles from its edge to build the Grim a fortress of rock. It was majestic, a battlement from which the Grim and his super heroic, adventuring friends enacted justice and protected the weak.

As he played, he soon became lost in the Grim's medieval journey. The sound of gravel crunching under boot and the stench of garlic and motor oil snapped him out of his imaginative trance. Returning to reality, he looked up to see a large man standing over him wearing a cowboy hat. By adult standards, the man would have been considered short, but to Oliver he was downright gigantic. Oliver saw the Ghoul. Oliver's instincts told him for sure the man was a villain, until he spoke.

"You best be careful buddy," the man said, grinning. "Else you'll end up in the road."

After the man spoke, Oliver knew he'd been mistaken. This man could not be the Ghoul. The Ghoul would not be thoughtful. The Ghoul would not look out for anyone other than the Ghoul.

The man continued. "Road's dangerous. It's not nice to little guys who get lost to it."

He hunched over Oliver, casting his shadow over him and the Grim's fortress. Oliver flinched away from the man's uninvited proximity. As if sensing the intrusion, the man leaned back a few inches, not stepping away.

"Road's a snake that'll bite off your little head clean off." The man snapped his teeth together with a hiss and smirked at him playfully.

Oliver had had enough. He jumped to his feet and fled into the house, leaving his toys behind. Once inside, he swiftly locked the door behind him. He sat on the floor next to his mom's chair, hoping she would come and comfort him, all the while knowing she would not.

Outside, the man knelt down and carefully reinforced the walls of the Grim's stone fortress. The neighbor stepped through his front door and the man froze for a moment as the neighbor peered at him. Ignoring him, the man soon resumed his reinforcement. The neighbor shook his head, turned and popped the Trans Am's hood.

The man gathered the Grim and the other action figures, walking them up to the house. The neighbor glared at him as he crossed the yard.

Back inside the trailer, Oliver watched as the Special Company stepped out of the bathroom down the hall. The man sneered at him, and he felt judged. Oliver didn't like the feeling, didn't like the man. Despite his disgust, Oliver wished for the day the Special Company people would be nice, the day one would stay and maybe be his dad. But they were never that nice, they never stayed very long, rarely came back, and deep down he knew they would never be his family.

After using the bathroom, the Special Company stopped

in the hall, looking at the boy through small, dark eyes. He entered the bedroom, and a moment later Oliver's mom started to shout. "What? No! Go outside, Oliver! Mommy's got special company! Go play in the yard!"

Oliver opened the door and fled the house, seeking the safety, familiarity, and acceptance of his toys. He stepped through the door and froze. His action figures greeted him on the porch, lined up in a row with the Grim at the center.

Oliver smiled. He checked the yard, and looked down the street. No sight of the giant man, only the neighbor leaning over his Trans Am's engine. Oliver scooped up his action figured and returned to his fortress, somewhat shocked to find it in better shape than when he had left it a few minutes earlier. Twice as tall, twice as strong, and infinitely more glorious.

Each day after that, the strange man would pass by, and each day he passed he would step closer and closer, finally crossing through the yard itself. Prior to that, the only one who crossed into the yard was the paperboy. Eventually the man passed through daily and freely, as though he were strolling through a park. The only exception being if the man saw the neighbor working on his Trans Am. On those days he would walk on the other side of the street, going out of his way to avoid Oliver.

One day the man stopped and stood over Oliver. "I know your name," he announced.

Oliver glanced up, saying nothing.

"Is it Glen? Maybe Reuben?"

Oliver scowled and looked away.

"Maybe it's Huey, Dewey, or Louie?" The man paused, his grin growing wider. "Nah, I know what it *really* is. Your mom told me. She's my friend, you know. She said it's… Oliver."

Oliver smiled, and moved the Grim.

The man continued. "My name, I had to give it to myself. See, your mom named you, but my daddy named me, and he was a villain. So one day I named myself. I'm Cowboy." He tipped his hat at Oliver. "All the greatest heroes and warriors were cowboys, you know, so I became a good man that day, when I gave myself that name."

Oliver's hand flinched. The action figure dropped into the dirt beside him.

Over time, Cowboy's random comments expanded beyond broad greetings and generalities and became open doors – doors which Oliver refused to step through. Invitations to conversations the boy did not want to have.

Day after day, Cowboy persisted at trying something new, making random conversation about the neighborhood, his favorite cartoons and superheroes, even Oliver's mom. With each crossing, Cowboy always came a kind word, a warm greeting, a comment on Oliver's toys or the cartoon or superhero t-shirt he was wearing.

Oliver didn't like it.

He didn't like Cowboy, even if he couldn't understand why. The man was always so polite, and knew the names of all his toys. He should've liked him, but he didn't.Until one day Cowboy said something so utterly insane, Oliver had no choice but to respond. "You know," he said, shaking his head, "The Grim really isn't the hero. He's the *villain*."

Oliver looked up at him, frowning.

"The Ghoul's the hero," Cowboy continued, "but the Grim stole his identity and does evil in a good man's name."

With his eyes as big as hubcaps on the Trans Am next door, Oliver was aghast. His passion for his hero flared within him, and he had to right this wrong. Immediately.

"No he isn't!" Oliver snapped. "The Grim's a good guy!"

Halfway through his second sentence he teetered a bit. His stance wavered as the innate fear of talking to Cowboy overtook him once again.

"I wish it were true," Cowboy said, shaking his head. "But it's not. Listen, back in my trailer I have the proof. I got *all* the comic books, the original issues, Goin' way back into the sixties. Goin' all the way back to I was little, a fresh little superhero, just like you." He licked his lips and lowered an arm toward him.

Oliver shuffled away, gripping action figure and running up the sidewalk until he was safely inside the trailer again.

Several weeks passed, and during that time the only person to cross the yard was the paperboy. His mom had no company, special or not, and Cowboy did not return. Even the neighbor failed to make an appearance, having abandoned the tarp-covered Trans Am. Until, one day, Cowboy stood across the other side of the road.

He acknowledged Oliver with only the slightest of nods. Oliver stood, paralyzed at the sight of him, but holding his position in the yard. He did not wave back.

Weeks passed, and summer soon turned to fall. The days grew colder and more damp, the papers arriving later each day even as the sun would start to set earlier. Cowboy's visits became more frequent as he once more inched closer and closer to the yard, soon crossing the yard like he had before, returning to general pleasantries. Now thoroughly the heart of fall, the leaves were a dying rainbow of reds, yellows and orange. Oliver grew complacently comfortable with the routine. The moment of encroachment, a long-forgotten memory, Cowboy's passing eventually became the lone high-light among a monotony of remarkably uneventful days, greater even than the delivery of the newspaper.

One afternoon, mere moments after the neighbor parted from his Trans Am and disappeared into his shed, Cowboy stepped into the yard. "Hi little friend," he greeted Oliver. In his hands he held a comic book, the cover of which featured the splash title, "THE GRIM AND THE GHOUL." Oliver did not know the comic book, but he knew the characters.

Entranced by the cover, Oliver reached out and eagerly yanked it out of Cowboy's hands. It featured a weeping Grim standing over a grave that read "Here lies The Ghoul." The title at the bottom read, "Brother's Keeper."

Oliver had no idea what the words meant, but he knew they were beautiful. With greater desire than he had ever before known, Oliver wanted to open that comic book, to step through the doorway of the mylar bag and live in abetter, more vibrant world of truth and love.

"You like it?" asked Cowboy.

Oliver nodded in silence.

Cowboy leaned over Oliver's shoulder, his beard brushing lightly against Oliver's cheek. The coarse hair scratched his soft skin , but he care as his eyes took in the cover's delicate details. Despite the discomfort, he felt a sense of closeness he'd never once felt with a grown up before. A warmth that the Special Company nor his mom ever showed him. Oliver wondered if this is what it felt like to have a dad.

Cowboy's breath was soft and ragged when he next spoke. "Do you want to see more, Oliver?"

This time, Oliver found his voice. He spoke clearly, loudly, full of unbridled anticipation. "Yes!"

Cowboy smiled and leaned closer to nuzzle against him. Oliver wanted to inch away, to flee the grotesque encroachment, but again froze in the unexpected intimacy.

"I'll tell you all 'bout the Ghoul and the Grim, the whole Fabulous Thunder Family, Star Spangled Soldier, and Hero, and his son Hero II. Even Vigilance. *All of 'em*. I know *all* their stories. I have *all* the comics, and toys! I have more than you even!" he said. "But I'd love to share them with you. Even give you some, if you want some more toys." He paused, as if standing on the precipice of a cliff, watching the scene unfold before him in slow motion.

It all confused Oliver. He didn't understand why Cowboy knew about action figures, or how he knew so much about comic books and cartoons. It didn't make sense, but he ignored the inner voice of worry, happily trading it for the sake of this strange new friend.

"Come to my trailer, Oliver," Cowboy said. "I have boxes of 'em." He leaned back and extended a hand toward Oliver.

Oliver lifted the comic up to his hand, but Cowboy pushed it back and shook his head. "No, no, you hang onto that one. That one's just for you. Just for Oliver."

With the comic book dangling down behind him in his free hand, Oliver walked hand in hand with Cowboy. He was elated. He'd not only made a new friend, but his friend had given him his very own comic book! To keep! Nobody had done that, not his mom and definitely not any of the Special Company.

OLIVER AND COWBOY strolled onto the road and disappeared over the crest of the hill. Just after they were out of sight, the neighbor returned from inside his shed, dragging a soiled, gray tarp behind him. Staring at the space vacated by Cowboy and Oliver, he shrugged and covered the Trans Am with the tarp.

Down they went, down to a spot, hidden behind neglected hedges and jagged shrubs. The yard was filled with car parts and mechanical junk and construction debris, a virtual wasteland. Near the door sat a pile of trash, mostly discarded pizza and take out boxes, riddled with flies and maggots .

Oliver pulled back on the man's hand, aghast at what he was seeing. "I..." he whimpered, "I want to go home..."

Before had had even finished his sentence Cowboy had swung a short piece of rebar down at him. The wind went out of his chest, it hurt, but without breath in his lungs, he couldn't scream. Clutching the comic book in his tightening fist, Oliver's eyes searched for an escape The large man yanked the blood-splattered comic book from Oliver's hand

and flicked it onto the porch. Glancing over his shoulder toward the street, he bent over and grabbed Oliver's foot, dragging him toward the house. Bright red blood dribbled from the head wound, trickling a ragged trail across the yard, the porch, and through the front door. Oliver's exposed skull bumped noisily over the screen door's metal base, jarring him back to consciousness. One eye drifted up to Cowboy, now standing over him, his breathing labored with exertion and excitement. Oliver wanted to vomit, instantly recognizing how the house stank even more strongly of garlic and motor oil than Cowboy himself.

Oliver blinked, and he no longer saw a man standing over him.

He saw the monster.

With dark, deep-set eyes and round shoulders, Oliver recognized him for who Cowboy truly was: The Ghoul. The villain who merely shared the *appearance* of a hero. Cowboy, his friend, faded away, and in his place stood the Ghoul.

IN THE DEAD of a crystal-clear fall night, under the light of the moon, the Ghoul took hold of Oliver, cradling him in his arms and carrying him out the trailer's back door. Pushing through the tall, dead stalks of corn and into the dark woods beyond it, the Ghoul lurked into the darkness, hiding his prey in his massive arms.

There in the woods at night, using an industrial steel wire, the Ghoul strung Oliver up, threading a noose of cold metal wire around his neck. When he released him, the wire's slack drew taut, slicing into the boy's thin neck, although he felt nothing as it did.

He hung there, swaying in the breeze, body rotating in a lazy arc, muscles twitching every few seconds.As Oliver hung from the tree, his life slowly squeezed out of him. He was aware something had changed, but didn't fully register his death. The image of the Ghoul remained in his mind, deeply etched as his last conscious memory. The Ghoul stared at him, grunted in approval and stumbled back through the forest, pushing his way into the corn.

The hurting stopped. Only one sensation remained, the pervading invasion of numbness, accompanied by a new realization: His mother didn't know where he was.

With everything inside him, Oliver resolved to find a way to let her know where he was, and not to worry.

THE BOY'S corpse hung by the tree, oscillating, waiting nearly two weeks to be found.

Suddenly a bright light cut through the darkness. Great columns and colonnades surrounded the courtyard to an ethereal trailer park. The sun beamed as though it came from everywhere at once, everything glowed, the world smiled. Thousands upon thousands of cartoon characters and human-sized action figures stood cheering at the center of the courtyard.

Oliver opened one eye and noticed his mom standing next to the Grim, together calling to him, beckoning him to cross over to them. He tried to move closer, but couldn't, as if he were paralyzed.

The Grim cheerfully walked to where he was and cheerfully heaved him onto his shoulder. Overhead, several fighter jets darted through the sky, leaving behind a wake of fireworks, spelling, "Happy Birthday Oliver!"

A whimper on the wind, and everything disappeared.

Confused, Oliver blinked and realized he was on the forest floor, looking up at the sunset sky overhead. He pushed himself to his feet and stood for a few seconds, staring at the tree trunk beside him. Slowly, he moved his gaze higher and higher, until he saw himself.

He hung in the air a few feet overhead, an early frost

forming upon his shoulders. He knew he was dead, but for some reason that was okay with him. He didn't hurt anymore, and he was okay with that, too. Oliver was kind of like a superhero now, a Corpse Boy. Concentrating, his new body glided above the snow, hovering in the air with but a thought.

Glancing over his shoulder, he watched his body left behind, the leaves trickled down around his corpse, and he frowned as he realized a single, looming question had become lodged inside his mind.

How did he die?

CHAPTER 18
IN A LION'S DEN

Daniel and Oliver sat high on the side of a hill. They overlooked everything in the world. At least, it felt like everything to them. As the sun rose, they could see most of the trailer court, down onto Popeye's across the bridge and, if you looked carefully, Daniel's house. The sun rose behind the hill opposite them, where Daniel lived. The hill his Pap used to call, "Danny's Hill."

It was a beautiful moment.

As Daniel began to drift off, his companion stared ahead, as if keeping a vigilant watch with his one good eye. He wasn't sure why he'd come here in the first place, and was equally unsure why he'd stayed so long. Maybe he was avoiding the truth again, avoiding what he knew needed to be done.

"I think I know why you're haunting me," he sighed.

Oliver smiled at him.

"I'm supposed to tell people what happened to you, but..." Daniel held his breath. He let it out in heavy sigh. "...I don't want to."

The clock struck sunrise, the universal signal it was time to go home. Gathering himself, Daniel stood to his feet, putting his hands in his sweatshirt pocket to warm them. He felt the empty, leathery sheath inside, and remembered he'd jammed the knife in the tree earlier. He bit his lip. There was no way in hell he was going back to get it.

Daniel increasing grogginess was in stark contrast to the surprisingly chipper and upbeat Oliver displayed as they walked out of the corn field. Without realizing where Oliver had led them, they parted the corn and stood at the edge of Cowboy's backyard.

"Crud," Daniel muttered.

Just as he spoke, a police car pulled to a stop in front of the trailer.

Crouching lower behind a the ancient front end of an Ford F-100, Daniel watched, wide-eyed and suddenly alert. As a dutiful sidekick, Oliver hid alongside him. Daniel failed to notice Oliver was most definitely not watching the scene unfolding before them, but looked longingly behind them, back beyond the cornfield, back to his final resting place, back to the tree.

A police officer stepped out of the car and walked to the passenger side, opening the cruiser's back door. This was a new someone Daniel had never seen before. After a moment of quiet discussion, a pair of grease-stained hands gripped the roof and out swung Cowboy.

Daniel wanted to swear, but said nothing.

Cowboy sauntered through his junkyard front yard with an exhausted, arrogant strut. The officer appeared to stare darts, daggers, knives, swords, and lightsabers into the man's back as he went, all the way until Cowboy entered his trailer.

Daniel ducked down, making sure Cowboy wouldn't spot him in the yard. He listened, holding his breath. Punctuating the silence, there was the click of a lock, the slamming of car door and a vehicle driving away fast enough for the loose gravel to spit across the trailer park road.

Safe, Daniel thought.

Sneaking like he did when he walked down the spiral staircase at home, albeit now with shoes on, he carefully crossed Cowboy's yard. Step over and around discarded carburetors and radiators.

Exactly as Daniel crossed the midpoint, the front door opened and he glanced over to see Cowboy standing in the doorway, a bag of trash in his hand. Their eyes met. Daniel swallowed. Cowboy smiled.

"Hey paperboy," the man said with a hoarse, worn voice. Clearly he'd been doing a bit of yelling during his time talking to the police. He tossed the trash bag out into the yard between them. The untied bag spilled open a few feet away from Daniel, and he scowled at it.

*Who does that? Throwing around trash in his own yard?*His eyes on the ground, Daniel meekly squeaked out a. "Hi."

Cowboy sniffed. He reached up and rubbed his temples aggressively, saying nothing.

Daniel so badly wanted to not be there right now. All Cowboy had to do was think, *now why am I talking to my paper boy at 6 AM? I should tell the kid to go home or to school or whatever and go back to sleep.*

Cowboy ruined it. "I have that thing for you." He paused for a long time, staring at Daniel. "You know. That thing..." Daniel waited. He didn't want to speak. Didn't want to breathe. In his mind, he hoped Cowboy would literally forget they were even having a conversation, turn around and just go back inside.

Cowboy glared at Daniel, as if he were using a Jedi mind trick, trying to coax Daniel to explain to him what he was thinking.

"What thing?" Daniel asked as he took a step away. "You know." Cowboy's accusation hung in the air, halting Daniel's steps. "That thing. For the newspaper."

Dang, Daniel thought to himself, shaking his head *why do I have to be a nice person?*

Cowboy continued. "For them free papers. They're free, right? You weren't lying, were you? 'Cause I've had just about all the liars I can handle today."

Gulp. "Yeah, they're free."

Cowboy grunted and turned for his door. He stood there, holding it open and looked back at Daniel. "Well, come on, then."

The door was a portal into the horrible unknown. Daniel knew, or at least strongly suspected, this was where Oliver had gone ghost. He couldn't begin to imagine what happened before his death, but he didn't need to. He only knew he didn't want to go inside. *At all.*

But he *had to* go inside. He was an employee of the newspaper, and it was his responsibility to deliver the papers to customers, *including* seasonal offers. It sucked, but there was nothing else he could do.

Petrified, Daniel looked for Oliver, but he was long gone.

"Come on, man," Cowboy scolded. "You're lettin' the flies in."

Daniel shuffled forward toward the door before him, an ominous black void. Inside he heard flies buzzing, waiting for him to join them. Cowboy gestured toward it in invitation. Reminding himself to be courageous for his friend, for the truth, Daniel entered. Once he'd crossed the threshold, the house seemed to come alive, as if an invisible hand had reached through time and space, grasping his throat.

Cowboy stepped inside and stepped aside into another room, leaving Daniel in the living room. As his eyes adjusted to the darkness, he took in the room. It was full of things, but somehow devoid of humanity.

Filth and dust covered everything. Between the stacks of junk, open crusty trails led to various areas of significance in the trailer – a TV, a couch, the kitchen and beyond. A light flickered on in the kitchen, allowing Daniel to see more filth ahead of him.

"Here it is," Cowboy announced aloud. "Got it right here."

Returning to the living room, Cowboy clapped twice. In the corner a shadeless lamp sprung to life. The sudden bright glare combined with the unexpected use of The Clapper caused Daniel to flinch, but he held his ground. The lamp burned hot and bright, as if Cowboy had installed a higher wattage bulb than it could handle. The light's truth exposed even more garbage around Daniel. Discarded food and what looked like trails of rat and mouse feces filled the place. He thought he was going to throw up.

Cowboy plopped himself down on the couch adjacent to the mirror. "Sit down, little man," he commanded. With the menace of some yet unimagined evil Wookie, Cowboy glared at Daniel. "Stay awhile."

Daniel's eyes narrowed. Cowboy didn't have the paper with him. If he had found it in the kitchen, he'd purposely left it in there. Planning his escape, Daniel cleared his throat.. "I have to get back home," he said. "It's late. I mean, early."

Cowboy smiled. "Well, which is it?" he asked.

"Kind of both."

"Nah. You can stay," Cowboy cooed softly, shaking his head.

Daniel hesitated.

"Sit down."

Daniel felt as if he were having a conversation with two different people. It was bizarre. "I'll stand," he said. "I sit all day at school."

"Uh-huh. You and all the other little boys," replied Cowboy.

"Middle school." Daniel struggled to breathe. "I'm in middle school."

Cowboy's smile widened into what Daniel easily recognized as a sinister grin. He'd seen it in enough movies and comic books to spot it in an instant. In the past, Daniel had always thought of Cowboy's smile as friendly and cordial, even if he was a bit odd. Now Daniel's eyes had been opened, and he saw in retrospect what it had always been: menacing.

Something was there, just beneath the surface, and try as it could to hide, it wasn't quite right. *True evil*, Daniel thought, *hides its true face in plain sight*. He stared at the man, stared into the face of evil, an evil whose eyes were black, cavernous abysses, not a glimmer of humanity behind them.

"So paperboy's in middle school." Cowboy shrugged, eyes locked on Daniel. "Little paperboy. Not so little, but not so big, are you, Danny?"

Daniel steeled himself, despite the crushing fear threatening to consume him. "I don't like being called Danny. *My name is Daniel.*"

Flaring his nostrils, Cowboy glared at him, saying nothing.

"Dan's okay," compromised Daniel. In his mind, Cowboy now looked like an evil Wookie, which would make sense, considering he already smelled like the inside of a dead Tauntaun.

"You need a nickname, a special name! Just between you and I," Cowboy said. "Just between us men."

Daniel saw through his games with laser focus, and he was suddenly alert and aware of Cowboy's ploys. "I don't like nicknames."

Cowboy leaned over and picked up an empty crinkled hamburger wrapper off the floor. He balled it in his fist and rubbed his eyes, rubbing so hard Daniel thought the flesh might tear right off his face. "I have a headache," he said, opening his eyes and looking at Daniel.

Is he...crying?

Daniel saw some humanity there, deeply hidden behind pain, hate and suffering. *Was there a man beneath the monster?*

"Do you ever get headaches..." he slurred, "Daniel?"

"Sometimes."

"I need some medicine." He leaned down as he spoke, and Daniel jerked back, out of reach. Cowboy didn't care about him, at least not at the moment. Rising from the couch, he loomed over Daniel facing the kitchen. For a moment Daniel could have sworn it was the Ghoul standing over him.

Fighting back the shards of humanity, Cowboy spoke again. "You should sit." Something far worse than the Ghoul, more inhuman than any comic book villain, reached out and pushed Daniel down into a trash-covered armchair.

"Bet you heard some things... about me."

Cowboy's sounded like a mixture of two voices to Daniel. Possibly more.

"No body, no proof. An' they ain't got no body." Cowboy became more and more irritated with each word. "They even told me they don't. The police said it's in the paper, but the dumb idiots didn't even search my house, *or* the woods. Soon as they walked into the corn they got lazy when their shoes got a little muddy." He sneered at the thought, shaking his head in disgust.

Daniel's eyes darted around the trailer. He didn't know what he was looking for, other than a clear path to the front door.

"You read the paper?" Cowboy asked, legitimately forgetting that Daniel delivered the paper.

"Sometimes," Daniel said. "I mostly just read the comics." He'd decided to play the man's game, baiting the beast with a big fat, four-colored world.

The monster took the bait. "The comics? Yeah, the comics! I *like* the comics." His gaze searched the room. "Boys *love* comics. Do you like comic books?"

Daniel was about to answer when Cowboy thrust his hands in the air, fists clenched tight. Apparently unable to find his comic books, he slid into a minor rage. "I hate this mess!" he yelled.

"I do like comics," Daniel said, hoping to calm him. It seemed to work, or at the very least redirected his attention.

"I even have a ping-pong table." Cowboy's voice sounded almost cheerful, but Daniel knew it was a false face.

"I know." Daniel felt strangely confident and decided to double down. "I don't like ping-pong," he announced.

Cowboy cringed at the statement, and Daniel wondered if he felt as if he'd lost his latest prey. Daniel actually had the upper hand, whether this monster knew it or not.

In an effort to make nice, Cowboy said, "But you like comic books, an' I *have* comic books. I can show them to you, if you'd like. I have The X-Men, even The Fabulous Thunder Family. Those books are hard to come by!"

"Fabulous Thunder Family," Daniel muttered as he put together the puzzle pieces.

"Yeah! You know them? You wanna see my comic book collection?"

Daniel saw the situation with a renewed sense of clarity. This was it. This was how Oliver had become the prey. The comic books had been the bait, irresistibly luring his friend to his death. Fighting his growing sense of fear, Daniel tested the water. "I would," he said, forcing a smile

Cowboy smiled back. Sinister wasn't the word for it, it was beyond that. Daniel thought his teeth looked like yellow saw blades, buzzing in the air between them. "They're in the back room," Cowboy said, slowing down his words. "You'll have to come to the back room to see them."

Daniel sucked in a breath. He knew all he needed to know now. He also knew he desperately needed to get out of there, or he'd soon be joining Oliver in the woods.

"I won't go in the back Mr. Cowboy."

He'd said it with such confidence, but truthfully he also wanted to see the comic books. After a moment of hesitation, he gave into his curiosity. "Bring them out here." He was close to assuming there were no comics, but if there *were*, hey, why not take a look? It wasn't every day he got to see a genuine silver age Thunder Family comic book.

"No," Cowboy said, shaking his head. "You have to come to the back to see them."

Daniel stared back at him, saying nothing.

The man winced as if in some unspoken pain, contracting his face. Clutching his fist in front of his face, he spoke again, but with a different voice. "There's a demon inside me."

Daniel wasn't interested in the comics anymore.

As he eyed the door, he mentally curled into himself a little. He couldn't run for cover. He couldn't hide from his fear, which breathed hot breath on his neck like the predator it was.

No. Fear couldn't win. He had to find a way out, had to remain brave. He had to grow up. For Oliver's sake. Daniel stood to his feet, making himself as tall as his 5 foot 3 inches would stretch. He lowered his voice as deep as he could. "I need to go. I want to have breakfast with my dad before he goes to work."

"You can't leave," Cowboy roared. "I didn't give you the form!" Pulling it from God knows where, he held up the wrinkled form between them.

The last thing Daniel wanted was that damn form. He now recognized that his being a nice guy might actually get him killed. Well, that and the blatant stupidity of ever stepping foot into the house to begin with.

"I need to fill it in," Cowboy said, trying to come up with a way to keep Daniel in the house. He shuffled and shifted various stacks of paper near the coffee table, digging around until he found a pen. Crouching down next to the table and filling out the form, he pressed the drying pen so hard against the paper he nearly tore through it. "I'm gonna write down Cowboy as my name," he said. "That's the name I was *supposed* to have. It's the name... the name the demon doesn't want me to have."

He spoke, but not to Daniel as much as he were talking to himself, as if he were trying to convince himself of something. When he finished writing down his name, leaving the rest of the form blank, he looked up at Daniel again. "You want me to show you those comics now? Those comic books? Just come to the back room with me." His voice alternated in pitch when he spoke, like a kid going through puberty.

"No!" Cowboy yelled, His voice was like a small boy's, anguished and strained. "That's the demon talking! The demon!" He looked like he was about to burst into tears. "Do you believe in Jesus, paperboy?"

"I go to church every Sunday," Daniel lied.

"Do you like it?"

"It's okay."

"Just okay?"

Daniel shrugged. "Is okay somehow bad?"

Cowboy sniffed. "I guess not."

"My dad plays guitar at church. The music's okay."

"But do you believe?"

"I do. I do believe." He was becoming increasingly certain he was about to meet Jesus face-to-face, something he was absolutely *not* ready to do.

"That's good." Cowboy sounded as if he truly believed what he said. "As a little boy I never went to church. Before Jesus saved me, I worked in the Sunday school." He seemed filled with very real regret. "Now... well, now I'm not allowed there." Cowboy paused, a lament. "Not allowed back at church. They said I can't go back." Clearly he wanted to go, maybe even *needed* to go, but the demon's sway over him was too great.

"But Jesus saved me, you know. See, he doesn't care if I go to church or not. He saved me. I... I used to do wrong, you know. Terribly wrong things, but now I don't. Jesus tells me not to, see? Even when the demon is so damn loud that I can only hear it. Jesus still shouts, shouts loud enough for me to hear him." He locked his eyes on Daniel. "He's shouting now."

"I'm glad he's shouting," said Daniel.

"They're both shouting."

Daniel watched as the contrite, remorseful mouth slowly twisted into a smile. A hungry smile. He balled his hands into tight fists, preparing himself for the fight of his life.

Weeping, Cowboy thrust the form between them. ""You know, there are hundreds of comic books in that back room."

"I don't want to see them," Daniel lied through gritted teeth.

Cowboy straightened himself back up, speaking with a cacophony of voices. "Home. You may go. Go home. Eat with your Daddy. He's a good man, not like mine. No, not like mine. My Daddy was an awful bad man." Cowboy's face grew solemn, almost peaceful. "My Daddy gave birth to the demon."

With nothing left to say, Daniel sprinted out of the room, through the foot door and down the sidewalk, running all the way home.

CHAPTER 19
WRATH

Moving as fast as his ungainly legs could propel him, Daniel ran past the USA Gazette Guy's trailer. The gruff, kind old man watched him dart past his window from inside his trailer.

His eyes followed the boy as he chomped on his wad of chew, ratcheting his jaw with each bite, as if he might dislocate the rickety old thing. Angrily he spat the chew into a tin cup with a resonant *ping*, followed with a hacking clearing of his throat. Looking down at his end table, he shook his head, staring down at the cover article about Cowboy.

The mantel above the gas-operated fireplace sat full of items celebrating the second World War. The memorabilia included a picture of the USA Gazette Guy as a young man. Evgeni Petrov, when people could pronounce his name properly. He was fit, athletic, and a good three inches taller back then in the prime of his life. Happily killing Germans for the protection of his homeland, a land that would be lost to time. Lost to him.

At the end of the shelf, the Sh-40 helmet. In the picture, he held it proudly under his arm. It had been years since he'd held one; it made him feel young again. He tapped the

172

helmet. Rhythmically, he drummed his fingertips on it in sync with the crackle of his jaw. In a strange way, it gave him strength, but it wouldn't be enough. With a grunt, he stormed out the front door on a new mission.

He marched down the street, gravel crackling and retreating from his loafers as he walked in stiff determination. With each step he lost an ounce of his strength, his resolve melting just a bit as he became less and less of the young man in the picture and more of the old American who lived in a trailer. An old man with no teeth, and just as little backbone.

If anyone asked, he would tell them he was long ago Russian. He'd also remind them that he was now a proud American. That he'd fought as an ally in World War Two, fighting for what was once upon a time mother Russia, but was now the old country.

Today, he would fight for his new country.

As he walked, he became colder. Laughing at himself he shrugged it off. He had known cold and winter like few in the world ever would. He once watched brothers freeze to death before they bled to death. When they did bleed out, the blood froze black into the snow. It was a long, bloody winter at Leningrad, the winter that won the war, because he and his people were stronger.

It was time again to be stronger than the enemy. Then as now, the enemy was a neighbor, and the enemy had to be forced from his home.

He approached Cowboy's trailer with an old man's limp a soldier's determination and a Russian's fury he hadn't let himself feel in years. Reaching the door with a screaming indignation and a pounding fist, Evgeni yelled. "Come on out here, you son bitch!"

Within the trailer, a curled up Cowboy wept on his couch. He felt his humanity inside him, a deeply broken little boy, and he hated how weak he was.

The pounding continued.

Cowboy's head throbbed.

First the door vibrated, then the entire trailer violently thrashed and shook. The roaring vibrations continued, colored light flitting through the windows, although Cowboy heard no sirens. Judgment had come for him at last.

USA Gazette Guy stood outside in the dim coolness of the morning, laying into the door with all his old man might. "We want you out! You no good!" He repeated this mantra over and over, pounding it against the door over and over.

Inside, the vibration became downright violent within Cowboy's mind. Glass cracked, walls crumbled, and the brightness of the flashing lights overwhelmed him. He rose from the couch and walked into the kitchen, where he stood on a wobbly old dining table and pushed aside a mold-stained ceiling tile. Feeling around in the dark, his hand finally rested on the cold steel and he pulled out a lightweight handgun, a silver Colt Double Eagle.

Evgeni pounded at the door. He shouted until he began to wear his voice hoarse. "Out! *Want you out!*"

Gun in hand, Cowboy stared at the door. He exhaled slowly, then raised the weapon and pulled the trigger. Bullets peppered the door as his arm swung down and around.

Five shots fired, all went through the door. Four of those hit Evgeni. One shattered his right wrist; he bled profusely from his ulnar artery. The final three bullets shredded his abdomen and popped his lungs. He wasn't dead. Not yet anyway.

Amidst the trash strewn on Cowboy's porch, Evgeni writhed violently, gasping for breath. Grasping at the garbage near him but failing to muster enough strength to even pull himself upright. He looked up at the door, mirroring his body's bullet holes. Thrusting himself up on one arm, he finally let out a prolonged groan and fell in a bloody heap.

Inside, Cowboy flipped on the surge protector. Noise consumed the trailer, inside and out.

Evgeni gritted his teeth. He tried to speak, but couldn't. Painted with blood and agony, his body hidden by the plethora of car parts, he writhed in fresh waves of anguish. He breathlessly muttered and wheezed, cursing both himself and his killer. Evgeni coughed a thick, wet cough, spitting out a wad with a whole lot of phlegm and a little bit of blood. His heart was still beating, but for how long?

CHAPTER 20
THE CORPSE BOY SPEAKS

Daniel approached the house, not by way of the driveway, but cutting through the woods so as not to be seen. It was a tactic his brother perfected, and it worked. Once his brother tried driving up the driveway with the lights off, but got stuck in a ditch. He had to wake their dad up and there was absolute hell to pay for that. Like, Uncle-Owen-from-*Star-Wars* levels of hell to pay. After that fiasco he'd have a friend drop him off at the edge of the woods and then sneak through Daniel's room. Most nights Daniel buried his head under a blanket, although some nights they'd talk for hours. He'd do anything just to be able to talk to him again for a minute or two. The house, built by his dad when Daniel was quite small —little more than ten years ago, was built into the hillside. This meant when Daniel approached the back of the house, he was actually entering the second floor. There he climbed through his open window. He did so rather clumsily, but without any major disaster and minimal noise. He landed on Mac, who didn't bother to get up, but raised his head and groaned in tired annoyance. Mac relented and plopped his head back down. Oliver resumed his typical throne on the toy chest.

Exhausted, Daniel hopped on his left foot, struggling to remove his right shoe. Success! Daniel tossed the first grody shoe aside just as the door swung open.

"Aaahhh!" He shrieked.

"You're up!" His mom said with a great deal of surprise.

Daniel's glanced at the toy chest.

Mom's eyes followed.

She seemed poised to speak just as Daniel interjected. "Yeah. just getting dressed." He hoped she wouldn't have any of a number of potential comments, corrections, or criticisms, all of which he was sure he deserved.

"You're going to wear that?"

He grinned. He'd happily take that, as he was, after all, covered in dirt. "I'll change," he said, knowing he seemed like the good guy by doing it before she asked.

"Would you like breakfast? You actually have time for it today."

"No, I'm not hungry," Daniel lied. "Thanks." He didn't really know why, but he didn't want to be around anyone. Particularly not a mom who might ask questions he either didn't want to or was unprepared to answer.

"Okay…" she hesitated. "Maybe you should shower, then."

"Uhhhh…"

"Just make sure you dry your hair. It's chilly this morning. Not cold enough for ice, but we don't want your hair to freeze again," she said, attempting humor.

Yes, this had been an issue a few years ago. Daniel hated showers and baths with equal loathing. Mom hated that he wouldn't take them. Daniel's creative mind soon found a way around it. He'd go into the bathroom, turn on the water, and sit on the toilet reading a comic book. He'd even wet his hair, but he'd never use soap or do anything to actually clean himself.

"I did," lied Daniel.

Mom thought they'd worked through that. She believed Daniel now took baths, where he could read or play his Game Gear in the tub. All of which were true. However, maybe he'd just become better at covering things up. "Did you?" she asked hesitantly.

"Yes, Mom! Geez!" he snapped. "I just picked out a dirty outfit. It's my favorite shirt and jeans." He hated lying to her, but he had a good reason why. He wanted her to know he was okay, despite the fact that he was, absolutely, *not* okay.

Mom looked at the shirt, a hand-me-down Deer Lakes National Honor Society shirt. It had belonged to his brother, and she knew very well it would never be on Daniel's Top 20 favorite shirts list. (Which, yes, he did have. And no, it wasn't on the list.) She smiled the smile of a worried mother. He used to tell her everything, now he bottled it all up. Turning to leave she stopped at the door and looked back at him. "Are you alright?" Her voice was thick with all the love she knew he would allow her to give.

"I'm fine," he lied.

"Okay," she replied, knowing he was lying, but not wanting to push him any more than that, for fear she would in turn, push him away. She nodded and shut the door behind her.

Oliver reappeared. Without a word, Daniel stared at him for a good long time. Finally, he found something to say. "Do you want to play with toys or something?"

The boy looked around the room, then back to Daniel and shook his head. "No," he said softly.

Daniel's eyes snapped open, and he backed up, falling to the floor. "Holy freaking crap," he said. "Did you...? Did you just...?"

Oliver nodded, a wan smile crossing his face.

• • •

DANIEL CLOSED HIS EYES. He shook his head and held up a finger between them. "Dude. Could you talk the entire time?"

Oliver shrugged. "I… don't know," he whispered. "Maybe?"

Pushing himself up, Daniel crawled over to his friend and balanced on his haunches, Spider-Man style. He studied Oliver, breathing in deeply, and finally stood up until he was eye to eye with his friend. "Why talk now?"

"I need you to listen," Oliver said. He sounded like a little boy, but his words and the way he said them made him sound more like a man. Not a grown man, but an older one. An eternal one. One who saw the creation of the universe and who'd already seen the end, at least that's what Daniel now saw before him.

Daniel sat cross-legged before his best friend. "Okay, I'm listening."

Feeling put on the spot, Oliver the ageless man again became a little boy. He didn't know what to say, but he knew he needed to say it. They stared at each other for thirty seconds, but Daniel could have sworn it was thirty minutes.

"Daniel!" his mom called from downstairs. "Come on! You're going to miss the bus."

Hurriedly changing his shirt, Daniel attempted to console his friend. "Look, we'll talk later. I promise."

During homeroom, Daniel sat in his assigned seat, saying nothing. The other kids were all about the room enjoying conversation and friendships, but he remained oblivious to it all. Oliver sat next to him, looking longingly, desperately at him.

Jimmy walked by. He sneered at Daniel, but went unnoticed.

On the bus ride home, the air was filled with the roar of excited children, finally free from the confines of school. Oliver sat next to Daniel. The other kids goofed around, were downright joyful, Daniel couldn't even remember what that felt like. Daniel suddenly admitted to himself, Oliver never really went away. Oliver was always there, no matter what. No matter who Daniel was with or talking to, Oliver, and that ever bulging purple eye, remained.

Nobody noticed Daniel, just the way he wanted it. He also felt a strange sense of guilt. How could he be part of the world, yet feel so far away from everyone in it? He didn't like the question. More than that, he didn't like the answer.

At the end of his driveway, as the school bus pulled away, Daniel stared at his feet as he shuffled through the crunching gravel. The newspapers were already there with Oliver standing next to them, waiting. Finally scooping them up, Daniel made his way a quarter of the way up the driveway before moving off into the woods. Heaving the bundle of newspapers as high as he could, he tossed them into a gully.

Stunned, the always wide-eyed Oliver's eye went even wider. He raised his hands in confusion. Heading down into the gully, Daniel did his best to cover the bundle with nearby leaves and debris. He stepped back, checking his work and looked back at his friend.

Oliver shook his head in soft disapproval.

Inside the house, Daniel passed through the kitchen as his mom was prepping dinner. She didn't notice him in his silence, and he kept his head down as he passed.

In the bedroom, Oliver sat on the toy chest, Daniel's dog at his feet. He watched Daniel move at a crawl.

Daniel didn't want to deal with anything, not even taking off his shoes. With an annoyed sigh, he popped his shoes off, one at a time. He snapped the blinds shut and crawled into bed, never bothering to change out of his clothes. Burrowing deep under the covers, he closed his eyes and shut out the world.

Oliver dropped his head and locked eyes with Mac on the floor, looking for answers the dog couldn't offer.

As the sun set, everything and everyone in the trailer

court rested. Outside his trailer, Old Man Mumbles sat in his lawn chair next to his paper box. Having drifted off a few times throughout the afternoon and evening he got up to check the box. Again. Every single time, he found only an empty box. Impatiently, he grumbled to himself and sat back down, fidgeting as he watched the sun set.

At her kitchen table, The Sweetest Old Lady Ever waited. Next to her an empty glass and a full can of formerly ice cold, ginger ale, growing increasingly warm with every passing second, as she read yesterday's Arts and Leisure section. She drifted off to sleep a little until the all gray cat with white paws and a white spot under its left eye hopped up on the table, waking her with a start. The cat sniffed the rim of the cup before she shooed it off.

His body now stiff and cold, Evgeni wheezed a final curse in Russian. Silently, he prayed. The wind howled. His wounds screamed back. The cold felt like that long-forgotten winter. Inch by inch, they held the city, survived the cold as only they could.

As a young man back then, hardly more than a boy, he had no fear of death. Now he saw himself as a fool. He'd nearly died a hundred times, if not more. In fact, he had barely survived., the cold and his pride nearly doing him in. Now, he knew death was hovering over him to claim its long-lost prize, and he wanted nothing to do with it.

He grimaced. Anger burned in his belly as he lay there in eternal surrender and died.

Peggy Hart stood in her doorway, a plump, dissatisfied silhouette backlit by the living room. Her face fixed on her stoop, where she saw exactly zero newspapers. Her left eye twitched in rage. Remaining in the door, her anger fixed on her front stoop, she picked up her cordless phone and began to dial, attacking each button with unnecessary ferocity.

Despite his head buried under a few pillows and his bedroom phone disconnected from the wall, Daniel somehow heard the downstairs phone ring. He lifted the pillow mountain with an arm and looked at Oliver.

"That's probably your mom," he said, frowning.

Oliver looked longingly at the stack of VHS tapes, zeroing in on a copy of *Jacob's Passage*.

Hearing the ensuing silence from downstairs, Daniel was now absolutely certain Oliver's mom was on the phone. Just as he buried his head under the mountain the door to his room flew open. "Daniel!"

Silhouetted in the doorway stood Mom, cordless phone tightly gripped in her hand. "That was Peggy Hart! She said she didn't get her newspaper!" she shouted, unintentionally transferring Peggy Hart's intensity to Daniel.

Daniel said nothing. He froze, hoping she'd think he was asleep or sick and leave him alone. Of course he knew she wasn't that stupid, or stupid at all. His mom was smart.

"Daniel!" she snapped again, all intensity now one hundred percent intentional. Stomping across the room, she reached down and yanked down the blanket.

"DANIEL!"

"Mom, I'm... sleeping," he said reflexively. It was the lie he'd planned, however, her pulling away the blankets threw him off his game. He did have a backup plan, one he'd perfected over the years. Faking sick.

"You're sleeping?!" she barked, visibly noting he was obviously awake.

"I'm sick," he added with a groany emphasis. "I don't feel good."

"Why didn't Mrs. Hart get her paper?"

It wasn't that she didn't believe him, but frankly at the moment she didn't care. Peggy Hart really had her rattled.

"Miss Hart." Again Daniel spoke reflexively, immediately regretted correcting his mom.

She ignored it. "Why didn't she get her paper?"

Daniel didn't want to deal with it, so he doubled down on

his sickness ruse. "I'm just not feeling good, I must have missed it." Well, at least the last part was true. He certainly *had* missed it, and in his own mind he was emotionally distressed, so faking a physical ailment to prevent the need to talk about it felt fair.

"Did you have any extra papers?"

Daniel's fingers traced the dirt under his nails, dirt from when he buried the papers earlier. "No," he lied. "I ran out."

"Tomorrow, I want you to go to Popeye's and get an extra copy of today's paper." She put extra emphasis on "today's paper," knowing Daniel would likely forget, and she'd be dealing with another mind-melting verbal assault from Peggy Hart.

"Fine," he sighed, covering his head.

"I'm not finished."

She pulled the pillow away from his head and tossed it onto his dirty laundry. "You will also give her a month's worth of free papers."

"Fine," he whined.

"Still not finished."

He knew he was in for it now, he just didn't know what 'it' was.

"And it will come out of your pocket."

"Fine." He smothered his own head under the pillow.

She stood over him, waiting for him to apologize, to argue, for anything other than quiet defeat, but defeat was all he had to offer.

"Please shut the door," he moaned from beneath his pillow.

As his mom closed the door, Daniel's eyes popped up. He saw her stop, and thought she saw him reach out, but thens she abruptly pulled the door shut. *Was she crying?*

"And you'd better believe you're going to school tomorrow!" She whimpered, Daniel whipped the tears from his own eyes with his blanket and quite literally buried himself and his feelings.

HOURS LATER, Daniel remained burrowed within the nest of blankets. He did so in part to hide from the light his mom purposely left on, but also to avoid a very necessary conversation. Across the room, still perched on the toy chest, Oliver watched and waited. Daniel finally emerged from beneath his cotton cocoon. "I'm guessing you still want to talk?"

Oliver nodded.

Looking for reasons to be annoyed, Daniel conveniently found this annoying. He made sure to let Oliver know it. "Look, if I ask you if you want to talk, you need to actually *talk*, okay?"

Instinctively, Oliver again nodded. Upon Daniel's deeper dissatisfaction, he spoke a single word. "Please."

Daniel shook his head and smiled. "I don't know how your mom, being who she is, raised such a polite kid," he said, genuinely perplexed.

They sat in silence for several minutes. When Oliver had spoken earlier, Daniel once again thought of him as some kind of timeless entity.

"What made time?" he asked shooting for the moon with his first question.

Oliver shrugged.

"Sorry, that's kind of a big question." Daniel paused taking in his room. "And a weird one, and probably an irrelevant one."

Oliver nodded.

Daniel thought he seemed a bit like Yoda, but also somehow a small boy. So, yeah, totally like Yoda.

Daniel relented on his standoffish attitude towards Oliver. He assumed it was his job to figure it all out, so he'd start by asking what he hoped would be more reasonable questions.

"What happened to you?" he asked, kind of knowing the answer and simultaneously fearing it.

"I'm... not sure," whispered Oliver.

This annoyed Daniel, but he smiled and repeated it in Yoda fashion back to Oliver. "Sure, I am not." He really was a kind of dead Yoda, but not how Yoda glowed all luminescent at the end of *Return of the Jedi*. More like Yoda with a decomposing body and wonky bulbous eye, staring at you and-"He tricked me."

Daniel blinked, not believing what he heard. "Who?"

"The... bad one."

"Mr. Cowboy?"

Oliver frowned, searching his mushed up memories. "It was... The Ghoul," he said, unsure of himself.

Daniel approached the boy. "The Ghoul isn't real, Oliver."

"I know, but I saw him. The Ghoul. I saw..." He looked as if there were more to say, but he was either afraid of saying it or couldn't possibly know how to say it. "Like... I had to see him."

"I don't understand," Daniel said, shaking his head. "You imagined the Ghoul?" He paused, leaning in closer. "Like, your minded needed to see him? To make it okay?"

"Yeah."

Daniel scrunched his face, his hand upon his chin as he pondered what he'd just heard. He reached out to touch Oliver, to comfort him, but stopped short. *Would he even connect? Or would his hand just go right through him? Or worse, what if it didn't?*

Oliver continued. "He said... he said he was my friend. Like you... are my friend. He said there were..." His eyebrows knit together as he searched for the word. "Comics."

Daniel snorted. "Yeah, he tried that on me, too." He shuddered, actualizing the very real danger he'd been in.

"I didn't want to go," Oliver sighed.

"With Mr. Cowboy?"

"No," he said. "I didn't want to die."

"I'm sorry." Daniel didn't know what to say to that. He stared at him for a few seconds before a new thought popped into his head. "How did you come back?"

Oliver shrugged. "Don't know," he said. "I just... I'm here."

"Did you choose to come back?"

"I don't know," he repeated. "I'm just *here*."

"Fine, you're here. I get that," Daniel said in exasperation. "But can... can other people come back like you?" He sucked in a breath, shocked that he actually asked the question, mouth dry as he waited for the answer.

"I don't know." It was clear Oliver felt bad with the answer, seeing Daniel's disappointment. He wanted to say the right thing. "I just came, I'm just... here."

"Can you be alive again?"

"I don't think I can be alive again," he said. "That's not... I don't think that's how being dead works."

To Daniel, Oliver seemed to have a deeper insight on death. He wanted to ask more questions. After a few more minutes he gathered himself, swallowed some snot and wiped away some tears. He had a role to play in this and needed to find out what it was. "What do you need me to do?"

"I don't know," Oliver said, disappointed at himself for not knowing. "I'm sorry. Daniel."

Daniel smiled, a part of him warming at the sound of his name on Oliver's blue lips. He also felt disappointed, but tried not to let it show. "I'll do anything."

"He has to... say he's sorry.""What?"

"Sorry," Oliver repeated. "He has to say he's sorry... for what he did."

"That's it? An apology?"

Oliver nodded.

"He *murdered* you, Oliver. So yeah, sorry but I don't think an apology is going to be enough." Daniel felt his neck growing hot with indignant anger at the idea.

"He doesn't have to say sorry to me," replied Oliver calmly, clearly.

Daniel didn't know where this was going, but he went with it. "Okay, who does he have to say he's sorry to, then?"

"Himself."

Daniel really didn't get it. "I really don't get it Oliver. He's a monster and a killer and... and... *a monster!* He needs to be punished. He needs to-"

"He will be," Oliver said, as if possessed by a strange, divine insight. "But now he needs to fix it in his heart."

"His heart is *black.*"

"No. It's not. Not totally." Oliver looked directly into Daniel's eyes, the timeless entity peering into him. "I don't hate him. I did, but not anymore. Death is... free of hate," Oliver observed.

"Okay. Fine. Then what needs to happen?" Daniel wanted to help his friend, but he wasn't even sure if he was still talking to the 5-year old version of him or if a ghost had somehow possessed his ghost body. The logistics and possibilities boggled his nerd mind.

"He has to accept what he's done. He's torn in his own mind. If he can accept it, he can forgive himself and..." Oliver paused, his face becoming slightly pained as he spoke. "...accept his eternal justice."

Daniel had no idea what to do. Well, he had ideas, but they all involved digging a very deep, very large hole and hiding there until the world passed by. Something like a fox or a World War 2 veteran, he wasn't sure. He was more confused now than before the conversation, and realized again why he'd constantly avoided it entirely. He now regretted having talked to Oliver. Daniel still had no idea what he needed to do, but he somehow knew he needed to return to Cowboy's trailer and confront him one last time. And that scared him half to death.

"So I guess we're going back there." Daniel intended it as a question, but it came out as an affirmation. Almost a rousing speech to bolster the team or something.

Oliver looked into Daniel's soul. Daniel felt his eyes glaring at his heart, and he squirmed.

"Not we," Oliver corrected. "You."

DANIEL KNEW little but horror awaited him at Cowboy's trailer, but after that would come The End. With that horror, with that end, peace would finally arrive for Oliver. He found that fact in no way comforting, yet he knew he had to go. It was right, and his mom always told him to do what was right, no matter what. To be honest, to be loving, to be kind, still tough enough to fight for things, but only to fight for the *right* things.

Another part of Daniel didn't want to do it at all, no matter what it would do for Oliver, and it made him feel guilty. Daniel liked Oliver, he liked the idea of The Paper Boy and The Corpse Boy together. A superhero and his sidekick. If he were being honest with himself, he'd admit he didn't want that to end. And he knew it would, after he did what he had to do.

That night Oliver watched as Daniel wept on his pillow. He cried for his friend, for his brother. He cried out of fear of what was to come, but mostly he cried for lost time. He suddenly felt aware of time, and its passage became a curse. He knew this time was about to end.

No. It had ended. It had ended with their last conversation, and soon it would end for good. As weird and scary and challenging as it had been, Daniel knew he'd probably look back on it and reframe it as "the good old days," and he hated that.

He hated knowing how someday he'd be an old man, and Oliver would be forever dead, just like his brother, frozen in time at five years old just like his brother would always be eighteen in his mind. Only eighteen when his Plymouth Turismo got ripped in half by that oak, and in a few short years Daniel would be older than his brother ever was. After that, after all this, Oliver would be forever in his past, fading farther into the back of his mind as Daniel's life became more and more crowded with new friends, lovers, children and grandchildren. And after that? Well, after that, he, too, would be little more than a ghost, wouldn't he? A fading memory.

Outside Cowboy's trailer, the long-dead body of Evgeni, "the USA Gazette Guy" to Daniel, grew colder and colder.

CHAPTER 21
A NICE, BUT PROBABLY BIGOTED CHARACTER, DIES

Western Pennsylvania in the fall is heavenly. Before the seemingly endless winter and the overly humid summer, fall is the perfect balance of chilly evenings and crisp, cool days. The kind of days where you may need a sweatshirt, but no jacket.

At least, that was the logic in Daniel's mind when he walked down the road. When the leaves crunched under his feet, he no longer had to cut the grass. Although he did have to rake those leaves later, that in itself wasn't altogether terrible, as it gave him a ginormous pile to destroy with a running cannonball later.

This particular morning a slight frost glimmered upon a bed of leaves on the ground. The wind pushed in a bit of a balmy breeze, not warm, but not especially cold. The kind of day fall was made for. A day, Daniel would've exploited a few weeks ago, but had now transitioned into the first morning of his adult life. His age still whispered *"child,"* but his recent life experience screamed, "ADULT!"

The Sweetest Old Lady ever went outside, a cat in her arms as she stepped onto the porch with a fresh, coffee-fueled spring in her step. Wearing a green and white tracksuit, she was wide awake and ready to handle the chores of the day. She made several trips back in and out of her trailer, each time tethering another cat to the leashes on her porch. After putting out the final porch cat, she retrieved and filled an old steel watering can. Starting on the porch, she watered the plants.

As she went about her way, a big brown delivery truck slowed and stopped just across the street. Package in hand, Big Bill strode out of the truck, hopped down to the damp grass below, smiling and waving. "Morning, Mrs. Parker," he bellowed from across the street.

Mrs. Parker? Daniel never even bothered to ask her name.

Mrs. Parker half-heartedly waved back. "Morning, Bill." She made her way around the porch, watering the plants as she went. Continuing her circle, she found herself on the backside of her trailer, adjacent to Cowboy's trailer. As she always did, she scoffed at the mess in Cowboy's yard, however, this time something else caught her eye. Unable to identify it, she moved closer. Her intention was to add it to her ongoing list, one she fully intended to file with the county one day when she'd make a formal complaint about "the junkyard next door," as she put it.

Across the street, Big Bill finished delivering the package. He glanced back to Mrs. Parker's porch to say goodbye, but she was gone.

Mrs. Parker, still carrying the watering can, moved stealthily forward, as quietly as an 80-something woman could in a loudly swishing tracksuit. Weaving her way past the familiar junk, she paused when she saw something new.

No. Not something... some*one*.

She blinked, trying to understand what she was seeing. Her eyes saw a man, plain as day, asleep on the ground, just lying there in the dirt. She took a few steps closer until she was standing beside him, frowning at the mess he'd made

Something was wrong. He wasn't asleep. His rigid body

lay cold and stiff, and covered in reddish motor oil. He scowl grew deeper as she realized what she was looking at wasn't oil at all, but dried blood. All around him. Prone and stiff, his jaw clenched to the side in a final defiant grimace. Evgeni's eyes remained wide open, but they lacked any light.

"Oh, dear Lord..." she whispered. Aghast, she convulsed, her left arm curling into her body. Her face contorted and she dropped the bucket with a loud *clang right* next to Evgeni's head. Inside the water sloshed about, threatening to spill over the edge.

Still looking for Mrs. Parker, Big Bill felt an inexplicable obligation to say goodbye as he stepped back up into his truck. He looked at her porch for a few more seconds before he shook his head and turned the key grinding the vehicle into gear. He drove slowly, passing by Cowboy's yard just as she fell to the ground.

"What the hell..." he whispered.

The brakes screamed as he pushed them into the flood and threw the truck into Park. Big Bill leapt out, sprinting over to the yard. He slowed when he saw her body, next to Evgeni's.

"Oh, no... *no*..." he whispered.

A shot rang out. A bullet whizzed past Bill's head. Throwing his arms over his head, he hit the ground and started crawling back to his truck, as bullets wizzed past his head.

CHAPTER 22
THROUGH THE BLACK GATE

At school a bleary-eyed Daniel sat and stared at the wall.

That is to say, he was blearier-eyed than every other bleary-eyed day. He held his face in a resting scrunch, and he looked even more disheveled than normal. Daniel strongly disliked school. Always had. He very much enjoyed *learning*, but just couldn't handle doing so at a school. He wanted to learn about things he found interesting, like how to make video games, or edit an action sequence, how comic books were created, how toys were developed and made. Useful stuff like that. Today he found himself in English class, and a remedial reading one, at that.

Daniel stepped through the door and shuddered up entry. He knew himself to be better than this, arrogantly, but accurately, better than them, at least at reading. He wasn't a better person or anything, well better than some of them, but that wasn't really saying a heck of a lot about either Daniel or them. Daniel just didn't care; Daniel just didn't try. He didn't know it, but his parents and teacher decided to place him in this class to motivate him. It hadn't worked yet. It would, and soon, but today he felt haunted by his future and his brother's expectations.

. . .

LOOKING to the front of the classroom, Daniel noticed his teacher, Mr. Grodin. Now, he was aware of his teacher, and even kind of liked him. However, today was the first time he truly noticed him as a person like himself. Mr. Grodin's eyes were heavy, and they sunk into the bags beneath them. Other students talked about him, Daniel didn't, mainly because he just didn't care. But the other students came up with a series of thoroughly wild, and of course completely fictional reasons for his appearance. In truth, Mr. Grodin had eight-month-old twins at home. He hadn't slept in months - at least not a really *good* sleep.

None of it mattered to Daniel. Sure, it could have been the killing spree that Jimmy suggested; Mr. Grodin's exhaustion from dismembering several bodies a night. It could have been his wife leaving him for that Philip kid that moved to Michigan over the summer. It was all irrelevant today.

All Daniel saw was a person struggling.

That he could relate to.

THE DAY WAS NEARLY OVER, a fervor of anticipation swirled around the room. Less than an hour remained. For kids in a remedial reading class, it might as well have been ten minutes. They were universally checked out. A perpetually exhausted Mr. Grodin didn't mind one bit. As long as they didn't get too loud, he'd let them do their thing. He'd assigned a simple exercise on context clues in sentences, fully knowing it would take some longer than others.

Glasses trudged to Mr. Grodin's desk. He slapped the paper down on the corner with a triumphant snort. Without looking up, Mr. Grodin said. "Thank you, Daniel."

Glasses had already turned to return to his seat, but froze

immediately. He swung around to face him, thoroughly offended. "What?" he snarled.

Had Daniel been a current resident of planet Earth, he would have laughed.

Mr. Grodin finally looked up. "Oh, I'm sorry." He looked at the paper, back to Glasses and finally found Daniel sitting absentmindedly at the back of the room. "You're not Daniel."

Glasses stood and glared at Mr. Grodin, whose face looked even more worn than usual. "No. I'm *not.*"

"You may return to your seat."

Mumbling obscenities to himself, Glasses compiled. Other than his general slowness, intentional clumsiness and those clearly audible obscenities.

Glasses continued his drawn out return to his seat. . "Pumpkin peach," he snorted as he passed

Daniel still had no idea what that meant, and was so exhausted from the night before he didn't even hear the agricultural insult.

"Dog's gonna eat you!" Glasses continued. "No cops or rat dogs'll save you." He finally arrived at his seat, plopping down with an angry plop and what might possibly have been a bit of a fart. The nearby students all turned and glared at him, unsure if they heard what they thought they heard, the entire lot fearing the associated smell.

Gawking at Daniel, Glasses mumbled to himself. "Fruit loop." He followed up with an offensive hand gesture. The other students looked on, appalled at his boorish behavior, but not surprised by it.

Daniel wasn't aware of Glasses passing comments or possible flatulence, and was equally oblivious of any gestures performed at his back. A few minutes later, after a handful of students completed and submitted their assignment, Jimmy stomped to the front of the room. Like Daniel, Jimmy didn't belong in this class, and just like Daniel, his parents and teachers decided he needed a challenge. Unlike Daniel, however, Jimmy always looked for an easy out and didn't mind being put in an easier class one bit. He'd learned all this stuff last year, so this was his favorite class specifically *because* it was so easy and he was getting an A. Normally Jimmy would ask to see Daniel's paper before submitting it, but not today. Jimmy walked by, scowling, saying nothing.

Glancing up for a split second, Daniel caught Jimmy's eye. He frowned. He secretly wanted Jimmy to stop, if only so he could come clean about everything. All the weirdness with Cowboy and Oliver, how he'd found the body in the woods and was now haunted by a friendly ghost, it was a lot to deal with. Okay, so maybe he was stretching it to say he was being haunted by a ghost boy anymore, but all the rest still applied. Daniel needed a friend, *his* friend, his only friend in the world. Heck they could just talk about movies and comics or copy each other's homework, he didn't care. All he knew is he needed a friend today, more than ever in his life.

Jimmy ignored him and continued walking to the front of the room.

Sliding as close to the floor as he could, Daniel slumped down into his desk. From within his backpack he pulled out a folder and opened it. Inside, the autographed Merkanary card greeted him. Daniel took a moment to admire the signature, gingerly tracing his finger over the texture of the official, embossed seal.

Suddenly the voice of the Principal cracked and popped over the loudspeaker. It was a highly unusual time for any kind of announcement. The students all hushed in unison. His voice sounded like some kind of clerical Stormtrooper. "Teachers, please send the following students to the office immediately. Jim Taylor, Wendell Yates, Laurie Bird, Sheila Rourke…"

Reacting to the names, Daniel suddenly perked up, recognizing them. He knew those names, and their relation with each other.

They were all the names of the kids who lived on Daniel's paper route. They all lived in Valetto's trailer court!

"...Rudolph Wurlitzer, Denny Wilson..."

Glasses rose to his feet, ready to bolt.

"...and Harry Stanton," concluded the Principal.

"I'm outta here, dummies!" shouted Harry "Glasses" Stanton.

"Harry!" Mr. Grodin yelled from the front of the room. He sounded angry, or maybe just surprised, Daniel couldn't tell which.

"What're you gonna do?" Glasses spat back, apparently feeling bulletproof. "You can't send me to the Principal's office! I'm already goin'!" With that accurate assessment of the situation, Glasses sauntered across the room and out the door.

Though it seemed impossible, Daniel slumped even more and melted into the seat. Nearly sliding through his chair, liquifying or at least oozing and pouring over it. He took the Merkanary card, returned it to its heavy gauge plastic protective sleeve and jammed it into the pocket of his jeans.

Riding the school bus home, Daniel sat alone, save for Oliver. Daniel restlessly tapped the plastic of the protective sleeve in his pocket, as if he were hoping to release some form of positive energy from the card within. The talisman in his pocket did nothing. Daniel knew it did nothing, but he nervously tapped away anyway.

He had no idea why all the trailer park kids were called down to the office. He didn't bother to ask any teacher or administrator in the school, first because he hated to ask people anything, and second - and far more significantly - he also knew they wouldn't tell him anyway. He was right. They wouldn't, but that didn't mean he shouldn't have tried.

Daniel also knew it had to do with Cowboy. He didn't know what the end would look like, but...

No, scratch that.

He *did* know what The End would look like, if he were honest with himself. The end looked like his sitting on a school bus, frantically tapping on a trading card like a talisman, thinking about The End he found himself in right now. He was frustrated the principal didn't think to call *the paperboy* down to the office with the others.

None of those kids even lived that close to Cowboy's trailer. Daniel, on the other hand, delivered the guy's freaking *newspaper*! Daniel and Oliver stood alone in the driveway, watching the bus roar away. It headed across the bridge passing the trailer park without stopping, and it made perfect sense. There were no more students to drop off.

Sighing, Daniel grabbed a single newspaper, folded it as tightly as he could and held it up to assess his handiwork, wielding it as a weapon. Granted, he'd rather have Anduril or even Sting, but a condensed, lethal local newspaper would have to suffice.

"The last newspaper I'll ever deliver," Daniel mused. The words manifested themselves in his mind, as if the newspaper itself had formed a headline deep within his soul. Oliver's eye went wide.

"No, not like that," Daniel stammered. "I mean, I'm not going to die or anything. What I mean is, I'm done. Like,

I'm going to quit after this."

Oliver continued to stare, unsure how to respond.

"I'm not going to die," Daniel said, trying to convince himself. "At least, I don't think I will." He glanced at Oliver and shrugged. "The chances of my dying are low. Probably."

Prior to that exact moment Daniel had not considered quitting. Now, however, he knew it was time to move on, time to get going, because under his feet, the grass was growing. Or whatever the expression his dad always said was.

Maybe he would die. He'd never really thought about it. Even though he felt his very life threatened when he spoke to Cowboy the last time, Daniel also somehow felt safe from death. Now, death felt… inevitable. He just hoped it wasn't inevitable for him. Although he also had to admit the sheer nature of death meant it was inevitable for everyone, and like it or not, Daniel was a reluctant part of "everyone."

At Popeye's Gas Station, the entire crew looked toward the trailer park. Momentarily, The Hat glanced over at Daniel, but then fixed his gaze back upon the chaos of the trailer court. Keeping his head down, Daniel soldiered on.

Crossing the line of shrubs at the end of Popeye's lot, Daniel struggled to be brave. He tapped the card in his pocket again.

Nothing.

He looked at Oliver.

Oliver looked sad as he always did, but somehow hopeful, almost pleasant. It was nice, but still sad. He was dead, after all, and nothing that happened the next few minutes was going to change that. Daniel saw something in his eyes, besides purple puss, he'd never seen before tonight. *Was that the sparkle in his eyes when he was alive?*

Daniel felt brave. For his friend, he felt brave.

They marched beyond the tall shrubs, coming around to the volunteer fire station. Police milled about and emergency lights flashed in jarring, rhythmic patterns. The parking lot buzzed, populated by countless police cars and emergency response vehicles. Daniel noticed the fire trucks, some were from Highlands and others were from Butler County. In Daniel's world that was a far and distant land, as far Hobbiton was to Minas Morgal.

With a whooshing roar, the wind kicked up, so strong it nearly knocked him over. Even the police officers held their hats and braced themselves. No one noticed Daniel. Glancing upward, Daniel shuddered as he watched the helicopters swooping in low circles around the fire station.

He felt less than brave, but he knew his quest was not only noble, it was necessary. Ahead of him, Daniel noticed a large blue truck. A deep dark blue, a serious blue. For a split-second he mistook it for Big Bill's delivery truck, but then he saw the bold bright yellow letters on the side: *Allegheny Valley S.W.A.T.*

A SWAT Team Member, eyes heavy and five o'clock shadow thick, paced. Clutching an automatic weapon that Daniel could have sworn was used by Hudson in Aliens. He spoke into a walkie-talkie on his shoulder, glanced over at Daniel and then back to his conversation, yelling to overcome the rumble of the helicopter.

Daniel looked at Oliver. "You know this is all about you."

Oliver shrugged.

"I'm not sure what that means."

Oliver shrugged again, equally unsure.

Daniel smiled, surprising both of them. "I'm not sure if I like you better talking or not talking."

Oliver shrugged a third time.

Daniel accepted the finality of the third shrug, but had to get in the last word. "Well, whatever, but this is definitely all about you." He paused to think. "I'm not sure how far you can come, but I don't think I can take you with me where I'm going. And I *know* you can't take me with you." Daniel stopped, narrowing his eyes at Oliver. "I mean, I really *hope* you can't take me with you. I'm not sure I'm ready for death, but I guess I might need to be, huh?"

The boys continued walking. Police and emergency responders seemed to be everywhere - behind every tree, next to every car, near every trailer. A few of the residents were present, but most were unable to cross the barriers. Daniel looked to his right and noted Oliver was still at his side. Nobody even appeared to be looking at them. It was all quite strange, surreal.

He wished they would look at him. He wanted to be stopped, but he knew they wouldn't be stopped. He knew they couldn't be stopped. He knew they shouldn't be stopped. This was a divine appointment, and Daniel would finish it for his friend. Despite his desire to be stopped, at least by being ignored he felt less alone.

"This is all really weird," he said to his friend. Daniel meant it in both the broad and the narrow sense, but more than anything he just needed to say it. He needed to hear *himself* say it. He thought it would help. It didn't.

Mithral would, but alas.

With one police helicopter hovering behind him, Daniel observed another helicopter on the horizon. He could see a large blue 4 on the side. The local news. Peering ahead down the main thoroughfare, he noticed barricades at each entrance into the trailer park. Each barricade was occupied by two police cars and four police officers. At the end of Valetto Lane, a few news vans idled.

"This is a pretty big deal," Daniel said, glancing back at Oliver.

The boys continued on past the mostly quiet ponds. The only person Daniel saw, Old Man Mumbles, was fast asleep in his lawn chair as they walked by. At the only house in the trailer court, the house at the end of Valetto Lane, there was another news van. The closer the boys got, the more they were able to see. This van was broadcasting a live interview.

The Queen of the Court, Mrs. Valetto, stood beside the news van, a camera man between her and the van, her house behind her. Everything had been positioned thus, at her insistence, and she began fielding questions from a square jawed reporter. Daniel named the reporter Mr. Clean, because he obviously looked a whole lot like Mr. Clean.

Very early in life Daniel had learned that the shortest distance between two points was a straight line. So he weaved between the van and the house. Directly behind Mrs. Valetto and her interview, directly in the line of the camera.

At home, Daniel's mom swept the carpet, or "vacuumed" as the rest of the world referred to it. She worked at a rapid pace, hoping to finish before Daniel came home. The TV glowed behind her, as usual. Her channel of choice - channel four. Noticing the bells and whistles of the breaking news, she turned off the vacuum and stared at the screen.

On the television Mr. Clean interviewed the Queen of the Court. The reporter asked. "Did you know of Mr. Harrison's background? His troubling history with children?"

"Oh, hell no!" The Queen of the Court responded as only she could. "My son handles that junk, blame that on him." She continued with her absolute evisceration of her son's once-somewhat-good name. "His name is Greg. He does all the maintenance, too, and we've had *plenty* of issues. But Mr. Harrison was always such a kind man. I could never have known!" She was lying, but she loved the attention and milked it for all she could.

"And why did no one call when they heard the gunshots?" the reporter asked.

"Well, there were some complaints of Mr. Harrison going back there, in the cornfield, and winging crows." She stopped, trying to cover for herself. "People just got used to it," she lied. In truth, people still complained directly to her, but she simply ignored it. "Besides, around here, people like to shoot their guns!"

Midway through her last sentence, Daniel strolled by in the background., head down and pace slow but steady.

"Daniel!" she screamed.

UPSTAIRS IN DANIEL'S bedroom Mac popped his head up and just as quickly put it back down with a groan.

Downstairs, Daniel's mom moved at a rapid, but frantic pace. She snatched her keys and darted out through the laundry room. Outside, gravel popped and flew from behind the car as she exited the driveway and drove out onto the road, narrowly missing a maroon minivan with an angry soccer mom at the wheel. The soccer mom laid hard into her horn but was intentionally ignored. Zipping across the bridge she saw a barricade being set up, with several police officers and firemen pulling barriers off of a utility truck. For a split second, she considered plowing through the barricade, but at the last second slammed on her brakes.

Her Chrysler screeched to a halt just inches from the central barricade and one of the cops. Behind her the soccer mom repeatedly blared her horn, as if she were punching her steering wheel in the face. To prove that she's a jerk, she ran the stop sign at the end of the bridge.

Gesturing downward with both hands, the officer ran over and shouted at the soccer mom. "Slow down!"

He then turned his attention to Daniel's mom. "I'm sorry Ma'am," he began, even though it was clear he wasn't really all that sorry. "We can't let you across. There's a situation."

"I know, I saw it on the news!"

"Live?" Piped in the fireman approaching the truck.

"Yes!' She put her car in reverse before shifting back into drive and pulling forward. She tried to wedge her car through the small gap between barriers, but stopped short of scratching her front end.

"We can't let you through!" shouted the officer hand resting on her car.

"You have to!" she shouted through her open driver's side window.

"Maam, we can't do it! Take Hart's run if you need to get around," said the Firemen, in an effort to be helpful

"My son's over there!" she yelled at them.

The police officer chuckled and shook his head. Both the fireman and her looked at him, aghast that he would laugh at such a statement. "Don't worry Ma'am," he said, smirking at her self righteously. "No kids are over there. I promise."

"Yeah," agreed the fireman.

The police officer glared at him. "Listen, lady-""You think

we'd let kids back there?" the fireman blurted out, "When the guy's threatening to blow the place up?!"

The police officer shoved the fireman, grabbing him by the lapels of his jacket. "That's not public knowledge, you idiot!"

The two men started arguing.

She hit the gas.

The barriers moved a bit, but upon hearing a metallic scratch she paused. At this point the men momentarily set aside their differences and physically blocked her car.

She swore quietly, opened the door and stepped out to confront them, further denting it,by swinging the door into the now crooked barrier.

"He's the paperboy!" she pleaded through fresh tears. "My son's *the paperboy*. He's in there delivering the newspaper!"

The fireman and the Officer looked at each other. "That's impossible, Ma'am. For their safety, all the kids who live in the trailer park are being retained at the school."

"He doesn't live in the trailer park!" she wailed.

Still at their normal places at the gas station, the Popeye's crew noticed the spastic woman yelling at the cop. She tried to push past the police officer, struggling to hold her back. The fireman held up his hands and stepped back, allowing her to gain ground until a second officer ran past and grabbed her. He muttered insults aimed at both Mom and the fireman.

"I'm sorry Ma'am," the first officer said, although it was still clear he was totally not remotely sorry. In fact, he'd grown downright angry. Angry at Mom, angry at the fireman, angry at the stupid kid that walked by, angry at the psycho with a gun threatening to blow up his trailer, but really angry at himself for being such an idiot. "You can't get through!"

"Please!" she begged. "I can't lose him too."

The officer didn't release her, but softened his grip. "Look, I'm sure that our officers will stop him and bring him back home to you," he said. "What's his name?"

"It's Daniel," she said. "Daniel."

During the time his mother attempted to force her way through the police barricade, Daniel had made his way through the majority of the trailer court. He neared his final destination, Cowboy's trailer. Since climbing the hill by the Queen of the Court's house, he had not seen anyone. No police officers and certainly no news people could be found. Although there were still many people in the trailer park, occasionally peeking through blinds and shutters, Daniel felt utterly isolated.

Even with Oliver at his side, he felt alone. Not because Oliver was dead and a ghost and therefore not really technically at his side, but because when he finally confronted Cowboy, Oliver would be gone. Forever.

Daniel would, in the end, truly be alone.

And that was scary.

He'd accepted the possibility that he might die, but he struggled with the idea of dying alone. That was something he just wasn't ready for. Being alone. *Well, I won't technically be alone; I'll be with Cowboy.* However, he felt pretty sure that being with just you and your murderer meant dying alone.

"I'm sorry you were alone," he said to Oliver. "I'm going to make this right, but I'm still not sure exactly what I'm doing to do. I don't really have a plan, here." Before Oliver had a chance to respond, he added, "You don't need to shrug. I get it."

With a sweet, somewhat devilish smile, Oliver shrugged at him.

Daniel froze when he saw movement ahead. At the bend sat two police cars, lights flashing but sirens silent. A police officer stood between the cars, peering down towards Cowboy's trailer. Seeing Oliver still at this side, Daniel marched on.

They moved stealthily through the yards of the trailers up and across from Cowboy's trailer. Halting, he took a deep breath before stepping into the street. They crossed the street together, but just over halfway across Oliver flickered twice and disappeared entirely. Daniel stole a glance toward the Sweetest Old Lady Ever's trailer, where an armor-clad SWAT officer stared back at him. He continued walking.

Hidden around the corner, another SWAT Officer peeked around down towards Cowboy's trailer. His gun was out, upright and ready to fire. He looked at Daniel. Their eyes met, but just like the first SWAT officer, the other cops and the fireman, he said nothing. Daniel frowned, but continued on, walking to the end of all things. *The end of my childhood*, he thought, the notion liberally dowsed with a heaping helping of melodrama.

He walked towards Cowboy's trailer.

Behind Daniel, the SWAT officers exchanged looks and shrugged. Neither knew what to do, so they did nothing. The obvious choice would have been to stop the kid, but they'd been told there *were* no kids. They were likely so surprised to see one that they were both paralyzed.

From the walkie-talkies on their shoulders their commander yelled. "What's the paperboy doing?"

Taking slow, measured steps, Daniel walked with extreme caution. He didn't know what might be in the yard, but knew something bad had to have happened. Then he saw it. The body of Evgeni Petrov, the USA Gazette Guy, rotting in the dead brown grass.

"Oh, crap..." Daniel whispered as he neared.

The dirt immediately surrounding the body was a deeper, richer brown from the now mostly dry blood. Crinkling and tearing the paper, Daniel nervously clutched the newspaper in his hands. He considered tapping the card in his pocket, but thought better of it. Besides, both hands were locked in a vice grip around the neck of the newspaper.

He wasn't even sure why he brought it, aside from it being his only excuse for coming here. He had to give the guy the newspaper. Maybe the cops would let him go by if he explained he had to deliver this single newspaper. Of course, that was back in a world where they might've actually stopped him or even acknowledged him. Regardless, here he was, standing beside a dead body with a newspaper, staring up at the most terrifying house in his entire life.

Daniel eyed the SWAT officers again, but only for a split-second. He turned his gaze back to the front door. At this point he honestly had no idea what to do next.

"I want to leave," he said, staring at the door, afraid to look at Oliver.

He grasped the newspaper just a little tighter, and then he heard a voice. The sound familiar, wonderfully broken English and a Russian accent.

"Deliver paper," he said.

Daniel scrunched is already scrunched face more and slowly turned towards the voice. The USA Gazette Guy stood next to Oliver.

"Be brave boy," he said. "You're a brave boy. Street fighting boy."

"I don't really fight in the streets, sir," said Daniel a bit disappointed in himself. "It's a video game."

"I know boy, I know. I know video games." He added, "No call me sir, I'm friend of yours, call me Evgeni. Now, you deliver the paper."

Deliver the paper.

Hey, he'd brought it as his pretty lame cover story, he may as well deliver the thing. He walked up the to the house and reached slowly for the door. On some level he wished he could actually move slower, like some kind of Reverse Flash, but it wasn't physically possible. His mind started to spin with the similarities between *Superman II* and this moment and wondered if he could run fast enough to reverse the spin of the earth and reverse time like Superman.

He gripped the metal handle on the flimsy screen door, and with great care pressed his thumb into the button and silently pulled it open. He extended his arm, preparing to drop the newspaper and bolt when the main door flung open. A thick, hairy ropey hairy arm lunged out of the darkness and yanked Daniel inside.

CHAPTER 23
MEANWHILE AT THE LEGION OF DOOM

In the trailer, Cowboy pulled Daniel into the living room. Daniel yelped, but noticed he wasn't being manhandled. Cowboy seemed to be handling him with a shocking amount of tenderness and care, as though by pulling him inside he'd saved him from some looming outside threat.

Daniel knew better. He'd just been pulled into the single most dangerous situation he would ever find himself in. He wondered, how short it would be? Not his life, but specifically his time inside the trailer. Seconds? Minutes? Hours?

Days?

With Daniel inside, Cowboy swiftly locked the dead bolt behind them, clanging shut with a heavy thud. To Daniel it reminded him of the jolting sound of gunshots when Cowboy shot crows. He'd hated that sound. He preferred the guns in spy movies, the ones with silencers that sounded more like the noises he would make when playing with his G.I. Joes. The "pew-pew" guns, as Jimmy called them.

Despite his fear, Daniel focused on the details of the pacing madman before him. Stained black Harley Davidson T-shirt with cut off sleeves. Surprisingly clean, belt-less blue jeans with a belly bulging over. Sweaty forehead that he kept wiping with his forearm. The man was disgusting, and Daniel couldn't look away.

Cowboy said something, quietly muttering to himself. His mouth opened and closed spastically. Daniel couldn't hear him as the radios and televisions were all playing their discordant song.

Daniel began to speak, then hesitated. He looked around. He knew Oliver was murdered here, but that wasn't the saddest thing about this place. This place *was* Cowboy. In the chaos of trash and waste, in the cacophony of the noise, Daniel felt he was gazing at the very inside of Cowboy's soul. The soul of someone who wanted to be recognized, maybe not as a good person, but certainly as a normal one. Eternity and the noise stood between them.

Daniel held out the paper. "Here's your newspaper."

After saying it, Daniel finally realized why he actually brought it. He'd brought it to give it to Cowboy. He brought it to come here and hand it to him, person to person, like some stupid, simple human gesture.

It wasn't kindness, really, but more like recognition. Treating him like a normal person, like the person he thought Cowboy *wanted* to be. He hoped Cowboy wanted to be.

He probably didn't deserve even the most basic of human gestures, but Daniel left judgment was best left up to God or maybe Superman. He did it because he thought Cowboy deserved one normal thing in a life of some seriously messed up stuff that he couldn't even comprehend.

Despite Daniel's effort to connect, Cowboy showed no emotion, his face remaining a blank slate. Daniel wanted to see Shelob or an orc fighting to manifest, but he only saw a person. A very messy person, but a person nonetheless.

In kind, Cowboy peered at Daniel, staring for a long time until he reached over and flicked a switch, shutting off the surge protector, silencing the noise.

"Thank you, Daniel," he said in the silence. He smiled. "Thank you."

Say you're welcome. Say you're welcome. SAY YOU'RE WELCOME.

No words came out.

He fluctuated from utterly terrified and completely petrified to freak out of his mind. *Be brave and say something. Heck, just be nice and say you're welcome. SAY YOU'RE WELCOME.*

Cowboy glared at Daniel as the kid ran hurdles in his head. He likely expected the kid to say "you're welcome," but he didn't. Eventually he grew sick of waiting and took the newspaper from Daniel.

Daniel attempted to speak. He was going to finally not be such a weirdo and say, "You're welcome." But he stopped himself halfway and mumbled "Yerg."

Assuming Daniel had burped, Cowboy ignored it. Quickly, almost symbolically, he rifled through the paper. Glancing through it at rapid speed, only really taking in the pictures and a few of the headlines. Turning away, he tossed the newspaper into a corner, joining a much larger pile of other papers consisting of wrinkled receipts, bent notebooks, and torn and tattered magazines. He strolled over to the window and peeked through the blinds.

FROM BEHIND A BUSH at the corner of the house one of the SWAT Officers had his gun trained on the window. Narrowing his field of vision, he pulled his finger snug up on the trigger. "I've got a clean shot," he announced, never losing his target. "I can end this."

"Not with the kid in there," returned the second SWAT Officer. "We screwed this up."

"And I can unscrew it. Right now!" he shouted.

They both fell silent and focused on the house

Cowboy looked directly at them. He didn't close the

blinds, as if he wanted them to shoot. The officer lowered his gun away from Cowboy and shouted. "Let the paperboy go!"

Cowboy closed the blinds.

"They think I did something bad."

He was talking to Daniel, yet remained in front of the window, unmoving. "Awful bad. Bad, bad, bad." He sounded more and more childlike as he spoke, before suddenly snapping back into his adult self. "*No body*, not yet. How could they not find it? Is it in the paper?"

Daniel finally found courage through simple honesty. "I don't know. I haven't read it."

Cowboy pivoted, scooped up the paper and frantically turned the pages. Just as he did moments ago, he flipped through it too fast to really see or read anything. He didn't see a picture of himself or a picture of the boy, so he assumed he was still safe, at least for today.

He raised his eyes to meet Daniel's. For a sliver of a second, Daniel saw the humanity in them, but then they clouded over with orc-like rage. Cowboy screamed. "I didn't do what they say I did! I *swear* I didn't do it!"

Feeling more than out of his depth, Daniel silently struggled to breathe. It was as if a heavy, unseen weight was constricting on his chest, just like a demented symbiote or alien, and he found himself unable to think clearly. Daniel didn't see where it came from, but before he knew it, he was far too scared to register how afraid he truly was.

Cowboy held up a pistol.

Daniel recoiled, recognizing him as a villain in those boring old Western comics he found in Uncle Bob's garage.

Cowboy reminded him of a villain in an issue called "The Fat Rat of Rivertown." In the comic *The Saddle Bag Kid*, there was a young cowboy who did right, but always got kicked out of town for some stupid reason at the end of each issue. In this one he visited a town called Rivertown, where The Fat Rat ran things. The Fat Rat was a big, burly type with and handlebar mustache. Daniel couldn't even remember how the Saddle Bag Kid won, but he did. Wishing he remembered, Daniel thought it might be helpful in this situation. It wouldn't have been. It just involved a lot of punching and horseback riding along a river. Trying to figure out how that stupid terrible Western comic book from 1956 ended somehow made him less afraid, not not afraid, but certainly less afraid.

Noticing Daniel's wide eyes following the swinging movement of the gun, Cowboy felt compelled to justify himself. "I have to protect myself," he said matter-of-factly.

"You need to come clean."

The words came out of Daniel as if he were a puppet operated by some kind of external force. The words downright stunned him after he said them. He looked to the couch and sucked in a breath.

There, on the couch, sat the Corpse Boy. Behind him, arms folded but with a friendly yet fired smile, stood Evgeni.

He regarded Oliver. A little boy once known as the Corpse Boy, and right now Oliver's eyes pleaded with Daniel for help. The swelling on his eye had gone down, the color had returned. His eyes were bright and clear.

Cowboy looked at the couch and shook his head.

Daniel's eyes widened. *Can he see Oliver? How is that even-*

"I showed him my comic books," Cowboy said motioning to Oliver with the gun. "That's all." He looked over at Daniel, eyes narrow with intensity. "That is *all*."

Daniel said nothing, eyes darting from Cowboy to Oliver.

Cowboy approached the other end of the couch and plopped down. He tossed the gun on the floor at his feet, cradled himself in his arms and rocked from side to side. "I showed him my comic books. He liked the fabulous Thunder Family, he liked the Ghoul. I made the noises, from the pages." He stopped. He had truly wanted the boy to be his friend. For it to only ever be about comic books and wrestling moves, but it wasn't.

He continued. "The demon told me horrible things to do to him. Jesus shouted; Jesus tried to save me. But the demon...the demon put so much noise in my head, I... I..." He glanced at Daniel, tears in his eyes. "It hurts! It still hurts so much!" he screamed, and Daniel knew for sure the SWAT Officers outside had to have heard him, unless they were deaf.

"The demon's screaming now!" Cowboy continued. "But I can hear Jesus! I can hear Jesus!"

Daniel's true bravery came from just being totally freaked out. He became brave because he had to get out of there and he had to save his friend. Or at least redeem him. Strangely, he found a way to relate to Cowboy in the midst of this madness. He stood as tall as his well-worn Nikes would let him and spoke. "I know what it's like to have a demon!"

Cowboy's rocking and ranting came to a dead stop. Apparently he hadn't expected Daniel to say that, hadn't expected anyone to ever say anything even close to that. "You know a demon?" he asked, visibly afraid.

"Well..." Daniel struggled to make the connection he so easily just made in his head. He processed it through his words. "Not a demon, I guess. More like a friend that isn't you." That really wasn't where Daniel wanted to go with this. Again, in his head it just made perfect sense. "A friend that nobody else can see."

Cowboy frowned. He clearly didn't like these words, shaking his head in disbelief. He attempted to diminish it. "The demon is evil, it ain't nobody's friend."

Ignoring him, Daniel continued in his effort to make sense of things and to get through to the psychopath who had a demon screaming bloody murder in his ear. In his imagination, Daniel metaphorically hopped on Cowboy's shoulder to play angel to the mystery demon's devil.

"My friend wants me to help him," he said, looking over at Oliver. "He's... kind of like an angel, I guess. But he doesn't have wings. He came to me a few weeks ago. I think he wants me to tell his mom what happened to him. To tell the *world* what happened to him. He wants it set right."

"His mom?" Cowboy asked, thoughts drifting back to his own, long dead mother. "My mom loved me. She was a good woman, used to fight the demon, until the demon took her away from me. But... but she always loved me. The only one who did."

"Even bad moms love their kids," agreed Daniel. "He...my friend...wants the world to know what you did to him. It's the only way he can-" "I don't even know what the kid was really like," lamented Cowboy. "I wanted a friend. That's all. Really and truly, I just wanted a friend."

Daniel dug into his pocket. He pulled out the Merkanary card and offered it to Cowboy, who hesitated to take it.

"He liked Merkanary," explained Daniel. Cowboy finally took the card. He regarded it closely. "Merkanary was his favorite."

After sliding the card from the protective sleeve, Cowboy examined the signature and reverently slid his finger over the embossed seal of authenticity.

"Merkanary?" he whispered. "The Ultimate Rejects." He smiled. "I have Ultimate Reject comics," he said, seeming to offer them to Daniel. "Wanna see?"

"Pass," Daniel said defiantly.

The mania had snuck back up upon the man. In the honesty of the lunacy, he continued. "I've done so many wrong, awful things!" He clenched his fists tightly, inadvertently wrinkling and rippling the frail cardboard card. Not giving it a second thought, he tossed it aside like the rest of his trash.

Daniel avoided the compulsion to yell at Cowboy for destroying an invaluable Pete Pham autographed trading card. Mainly because he feared he would die if he said anything to trigger the monster any more than he already had. But inside, inside he mourned for the card and carefully held his tongue.

"I'm not the monster they say I am!" Cowboy wailed again. "I'm not the monster that the demon makes me." He looked at Daniel and sneered. "I. Am. Not. The. Monster."

"But you did something very terrible." Daniel moved closer. "You need to make it right. You need to tell me. For him."

They both looked at Oliver.

"His name was Oliver and he didn't deserve what happened to him. What you did to him."

A thin smile formed on Cowboy's lips.

"I killed him."

CHAPTER 24
THE GHOUL

I killed him.

The word bounced around the wall of the trailer and into Daniel's brain. Daniel clenched his fists at the words.

He wanted to kill him, but how do you kill a super villain? He saw the Ghoul, hulking over him, his rocky gray skin pulsing with each breath. Daniel shook it off, Cowboy was just a man.

He didn't know how, but he wanted Cowboy dead, and dead by his hand. The spoken words cut through him like no other words he'd ever heard. The anger settled itself into pain, and the pain became fear. He feared the reality of the situation, and now living in that reality, he wanted to vomit. For Oliver's sake, he remained composed. The truth - no matter how horrific, no matter how much he may not want it to be true, - must always come to light.

"Thank you," Daniel said. Despite his inner rage, he couldn't help but remain his mother's generally-well-mannered son.

Cowboy blinked rapidly. Stunned, his mouth agape.

"For admitting all that." Daniel attempted to course

correct and make the moment less awkward. "You finally did something right." He failed miserably.

Thoroughly pissed off, Cowboy stood and held his fist high over Daniel's head, ready to strike. He once again saw the Ghoul, a mass of muscle over him.

Daniel thought he was about to die. He turned his head and smiled at Oliver and Evgeni. A dead man has nothing to fear, so a dead man has nothing to lose.

Daniel looked up at Cowboy, unfazed. "You have to let me go."

"No, I don't." Cowboy looked over and regarded Oliver for a good long time

"You have to let me go," he said. "To get him. To make it all okay. Or at least as okay as this can be now." Daniel stepped away from Cowboy, toward the door, ignoring Cowboy's raised fist. He reached for the doorknob.

Cowboy's fist, still held high in the air, shook spastically. "BUT THE DEMON!" he roared, flashing into the form of the Ghoul.

Daniel turned and approached Cowboy, staring up at him with renewed, heroic confidence. "Tell your demon to get lost."

Cowboy smiled and laughed a loud genuine laugh. Almost instantly his smile disappeared. With that smile the man himself also faded into the background. What remained was not a man, not a boy, not even a monster. He was a void. Cowboy showed no emotion. His face revealed nothing, while inside Daniel remained convinced he raged against his inner demon.

Daniel turned and stepped for the front door again. He stopped, looking back at Cowboy, who remained bizarrely motionless, like a statue in a wax museum Daniel had visited in Niagara Falls. It freaked him out then and it freaked him out now even more. He reached for the door and turned the knob.

Grabbing his arm, Cowboy pulled him back an inch. The hand appeared rocky with scales, like that of the Ghoul.

Daniel shivered and cringed, fear cooking fresh goose bump boils all over his body.

Cowboy pulled Daniel's hand away from the door, stepped forward and flipped the deadbolt. It clanked with a menacing thud. He pulled Daniel away from the door and pushed him deeper into the living room. "It's not safe," he said.

"Clearly."

"The cops'll stop you."

"The cops?"

"They want to kill me!"

Clearly Daniel thought, but he held his tongue and waited for Cowboy to continue.

"They want me dead so they won't let Jesus allow you to show the truth!"

At this point Daniel finally felt safe. He realized the man he thought would murder him minutes ago, the man who had likely intended to murder him minutes ago, now protected him. Cowboy may have been the villain in the story, but like the best villains, he wasn't all bad and certainly wasn't a hero. And yet, he could actually be heroic, if given the chance.

A new kind of madness consumed Cowboy. "They'll kill you to protect the truth."

"Jesus will protect me," said Daniel.

Cowboy's eyebrows raised in shock. "He will?"

"He already has, hasn't he?" Daniel added. "If not him, Superman."

"I guess he has," Cowboy grumbled, almost believing, yet too deeply hurt to really believe anything.

"Heck, he even sent me an angel. Angels are kind of like God's superheroes."

Oliver smiled. He looked more alive than Daniel had ever seen him.

Looking past Daniel, Cowboy spoke. "Go out the back."

Daniel followed Cowboy's eyes and turned around. At the end of the hallway he saw a small, rear window.

Cowboy grabbed the newspaper and haphazardly folded it back up. He went wrong on the first fold and transformed it into a jumbled mess. He offered it to Daniel. "Here, you might need this."

"I won't," said Daniel, who nonetheless took the paper, because he was, after all, a paperboy.

"Hide in the corn, then the woods." He gazed through Daniel. Through the shuttered window, through the corn, through the woods, but he only saw the forest where the boy's body rotted, hanging from a tree. "The woods hide everything."

Having nothing left to say to Cowboy and feeling resolute in his divine protection, Daniel hurried down the hallway. He pulled the venetian blinds away and hopped up onto the narrow window ledge. Stumbling up and over, he fell into the relatively open section of the backyard, miraculously free of mechanical debris. Oliver stood there, waiting for him. Daniel threw a sideways glance to the Sweetest Old Lady Ever's trailer, smiling at the thought of her.

"Try to keep up, kid," Daniel said. He thought he was being clever, then immediately realized he was essentially speaking to a magical being who basically teleported from inside the trailer to outside the trailer as he, himself, had oafishly bumbled out the window.

Doing a small runner's stretch, Daniel bounced from side to side and then sprinted through the yard and into the corn. Rushing through the tall and dying corn, Daniel glanced over his shoulder to ensure Cowboy wasn't following him. Satisfied, he turned back and ran directly into a SWAT Officer, losing his footing and crashing through the corn.

Caught off guard, the SWAT Officer helped Daniel regain his feet. Reflexively, he dusted off Daniel's now dirty shoulder.

"Whoa," Daniel whispered as he did a double take. The cop looked almost identical to his brother. He had a beefy face and kind-but-judgmental eyes. The kind of eyes that automatically made you feel guilty even if you didn't need to feel guilty, but *especially* guilty when you had reason to feel guilty. The SWAT Officer started to speak when Daniel snapped back to reality and darted away, just out of reach as he disappeared among the stalks of corn.

"Crap!" shouted the SWAT Officer. He could hear Daniel, but could no longer see him. "It's the paper boy! Repeat, it's the paperboy! Don't shoot!" he shouted into his walkie-talkie. "He's in the corn!"

"Follow him! Find out if he's hurt," came the reply from the walkie-talkie.

Running faster than he had ever run and likely as fast as he ever *would* run, Daniel sprinted through the corn. He miraculously avoided several SWAT Officers peppered throughout the field, gathering a few scratches and abrasions from the dry stalks.

At the barricade between the bridge and Popeye's gas station, Daniel's mom attempted to push her way past the unyielding police officers. The officers were far from gentle, but held her back with a minimal level of force.

"Ma'am, please stop," one said.

"There's no kids back 'er," a second added.

"Just stop it lady," a third officer barked, having lost his patience long ago. Every now and then a few profanities colored the phrases, but overall they kept their cool.

She didn't say much, but eventually gave up pleading with the lunkheads. Like a tennis player seeking extra power on her serve, she'd only grunt when attempting to push past, occasionally shouting. "Get off me!" All the yelling garnered the attention of the gas station crew, who instead of watching a whole lot of nothing in the other direction had long since tuned in to the scene developing behind them. Hoping to help de-escalate the quickly escalating situation, the crew hurried over to the barricade.

With an ice cold Coke in each hand, Popeye wielded them like weapons. "You officers want some pops?"

"Cold pop," giggled Belly with a jolly rumble. Why he found that funny was beyond the humor of the other men.

"Plenty'a Choco-Shocko," said Hat, locking his eyes with hers.

She ceased struggling and the Officers released her.

"Sure, I'll take a pop," said the fireman with a hop off the back of the truck. He approached and reached for a Coke.

"Hold your horses bucko!" commanded one of the police officers. He stopped the fireman and grabbed both Cokes, tossing one to the other officer and guarding the other from the fireman's efforts to take it.

With a wink to Daniel's mom, Popeye patted both police officers on the shoulder and gave them a sort of hug. "I want to thank you for your service."

"Yeah, thanks for the pops," said the officer.

Just then, Mom ran between Belly and the Hat.

"Hey! Stop her!" yelled the Officer.

When she passed, the two men stepped together, innocently blocking the halfheartedly pursuing officer. He bumped into Belly's bulbous but surprisingly hard stomach.

Popping open his Coke, the second Officer sighed. "Forget her, let the crazy lady go."

"More cold drinks? Snacks?" offered Popeye.

"Ah, sure yeah," said the first officer. "I'll take a Choco-Shocko."

With the cold, hard glare of a very successful business-man, Popeye replied, "That'll be a dollar twenty-nine."

Stunned, the cop seemed really and truly hurt. "But...I'm a cop."

"And people in hell want ice water." Popeye paused, and then added. "And you fellas owe me a dollar fifty for those Cokes."

The Officer handed over his unopened can of Coke.

Oliver walked alongside Daniel.

Daniel reviewed their odd relationship in his head. Originally little more than a stranger he saw in passing on his paper route, then a rotting corpse in a tree, followed by a ghost haunting Daniel's every waking moment, and now, as The End neared, his friend. They walked through what had once been an unknown forest, now all-too-familiar for them both. They made their way to the nest of trees where Oliver's body still hung.

As Daniel approached the tree, Oliver stopped hard, bouncing back as if he had walked into an invisible, freshly-Windexed, sliding glass door Daniel looked back at him, confused.

"What are you doing?"

Oliver shrugged. He tried to push forward again, but some mighty external force held him back. He could go no farther. He held up his hands and pushed into the air, shaking his head.

"You look like a mime," Daniel said, smirking.

Oliver frowned at him.

"Force field. Fine, I get it," he said, nodding. "But for what it's worth, you'd make an awesome mime. And you're never going to hear those two words come out of my mouth again."

The Corpse Boy's mission, it seemed, had been completed, now it was time for the Paper Boy to finish things. Daniel still didn't know what that meant, but he had to admit he'd felt protected up to this point, and compelled to return to the forest. He assumed he'd figure out the end part too.

Daniel took several steps forward, deeper into the forest. He moved closer to Oliver's body, and although he could not see it from where he stood, he knew it was just a few yards beyond him. He turned back to Oliver. The boys regarded each other as friends. Friends that now recognized their friendship was about to come to an end. "I guess this means you're going to go away," Daniel announced, pausing with a desperate gulp. "For good."

Nothing lasts forever, but the Earth and sky.

Oliver nodded in an affirmative.

"I'm… I'm going to miss you."

Daniel wept."I'm sorry that you had to die and all, but I'm glad it meant we found each other. That we got to be friends. The first part really sucks, I'm not gonna lie. But the second part is probably the best thing that's ever happened to me. I mean it." Daniel took a long thoughtful pause, not because he was overcome with emotion, but because he was unsure if he should say the next part. He ultimately decided to tell his friend the truth. "You didn't deserve to have all that stuff happen to you, Oliver," he said. I know you love her, but your mom was awful, and… well… you deserved better. I mean, I won't blame her for this, but if she was a better mom, things probably would have been really different for you. The same goes for your dad. I met him and he's… well… he's sorry he didn't know you. But I think you're better off." He breathed in deeply, catching his breath. "You'll always be my friend, even when you go away, when you die for good. That won't change."

Daniel smiled, ruminating on their good times. "I'll always think of you when I read an issue of *The Borough* and Merkanary fights the Ghoul, or the Grim leaves the Fabulous Thunder Family. Or when Mr. Gorgeous does a suplex. And anytime I watch *The Omega Man* or *Jacob's Passage*. I know that movie is really special for you. I believe you'll go to Heaven, and in Heaven you'll be able to watch superhero cartoons and play with toys all day and all night, but I assume it's always daytime in heaven. Or maybe it's always sunset, or twilight? In movies they call it 'magic hour' because it has the best light. Eventually your mom will come and be with you and take care of you again," he said, although he didn't believe that last part but said it out of love for Oliver.

"And someday, but hopefully not for a really long time, I'll come and see you. Even though I'm not sure how all that stuff works after you die."

Daniel fell silent. He looked beyond them toward the tree line, knowing what had to happen next. "See ya Oliver."

He turned away and started walking toward the body. He wouldn't see him again for years, and it shook him deeply. Eventually they'd meet again in heaven, he hoped, but that meeting remained many, *many* years away. Ahead, Daniel finally caught sights of Oliver's body, held intact mainly by the recent chilly weather and the deep dark shade of the nearby pines. Approaching the tree and the body, Daniel noticed the tire and his long-lost duck boot.

He looked up at the dead body, rotting overhead, Oliver's flesh, pale and peeling.

At least he doesn't smell. He bent down, plucked the boot from the now semi-dry mud, regarding it. He examined it as if it were an artifact to a long-lost reality or civilization Which it technically was. It belonged to a version of Daniel that no longer existed.

It belonged to a kid.

Daniel wasn't yet a man, but he certainly wasn't who he used to be when he'd lost it a week ago. He placed the boot back down on the ground, as if marking the area as a sacred spot, his and Oliver's.

It no longer belonged to Cowboy. It no longer belonged to

pain, but to redemption. Also, it kind of smelled bad. Not rotting corpse bad, but like a dirty old boot left in the woods for a week bad.

Daniel kicked the tire and started climbing the tree. He awkwardly struggled upward , but finally made it to the branch across from Oliver's body without incident. Although Daniel did not see him, Oliver watched his friend from a distance.

Reaching over from where he stood on the branch, Daniel pulled the knife from the tree where he'd left it. He began the arduous task of cutting the wire, despite the dullness of the blade. Discouraged, but seeing visible progress, he continued sawing away, dulling the knife ever more with each pass, but also splitting the wire consistently.

It snapped in an instant, The body collapsing to the ground below with an unglamorous *thud*.

The Corpse Boy smiled in the distance and finally disappeared forever.

CHAPTER 25

THE CLEANSING FIRE

Back at Cowboy's trailer, some serious crap was very much about to go down or hit the fan, or however people prefer to say it. A SWAT Officer stood with his hand raised. His eyes remained fixed on Cowboy's trailer, ear trained on the radio on his shoulder. In the trailer park, several previously-unseen SWAT Team members crept forward. Likewise, the SWAT officers in the cornfield inched their way towards Cowboy's trailer.

The walkie-talkie crackled to life. "We have confirmation that the paperboy is clear."

"Paperboy is clear?" the officer asked. "All clear?"

"Affirmative. We have an all-clear," replied the voice. "It's a go."

"Let's end this screw-up," the SWAT Officer said, dropping his arm.

"All go," the voice said over the radio.

Several other SWAT Team members moved from their positions. Slowly and stealthily, they made their way to the trailer.

Inside, Cowboy gazed down the hallway at the window where Daniel had made his escape. Through the broken blinds, bent from Daniel's clumsy tumble through them, he noticed someone moving. At first thinking it had been Daniel returning to the trailer, he approached the window. Moving carefully, he timidly pushed the blinds open a crack.

Death was approaching him, in the form of a tactical SWAT Team assault.

"Oh, hell..." he whispered.

He hurried back into the living room, he stopped at what appeared to be little more than a large pile of trash and pushed away garbage and debris. Underneath the mess was a glorious old Magnavox console record player. The monstrous record player dominated the room with its wood grain beauty, and Cowboy grinned.

Shuffling through a few nearby crates full of sleeveless records, he started moving at a frantic, but careful pace as he thumbed through his record collection. He stopped and pulled out a record. Swiftly tossing it on the record player, he dropped the needle, which landed perfectly in auditory bliss. The record moaned a muted scratching as he slid the needle across the unforgiving vinyl. The opening guitar riff of *Layla* by Derek and the Dominos filled the trailer. Eric Clapton and his guitar screamed a mournful harmony as Cowboy retrieved a bulky old kerosene heater from a hallway closet.

Cowboy truly felt sorry for all the horrible things he'd done to Oliver, however, he never once asked for forgiveness. Not because he didn't want it, but because he didn't believe himself worthy of it. He felt worthless and resolved to die. He knew punishment eternal awaited him, the fires of hell for all of forever.

He decided to take control and start the fire himself. He'd burn in hell anyway, so he'd decided to start burning right here on Earth. At least then he would be the one to light the match.

Cowboy lifted the heater and poured kerosene throughout the living room and into the kitchen, where he opened the oven and turned on the burners. He paused, resisting the urge to ignite them just yet. The soft, pungent tingle of gas tickled his nostrils and filled first the kitchen and then the entire trailer.

Outside the SWAT Team encircled the trailer. They moved slowly, carefully, to avoid undue risk, but they did not stop. They pressed forward.

Exiting the kitchen, Cowboy left a trail of kerosene behind him. With the heater held in both arms across his chest, he let it pour around and over him as he walked into the living room. There he emptied out every drop of kerosene, heaving the heater over the couch, on the garbage, across every one of the already extremely flammable surfaces he could see. On the ground near the couch, he dug out a small, tin fuel can full of kerosene and calmly walked into his bedroom.

There he stood over the bloody and soiled mattress. When the police had visited, he covered it in junk, but they never even poked around back there anyway. After they left, he removed the junk. His shame couldn't be known to them, but he must constantly remind himself. That was his curse.

He'd suffered every bit of the torture he inflicted on that boy, yet also found immense pleasure in it. He knew he had to die. He had to burn, and he had to burn *forever*. The fire had to start there.

Dousing the mattress in kerosene and nearly emptying the container, Cowboy stopped. He grabbed a short box full of valuable vintage silver age comic books. From *Amazing Spider-Man* number one to the *Fabulous Thunder Family* number three, he unceremoniously dropped them onto the mattress and poured out the remainder of the kerosene over the pages.

As the SWAT Team engulfed the trailer outside, Cowboy retrieved a can of WD-40. He shook the can and sprayed it around the room, almost as if he were spraying a can of air freshener after a particularly nasty dump. He sprayed again, this time just a little, then popped the nozzle and squeezed out a little more liquid onto the lip of the can.

Producing a lighter from his pocket and flicking his wrist, he touched the flame of the lighter to the edge of the can. Flame and combustible liquid violently melded in a glorious chemical chorus, and he grinned.

The can exploded in Cowboy's hand, burning his chest and right arm severely. His kerosene-soaked chest caught fire. The mattress became engulfed in flames, and began burning with heavy, black smoke. Cowboy winced at the pain, coughed as it burned his lungs, but he refused to scream.

He looked down at the comic books. The bold, bright four-color worlds consumed by orange flame, turning quickly to ash. The thirty-year-old paper proved to be good kindling, and seconds later the mattress ignited fully.

Cowboy threw himself on the place of his sin.

This time he screamed.

For the only time in his life, except for as a very young child, he felt happy. His suffering was so great in the moment, he honestly felt atonement might be possible. If not for him, then possibly for others, for good, nice people like the paperboy.

He died in agony. His clothing and his hair burned into his flesh. Soon after his flesh was ripped apart by the fire, he turned into goo. His fire-weakened bones cracked and snapped under the weight of his melting flesh. His blood boiled as it poured out of him. The fire had already carried into the living room and through the kitchen, guided by the trail of kerosene.

Fully upon the trailer, the SWAT Team breached the windows and the doors. Battering rams busted through doors as batons shattered windows, only to unleash a torrent of the thick, black smoke, followed by a chorus of flames.

"Fall back," the lead SWAT Officer commanded. "He's torched the place!"

Pulling back, the SWAT Team created wide a perimeter to assure Cowboy would not escape. Little did they know he had no intention of escaping. After a few minutes, the men relaxed, removing headgear and lowering their weapons. They watched the trailer, now completely ablaze. The flames leapt upward, threatening to singe the nearby trees and lower limbs. They felt relaxed and relieved, like a group of friends enjoying a summer bonfire after a softball game.

It burned.

The crinkled Merkanary card.

The comic books.

The mattress.

It all burned.

CHAPTER 26
THE PAPER BOY

Cradling Oliver's body in his arms, Daniel ran through the forest as quickly as an out of shape 14-year-old carrying the dead weight of a corpse could. His mind drifted back to games with his brother. Being a football player, he was a beefy guy. Not necessarily muscular, but strong and certainly heavy. And being a big brother, he loved to utilize that beefy strength to mess with Daniel.

His favorite game, annoying but innocuous at the time, was "I'm a Dead Body." In retrospect, Daniel recognized it was less of a game and more of a way to infuriate his weakling little brother. He'd literally lay atop his brother and not allow him to move. "I'm a dead body," he'd say, insisting he was unable to move and yet any time Daniel mustered up the strength to free himself, the dead body would miraculously move to center its mass upon the squirming brother.

Daniel smiled as the image flooded his mind. He missed those days, yet continued to hate that game. Jeremiah had been right about one thing: dead bodies were heavy. Thankfully, this one didn't move.

"Jeremiah," Daniel said aloud.

He came to a sudden stop, looking down at Oliver. After a

few seconds he said it again. "Jeremiah." Daniel shuddered. He hadn't said his name in such a long time, hadn't even thought about it. Granted, he thought of his brother all the time, but never his name. "Jeremiah?" he repeated, as if calling out to him. "Miah?" he said softly.

The forest was completely silent, supernaturally silent, and Daniel sighed.

Now at the edge of tree line, Daniel trotted forward. He stumbled over an unseen log, but did not allow himself to fall and did not drop his friend. No matter what happened, he refused to drop his friend. After carefully maneuvering around the log, Daniel confidently stepped forward and slipped on a patch of wet muggy leaves. He slid backwards onto his butt, taking great care to not drop Oliver. After catching his breath, he struggled back to his feet and heaved Oliver's limp body up over his shoulders in a modified fireman's carry. Breathing through his nose, he forced a second wind.

Having looped around through the woods, away from the trailer court and back towards the fire station, Daniel saw his final destination. At the station, a plethora of people had gathered, more police officers, EMTs and firemen than Daniel had ever seen. He saw the stations and reporters and crew from all three local news stations, but didn't focus on them. He wasn't looking for them, but he knew they would help him find who he was looking for: Oliver's mother, Peggy Hart.

PEGGY HART MILLED ABOUT, having concluded her time with the news people, all of whom she now felt she knew personally. Most people disliked her, and that made them feel twice as sad for her.

Tonight Peggy Hart was a star.

It was like high school all over again, back when she had

her solo in the color guard. She felt justified in the attention. She *deserved* it. Deep inside, however, it sickened her.

She'd become famous because her son was missing.

Peggy attempted to sweet-talked a police officer, oblivious he interacted with her out of a sense of obligation to "comfort" the missing boy's mother. He'd drawn the short straw, so to speak. Constantly flipping her hair back and flashing a smile that came off more a grimace, Peggy failed to notice the Officer's obvious contempt. Watching with equal contempt, Oliver's deadbeat dad paced back and forth, digging a run in the uneven blacktop.

The undergrowth at the edge of the forest proved particularly thick and challenging for Daniel. He pushed hard, slogging through brambles and jaggers as they snagged onto his clothing with every step. Daniel had no hesitation to endure the abuse, wearing the remnants of the bushes and brush with pride as he protected Oliver's body from it all. When he broke through the edge of the forest, he was surprised to realize he now stood on the edge of the parking lot, still unnoticed.

Daniel picked up his friend, cradling him with the tender love and care of a parent with a baby. All he'd ever wanted in life was to be a good guy, in a literal sense.

To be a hero.

To be a *superhero.*

He wanted to fight crime by night and be an investigative reporter by day. Doing good on top of good, fighting for justice on two fronts. Even though Daniel knew his becoming a bonafide superhero wasn't realistic, it didn't stop him from taking actions to become the everyday kind of hero, the kind who go unnoticed until they finally get a street named after them.

Tonight Daniel didn't want any of that.

He knew he'd done something heroic by facing Oliver's killer, and it killed a part of him inside. The fear he still felt rattled his bones and shook his knees. He inhaled deeply, mustering up his most heroic stance as he approached the crowd, even as he had no physical or emotional strength left inside him.

A handful of the cops and emergency responders noticed Daniel's approach, but ignored him in the chaos of the trailer's blaze. With Oliver's body in his arms, Daniel walked forward.

The police officer who previously had the unfortunate duty of comforting Peggy Hart now had the unfortunate privilege of being the first to notice the boys. As Peggy prattled on, he caught movement out of the corner of his eye and stole a sideways glance before turning his head completely.

He said nothing, but stared at Daniel and Oliver's body in disbelief. "Oh my goodness…" he whispered.

Within seconds, nearly everyone in the crowd turned to Daniel, a collective hush falling over them one by one. Wide eyes followed Daniel as a wave of gasps erupted to his left, the sound of disbelief resonating like an unseen force. People parted like the Red Sea in *The Ten Commandments*, moving aside as if pushed by the invisible hand of God, all to let Daniel pass. They created a strange wall of silence around him and Oliver. Looks of awe and incredulity filled the crowd. In the back of his mind, Daniel heard the sirens screeching along with the helicopters and motors and distant grumblings over various radios and walkie-talkies.

Now firmly in the center of the parking lot, Daniel had nothing left to give. He collapsed, sinking to his knees, protecting Oliver as he fell. The crowd formed a massive circle around them, engulfing them like the walls of water crashing in upon Pharaoh's army. With great care, Daniel set Oliver's body down to the ground. He straightened Oliver's broken neck and lightly pulled open his swollen eye, trying his best to make him look normal again.

Daniel sat next to the body of his friend, looking around

apprehensively. he wanted to somehow protect him from the crowd, from the intrusive news people vying to take photos. Oliver's jacket fell open, revealing the image on the t-shirt beneath. Daniel smiled. The Fabulous Thunder Family stood strong, with the Grim at the center.

Suddenly hyperventilating, Daniel struggled to breathe. He reached down to close Oliver's jacket, then lowered himself to the ground, curling in and around Oliver's body, crying hysterically.

As the only person in the area to not notice Daniel and Oliver's arrival, Peggy Hart remained focused on flirting with yet another police officer she found cute.

Deadbeat noticed his son. He walked over tentatively at first, but then more confidently as he recognized Daniel. No one else in the crowd moved toward the boys. The crowd pushed and shoved into one another just inches away, but they remained untouched. The water had not fully fallen. The intimacy of their space had not been breached.

Oliver's father reached down and touched his face, just below his purple swollen eye. A drop of water fell upon them. He trembled as he touched the boy, then quickly snapped his hand away. He held it in front of his face, watching it shake violently, uncontrollably. He had never met his son before, and tonight, the first time he'd ever touched him, Oliver had been dead for a week.

Still crying, Daniel peered up, his eyes meeting Deadbeat's. Oliver's lifeless eye stared up at his father's face.

"Paper Boy, you're not afraid?" Deadbeat asked. He finally steadied his hand, bringing it to his mouth with a gasp. Stepping away, he disappeared into the crowd, overwhelmed with sorrow.

"My baby?! My baby!"

Peggy Hart she rumbled over to the boys. She stood over Oliver's body out of glaring down at Daniel. Ripping him from Daniel's gentle grasp, she scooped him up. The final torrent of water was no longer held at bay, and whether the grief was real or for show, Peggy Hart cried out. Daniel fell backwards, stunned by her arrival. The crowd formed around Peggy and Oliver. Daniel scooted away from the scene, his entire body wracked with sobs. The storm around him started to subside, even as the one inside continued to rage.

The circus now firmly fixed on Peggy, Daniel was finally able to breathe more steadily, hovering at the edges of the crowd, numbly watching. The news people pushed against the police officers, swarming Peggy like bloodthirsty, Africanized bees. Everyone passed Daniel and ignored him. Everyone but one.

"Daniel!"

His mom pushed through the crowd to get to her son.

Daniel reached out his arms, just as he did as a toddler when his mom could and did fix everything. She bent down to him, pulled him up to his feet and held him tightly. She hugged him with all of her strength, keeping him on his feet when he couldn't stand on his own. Her arms constricted tenderly as she squeezed every ounce of her love into him.

"Oh, thank God," she whispered, tears flowing slowly but freely. "Thank God you're okay!"

Daniel bawled, his hysterical crying returning with double the ferocity. Through his sobbing, he muttered, "I still play with toys, Mom. I still play with toys."

She held him tighter, smiling down at him. "It's okay Daniel, it's okay," she whispered, rocking him back and forth. "It's okay to play with toys. And I'm here, baby, I'm here."

CHAPTER 27

THE STORY IS OVER, BUT IT ALSO ISN'T

Daniel crouched over the newspapers at the bottom of his driveway. He wanted to quit, but his mom wouldn't let him. At least not yet, not until he'd found a replacement.

He shivered involuntarily. Theoretically, winter remained a few more weeks away, sometimes fall could suddenly decide to become winter when you call Western PA your home.

The cool air gave way to the frigid winds, and.he started to think he should have worn a heavy jacket. Yes, his mom had suggested one, but he just wanted to get the paper route over and done with. He felt that way about a lot of things lately.

Without question he had absolutely no desire to return to the trailer court. However, as his mom point out, being an adult sometimes meant you had adult obligations. Daniel envisioned that chestnut largely depended on the individual adult in question.

Moving slowly despite wanting to hurry through it, Daniel jammed the papers into his bag. Some were wrinkled, others folded, he didn't care. He just wanted to be *done*.

Sighing, he craned his neck and looked around the area.

He was alone. He felt colder. Slinging his bag over his shoulder he started plodding along the route.

In the time since Daniel brought Oliver's body out of the woods there had been long, draining conversations with the police. They asked him a million questions, asked his mom a million questions, they didn't ask his dad as many, but he still got peppered as well. The Pittsburgh news stations, on the other hand, had one question that they asked law enforcement over and over again:. Why didn't anyone check the woods?

The police had no answers.

Nobody had an answer for that, apparently.

Daniel didn't have the answers they wanted, either. He had to be honest with himself and ponder his own sanity. Had he really spent that time with Oliver, day after day? Or was it all the fall out of some kind of psychotic episode, a mental breakdown he experienced when he first encountered the body in the woods? He came close to sharing his secret with his mom, telling her all about him, but elected not to. He didn't want to worry her. She had been through enough already. Real or imagined, he was grateful to have had that time with Oliver. It would forever remain his.

The Pittsburgh TV news and the city papers kept calling, so much so that the family had to change their number and keep it unlisted. Daniel decided that, if he ever did an interview – and that was with a capital IF - he would do it with the Valley, keep it local.

Or maybe one day he'd write a book about it.

At Popeye's, Daniel passed the normal crew. They waved hello and Daniel waved back, but he did so halfheartedly. No one exchanged a word. Daniel kept on walking.

A few minutes later he approached Old Man Mumbles, who sat grumpily in his usual chair. Extending his arm,

Daniel stopped and quietly offered him a paper. Old Man Mumbles waved it off. Still silent, Daniel shoved it into the box, nodded and kept walking. Old Man Mumbles didn't bother to get up. He remained in his chair, curling his heavy Steelers Starter Jacket around him.

The gravel off the driveway crunched under Daniel's feet. Habitually, Daniel crouched down and picked up a small handful of sharp rocks. He selected the sharpest and most angular, the one most like a spaceship launched from the lower atmosphere down through the shielding much and into the subaqueous fortress. He cocked his arm back and threw it hard. It cut perfectly through the algae, but it was a child's game, and he knew it. This realization settled on Daniel hard, a heavy blanket of inconvenient truth. It wasn't fun anymore.

He wasn't a kid anymore.

Outside Peggy Hart's trailer, Daniel stood and stared, trying to compose himself. He regarded the trailer for a long time thinking of Peggy, of Oliver, of everything.

How she mistreated him.

How she mistreated Oliver.

His anger toward her faded a bit as he realized how much he missed his friend. His mind conjured up images of the little boy he used to see playing in the yard, a boy he'd largely ignore, with exception to his exceptional toys.

Oliver didn't have many toys, to be honest. By contrast, Daniel had so many. Too many, some would argue. He could have given him some, could have at least talked to him, could have become his friend when he was alive.

When he was alive.

Daniel disliked Peggy Hart, but he hated himself for failing to recognize the opportunity to make a friend when he had the chance. He condemned himself of this, because maybe if he had been a little less self-centered and little more considerate of those around him, he could have saved him.

If they had become friends, maybe he would have

somehow kept Oliver alive, even if only for a few more days. Daniel would have told him not to go with Cowboy, would have noticed when he was missing.

Something would've been different.

Anything would've been different.

No, *everything.*

Everything would have been different.

DANIEL'S EYES fell to his feet, tears staining the gravel beneath his sneakers. He knew this loop, this self-condemning sadness wasn't justified. Wasn't real. But he still felt it, he felt it so, so strongly right now.

Taking a deep breath, Daniel wiped his face and moved on.

Approaching the next double-wide, Daniel psyched himself up for the part of the job he hated the most. Asking people for money. He particularly hated it in situations like these. While the paper didn't cost much, but not everybody could afford it. The thing was, when someone didn't pay, it came out of Daniel's pocket in the end, and those pockets weren't particularly deep.

Sheila milled about the yard, doing her best to clean up the mess of toys from her younger siblings. Ever a soon-to-bloom-teenage-goddess, she wore a snug, pink polka dot sweater and cutoff jeans with sunglasses perched atop her head, nestled securely in her scrunched hair. In his head Daniel asked the question, "Aren't you cold?" a few times, mentally rehearsing for polished perfection before delivering the real thing. He visualized the staging and his positioning relative to hers, his vocal cadence and tone and syntax. It was going to be perfect. He was also a few inches taller than her in his imagination, when in reality she was the one a few inches taller than him.

She beamed when she saw him. "It's so cold!" she exclaimed with a grin. "I was just wearing this in the house."

Daniel's eyes widened at her words, experiencing the loss of his perfect line delivery. He had nothing. Said nothing.

His awkwardly long pause made her feel uncomfortable, and she looked away, like she was ashamed. As Daniel struggled to verbalize his thoughts, she filled in the silence. "I mean, I know it's cold for shorts, but they're just so cute and I'll do anything to hang onto the summer. Won't you?"

"I..." Daniel stammered, blinking twice. His mind conjured up a cool response, he opened his mouth and heard himself say, "You should live by the beach." He smiled, actually impressed with himself. What a sweet line that was! She'd be sure to like him for something so obviously clever.

"I *should* live by the beach!" she agreed, smiling at him. Her smile, terrible teeth and all, simultaneously swallowed Daniel's void of awkwardness and her void of nervousness.

Daniel's smile faltered as he remembered what he was there to do. He looked down at the ground between them and shrugged. "Is your mom home?"

It was the only line he didn't rehearse, the one he'd avoided, even in his own head.

The smile melted away from Sheila's quaintly pretty face. "She's inside," she sighed heavily.

Daniel felt guiltier than Dr. Doom. Guilty for attempting to collect money from a woman who obviously didn't have it. He swallowed and shook it off, retrieving his collection booklet. Walking past Sheila, he climbed up onto the porch and knocked a heavy and impressive knock on the door.

He waited. Knocked again. Waited again.

He repeated this process a few more times before he sighed and dropped his shoulders, looking back at Sheila.

"I forgot, she just left a minute ago," Sheila lied. "Burt had little league." She sounded earnest, really wanting him to believe her.

But Daniel knew Burt didn't even play baseball.

Nobody played baseball this late in the fall.

Daniel didn't even think about it. Didn't have the energy to care. Walking off the porch, he slumped off, making his way to the road.

"Come back later?" Sheila pleaded. "I'm sure she'll be home soon."

Daniel said nothing, walking away.

"Daniel...?"

He stopped dead in his tracks. He didn't turn around, but turned his head to the side to show he was listening.

"Come back, anytime."

He knew she meant it, despite how ashamed she was of their situation. She was trying, and he should have given her credit for it

He didn't. He just walked away.

Taking in the wreckage, Daniel stared at Cowboy's trailer, now little more than a burnt husk of jagged metal and melted plastic. The blackened trees overhead swayed in the fading breeze, empty and lifeless. Daniel's mind wandered back to before, to what had happened in that terrible place. The horrible things he saw, the even more horrific things he *didn't* see. He thought about his own bravery, with mixed emotions. Was it enough? Should he have acted sooner? Would anyone have believed him, if he'd told the truth right at the beginning?

He knew he should, but he didn't feel relieved that it was over, even with the evil husk before him burned to the ground. Sure, an evil had been purged from this world, but he didn't feel any more peaceful or comforted by this fact. He just felt... empty, as if part of himself burned up in that fire. He hoped one day he'd be able to identify it, maybe even find it, that missing piece. But even if he couldn't, he just wanted be be able to breath again, to not feel the ghost of constant pressure upon his chest.

His head down and his eyes only on his Nikes, Daniel neared the Sweetest Old Lady Ever's trailer. Briskly walking away from the house, very nearly stepping into Daniel, the Queen of the Court bolted past him, cradling a cat. Without looking back, she got in her town car and peeled away, never saying a word. He didn't even think she was aware of him, and even if she had seen him, he was pretty sure she wouldn't have cared.

Daniel stepped up onto the porch.

Without any cats around it, the sight depressed him. He didn't know a porch could do that. It never occurred to him that an empty porch, utterly devoid of accustomed cats, could be transformed into a thoroughly sad place when abandoned.

Like any other day, Daniel approached the door. Like any other day, Daniel dropped a paper in the slot. Unlike every other day, Daniel walked away without saying a single word to the Sweetest Old Lady Ever. Months before this would have been a relief. On a normal day, it'd mean he'd be home twenty minutes earlier.

"Wait! Paperboy, wait!" a kind voice shouted.

Confused and very much rattled by recent experiences, Daniel crossed the yard, unsure if his imagination was playing tricks on him again.

"Please," the voice pleaded, closer this time. "Wait."

Daniel turned slowly as a middle-aged man approached him from the house. His face was filled with concern and determination. A familiar face – a kind face.

"Here." The man reached out and pressed something into Daniel's hand.

Daniel frowned and looked down. It was a crinkled piece of paper, with a portrait in the center featuring a president. *No, not a president*, Daniel thought. A founding father named Ben.

He regarded the hundred-dollar bill with pure confusion. "No," he stammered, shaking his head. "I can't take this."

"Please. I'm sure Mom owed you money," clarified the man.

"What? No, she… she was all paid up," corrected Daniel. "Paid *ahead*, actually."

"Well, then you can keep it." The man smiled, and Daniel recognized the dimples and joy of The Sweetest Old Lady Ever, hiding within his facial features. "That's for you."

Daniel's eyes welled up with tears at the sight, taken off guard at experiencing such a familiar sight, one he thought had been forever lost. "Thank you," he whispered, wiping a tear away.

The man just continued to smile at him. Aside from the smile, Daniel couldn't see much of a physical resemblance, but this man had unquestionably inherited his mother's soul.

Unsure of what else to say, Daniel defaulted to business mode again. "Should I cancel the paper?"

The man shook his head. "I'll be staying here, the next week or so. You can keep on bringing them by for now."

"Okay." Daniel nodded, choking back tears.

"I'll let you know when it's time to stop." The man turned to go and then paused. "You wouldn't by chance want a cat, would you?"

Daniel smirked. "I have a dog."

In the window behind the man, the all gray cat with white paws and a white spot under its left eye perched regarding Daniel.

"Ah. Well, I had to ask." The man nodded and left Daniel in the yard, fighting the urge to break down in tears.

Strolling away down the road, Daniel regarded the money. Only a handful of times in his life had he even seen a hundred-dollar bill, much less been given one. Two handfuls, to be specific - one each Christmas since he'd been born. He loved nothing more than taking that money to Ross Park Mall and then down the hill to Toys 'R Us the day after Christmas. After all, even though he'd been given a hundred dollars' worth of toys the day before, he could always use a hundred dollars' worth more.

He grinned with the idea, but then slowed down to a stop staring at the bill. Something about it looked different to him. No, it wasn't the bill, it was him. It was the way he was looking at it.

This isn't about me. About getting more toys.

This is about something… bigger.

Daniel looked up the sky and exhaled slowly, lamenting the loss of a part of his childhood, while at the same time welcoming and recognizing the opportunity to step into adulthood. *On purpose.*

"Be a superhero," he whispered.

It was partially to himself, but he also said it aloud to an Oliver who no longer walked beside him. Who knows? Maybe he could still hear him, could still somehow see him? And if Oliver couldn't, maybe Jeramiah could.

He turned around, heading back where he'd come from.

A minute later he found Sheila, still cleaning up the yard. She still wore the same shorts, but had added an overly large Penn State hooded sweatshirt. In Daniel's eyes, she looked like a stereotypical college freshman. Granted, he didn't much care for Penn State. His brother went to Pitt, so he assumed he must therefore dislike Penn State or he'd be considered a disloyal brother, and the fact was he loved his brother very much. Daniel wondered if he could he still love someone who was dead? Would the empty void of loss, the lingering pain ever stop? And if it did, did it mean you had to stop loving them?

Sheila's sunglasses now covered her yellow-green eyes, and she continued her seemingly endless effort to clean the yard. Daniel briefly thought of the real possibility her brothers would grow up and eventually make the yard look like Cowboy's. He shuddered at the thought of another Cowboy springing from the well of a junk-filled yard.

The closer he came to the yard, the more he overthought what to say. He'd settled on his greeting, appropriately, "Hey, Sheila." His issue had now become *how* to say it. He practiced in his head with different emphasis, different tones, different speeds and delivery. Before he had a chance to test any of them out, she raised her glasses up and greeted him with a toothy grin, full of mischief and unintentional romance behind it.

"Daniel," she said sweetly, face flushing at the sight of him.

His heart fluttered. *Holy bleep. It actually fluttered!*

She glanced back at the trailer, biting her lip . "Sorry," she said. "My mom's not home yet."

"Oh, I know," his words fumbled out of his mouth. "I mean, I don't *know*, but I don't care."

She looked at him in confused amusement.

"I mean, I don't care about your mom." He felt his face fill with flaming flames. "No! I *do* care about your mom! Very much!" The fire burned brighter. "Oh, man..."

Sheila laughed.

Relieved at her response, he eased back on the throttle and spoke more deliberately. "I, ah...forgot to give you your newspaper."

He offered her the paper and she reached out for it. Their hands touched. It felt like a fresh jolt of electricity shot through Daniel's arm, coursing throughout his entire body. Now his heart really *had* fluttered for Sheila, an electricity and fluttering that he was pretty convinced was mutual.

"Thank you, Daniel," she said, grinning at him.

Daniel felt a compulsion well up inside him, the irresistible urge to suddenly do something honestly, genuinely heroic. "Hey," he began, "Tell your mom not to worry about the newspaper."

She frowned. "Really?"

"Yeah. You see, Cowboy..." Daniel stopped himself, swallowing the word, the bitterness of it turning his stomach sour. He didn't have to say that name again. That name burned with the rest of the man, consumed in the fire. *"Mr. Harrison has a bunch of free ones coming. I'll let you guys have them."*

Sheila swallowed, visibly choked up a little. "Thank you," she whimpered.

"And here," Daniel reached out and pulled up her free hand closer to him. He gingerly placed the folded hundred-dollar bill into it, closing his hand over hers. "I want you to have this."

She stared down at it, thinking of a thousand excuses as to why she shouldn't take it or didn't need it, how Daniel wasn't really a rich kid and on and on. Before she decided on the best response, Daniel interrupted her thoughts.

"I know you need it," he continued. "While I'm not exactly rich or anything, I have enough. *More than enough.*"

He took in the chaos of broken toys in the yard.

"I also have a bunch of toys the kids can have. They aren't new, but I took really good care of them," he said. "So, not mint condition, but 'very fine'." He smiled. He'd actually surprised himself. He hadn't expected to do that, but it felt right. Doing good felt... well... really good.

He let go of her hand. It hung in the air, suspended by Sheila's sheer disbelief at what was happening. Daniel took a few steps away. "Bye," he said.

"Daniel," she called after him.

He stopped and looked back. "Yeah?"

"Did he...?" She struggled through every horrible syllable simmering in her mind. "Did Mr. Harrison ever... touch you?"

Daniel very nearly found this funny, but held his smile at bay. Laughing seemed like it would be really, really inappropriate right now. He shook his head. "No," he said. "He never did. Not me." He pointed to the heavens and thought of Oliver. "I guess you could say I was protected."

She nodded, then started to cry. Walking forward, she

wrapped her arms around him and clung tightly, despite his discomfort.

"My little brothers," she blurted out, breaking down more with each word. "My little brothers." She sobbed in his arms, pouring her fear into him. Daniel held her. He pulled back, she remained in his embrace. "Daniel, do you...do you think he...?"

"I don't know," he said. "But I'm here, for all of you, I'm here."

Sheila nodded, nuzzle closer into his neck for a second before taking a step back. She wiped a tear from her cheek, then placed her hand back on his shoulder, keeping him within arm's reach. "I heard you're quitting the paper route." She sounded sad. "Are you still going to come across the bridge? To see us?"

To see me, Daniel translated in his head.

"I'll be around," he reassured her. "I'm always around."

They gazed into one another's eyes. The moment simultaneously destroying and defining them. Momentarily, both were frozen in place, mannequins in space. Daniel found himself beyond words. He wanted to say something to comfort her, to assure her nothing had happened to them, but he couldn't. In the moment, words were woefully inefficient.

She leaned in. He inched closer and kissed her.

It was an utterly sweet, awkward, perfectly imperfect first kiss for both of them.

And just like the first comic book he'd ever read, he'd never forget it.

CHAPTER 28
POST SCRIPT, FRIENDSHIPS DON'T END, BUT THEY DO CHANGE

On Daniel's bed Mac slept a deep, albeit whimper filled sleep. Snuggled next to him the all gray cat with white paws and that white spot purred in its sleep. In the center of the room, Daniel and his dad packed up a handful of egg boxes. Around the room the majority of Daniel's toys were gone, now residing in the boxes. The room now looked… different. Not yet adult, but not a kid's room, either. It was far more teenager, in Daniel's mind.

On the television an episode of *Space Missionaries* played. Daniel always hated the show, but his dad swore by it, insisting it was a big deal when he was a kid. Daniel chalked it up to the fact that some things kids just won't ever understand about their parents. His father placed more toys in the last egg box, distractedly watching the show.

In the show, the Missionaries of the title were surrounded by strange lizard aliens. Dad was riveted, but Daniel only saw the flaws. He held his tongue, deciding not to point out he zipper going down the back of the space lizards.

"Dad," said Daniel with a handful of 80s action figures in his hands.

His dad was enthralled as the crew of the Kopiko boarded the cardboard shuttlecraft.

"Dad! He shouted finally breaking his dad's 60s sci-fi trance. Daniel held up the action figures.

"He-Man and bug guys," said his said with a bit of pride.

"Sectars," corrected Daniel. "And technically, it's the Masters of the Universe."

"Miah called them bug guys," he said softly.

"They were his toys," said Daniel sadly, "not mine. In the box?"

"Up to you."

"In the box."

The figures crashed and fell with a clank of plastic in a heap of lost memories of play.

Next, Daniel handed him a Mr. Gorgeous action figure. His dad stopped and examined the toy, then touched Daniel on the shoulder. "Your brother gave you this?" he asked.

"Yeah," responded Daniel.

"You know, I bought this for Jeremiah," he snorted, holding back his emotions. "We actually went to a wrestling match. Can you believe that?"

"You did?" Daniel was genuinely intrigued.

"Yeah," his dad continued, drowning in once-happy, now brutally-painful memories. "Not like seeing Bruno Sammartino, but a big event. In the city, the Civic Arena. Where the Penguins play."

"I know where the Penguins play," Daniel snorted back. He wasn't trying to hurt his dad, but instead protect himself from his feelings. To help him continue to deny his sadness about his brother, as they all had. They thought that would be easier. It wasn't, and Daniel was starting to see that now.

The levee broke inside him, and Daniel's facade broke along with it. "I miss him, Dad."

His dad inhaled deeply, nodding his head. "I do, too," he said.

"I'm sorry..." Daniel started, then closed his mouth. The words were too much

"What do you have to be sorry for?" his dad asked.

"I'm sorry... I'm sorry you're left with me." Daniel choked, shaking his head as the realization of what he's just said, what he had finally given voice to settled on him.

"Dan..." His dad stammered. "No..."

"I'm not him. And I'm sorry for that, I'm so, so sorry I'm not him. I'll never be him. But..." Daniel struggled for a breath.

"No, Dan, you're not him."

Daniel closed his eyes, his father's words punctuating him like the sharpest, hottest poker. He shook his head in resignation.

"But you're Daniel, and that's exactly who I need you to be." He reached out and placed a heavy hand on Daniel's shoulder, giving it a light squeeze.

"And I'm sorry I didn't go to the funeral," Daniel said as he whipped away tears with the sleeve of his sweatshirt.

"I know."

"No, you don't." Daniel said, "I think if I went I could have seen him again." Upon his dad's bewildered expression Daniel stopped. How could he explain the whole casually hanging out with the ghosts of dead people he sees thing to his dad?

Reaching Daniel squeezed his dad's hand. Instead of retreading from the intensity of the moment he pointed at the television, Daniel said. "This is the good part. When Captain Hunter finds the sonic frequency to defeat the lizards." He grimaced. No question, he still thoroughly hated the show, but he'd seen the episode a dozen times over the years alongside his dad. All those years he'd pretended he wasn't paying attention.

Daniel's dad smiled. He knew Daniel hated the show, but the fact that he recognized the moment wasn't lost on him. He held up the Mr. Gorgeous action figure. "Mr. Gorgeous is a jerk, by the way."

He tossed the toy unceremoniously into the box. "You know, you don't have to do all of this." He motioned to the rest of the room, eyebrows raised in expectation.

"I want to, Dad."

"You might regret it later." His words hung in the air between them, obviously spoken from experience.

"Then I guess I'll regret it later," Daniel said, conjuring up as much youthful wisdom as he felt in the moment. "But now, I feel it's what I have to do. What I *want* to do." He looked around the room, taking in a deep breath, processing the loss of the previous week, the past few years. Glancing back at his dad, he smiled. "Plus, I think I'm starting to think that regret is just a choice we make in life. So... I guess I'll make that choice when I come to it. Or not."

His dad nodded, silently stunned by Daniel's words.

A quiet rapping at the door cut through the silence. Mac popped his head up, growled and instantly dropped it and went back to sleep. The cat stirred, stretched a long glorious stretch, and hoped off the bed, making a pile of dirty laundry its new bed. The door cracked open to reveal the face of a subdued, contrite Jimmy. He looked in on them, eyes raised expectantly, saying nothing.

"You okay?" Dad whispered to a now calm, but ruddy-faced Daniel.

Daniel nodded.

Taking his cue, Dad quietly left the room, patting Jimmy's shoulder as he passed.

Jimmy stepped into the room and shut the door. "New cat?" he said quietly.

"New cat," echoed Daniel.

"Does it have a name?" Inquired Jimmy.

"Not yet."

"Were you crying?" Jimmy blurted out bluntly.

"Yes. Yes, I was," Daniel said, matter-of-factly.

Jimmy pursed his lips. He looked around the room and shook his head confidently. "Takes a big man to cry."

"Does it?" He genuinely hoped Jimmy was correct.

"I have no idea."

They both burst out laughing, the tension between them starting to crack at the shared awkwardness of the moment.

Jimmy looked up and noticed the TV for the first time. "Watchin' Sci-Fi, huh?"

"Yep."

"*Space Missionaries*? Ugh," said Jimmy. "Your dad's choice?"

"Yep."

Jimmy plopped himself down on the bed next to Mac, who totally ignored him. "I don't get it. My dad loves that stupid show too. It's an old people thing." He shook his head. "Old *man* thing actually, 'cause my mom hates it." Jumping up from the bed, he moved closer to Daniel and inspected the boxes at the center of the room, digging through the nearest collection. "Giving this stuff away?"

"Yep."

"Your comics, too?" Jimmy asked, equally appalled and hopeful at the idea.

"No!" shouted Daniel.

Jimmy grinned. He reached into his bag and dug out a stack of comic books, holding them out to Daniel. The Valor Vendetta and Spawn comics. "Here," he said, extending his arm and starting a well-rehearsed speech. "It wasn't a fair deal. And with everything you've gone through, my mom kinda thought I should give them back to you. And you can keep the Pete Phan Merkanary card."

The card.

Until then Daniel had forgotten all about it. He couldn't bear to tell Jimmy it had burned to Hell along with a child molesting murderer. "Thanks."

"My mom says you're welcome," Jimmy smirked.

Daniel wanted to smile back, but he honestly felt bad. "I think you got the raw end of the deal."

Jimmy smiled the toothy smile of a future lawyer. "We'll work something out." He poked around in the other boxes. "So you're giving *all* of it away?"

"Yep."

"Wow," Jimmy said. "I'm flabbergasted!"

Daniel laughed so hard he nearly rolled on the floor. "Flabbergasted?" he snorted, trying to stabilize himself. He was pretty sure something like this only happened in cartoons, but yet there he was, very nearly rolling on the floor.

Jimmy lifted his eyebrows in mock surprise. "It means 'amazed'. Go to the library and read a book someday, dude!" Daniel was about to protest when he pointed at the Grim action figure on the shelf. Jimmy jumped up and removed the weathered action figure. "What about him?" he asked, holding it up.

Daniel's face grew stoic. "I'm keeping that one," he said.

Jimmy nodded, carefully placed it back up on the shelf without a word.

ACKNOWLEDGMENTS

Within this book there is a great deal of reality and even more fiction. Shades of real people and moments. The wellspring of this story is all the toys I played with, comics & books I read, cartoons & movies I watched. All that has blurred together in my head, I'm glad it resides there.

I must also acknowledge the people who toiled behind the scenes so kids like me could dream dreams like this. I'm grateful for the two people that started it all, my mom and dad. George and Joann drove me on Sunday mornings when the papers were too heavy, with our dog Mac in the back of Dad's extended cab Ford F-150. I'm grateful to my brothers, 2 of whom were paper boys before me. I miss my teachers Coleman Hough and S.L (Sid) Stebel. Coleman challenged me as a writer, and stopped me from forcing my will upon a story and allowing me to find the heart of a story. Sid taught me, well he taught me how to write. Without Coleman The Paper Boy would not exist. Oliver would still be lost in the woods, without here Daniel would not have found him.

Judy, my wife, my darling, my girl, without whom, I would not be here to have written this book. We've had more hard times than we care to, but we've had them together. Penny and Prim, my daughters, my little girl versions of me, the final piece to the puzzle of understanding why I needed to write this book.

My deep gratitude to Laura and Stag Beetle Books for having faith in the story of a paperboy and his ghost companion. Finally, Kevin, THE editor of all editors, without his understanding of the soul of this story The Paper Boy wouldn't have found his way home.

FROM THE PUBLISHER

Thank you so much for reading *The Paper Boy*!

We hope you enjoyed the journey and characters as much as we loved bringing them to you. Please leave a review on Amazon and Goodreads while the story is fresh in your mind. Reviews are writing fuel for authors and help their books get into the hands of other eager readers.

If you're a big fan of speculative young adult and middle-grade fiction, we invite you to join our street team. Get copies of our books in advance, early access to covers, and other freebies!

Stag Beetle Books

www.stagbeetlebooks.com